# The
# Home Secretary
# Will See You Now

Also by Graham Ison
*Confirm or Deny*

# The
# Home Secretary
# Will See You Now

## Graham Ison

St. Martin's Press
New York

Library of Congress Cataloging-in-Publication Data

Ison, Graham.
    The home secretary will see you now / Graham Ison.
       p.   cm.
     ISBN 0-312-04329-5
     I. Title.
    PR6059.S6H6   1990                                          89-78004
823'.914—dc20                                                   CIP

First published in Great Britain by Macmillan London Ltd.

First U.S. Edition
10  9  8  7  6  5  4  3  2  1

# The
# Home Secretary
# Will See You Now

# Chapter One

Alpha Two, a red Ford Sierra of the Diplomatic Protection Group, was waiting in Cutler's Mews when Inspector Franklin arrived. Its roof beacon was still revolving lazily, bathing the mainly white walls in a rich blue light.

'Turn that damn thing off,' said Franklin testily. 'You'll have everyone in the mews complaining that there's blue light bouncing off their bedroom ceiling.'

The driver grinned. 'If they see a blue light in this part of London,' he said, 'they're usually too busy flushing their cannabis down the toilet to complain.' But he turned it off.

Franklin glanced at the door of Number Seven. 'Is that it?'

'Yes, sir.'

'Have you rung the bell?'

'No, sir, we waited for you.'

Franklin pressed the bell-push with his gloved thumb, and heard a corresponding ringing somewhere in the house. After a third attempt had brought no response, he stood back and surveyed the door, hunching his shoulders against the snow and wishing that he had brought a topcoat. 'Well,' he said at length, 'I suppose we'll have to break in.'

'I'd better let control know, sir,' said the radio operator. 'The house is alarmed, and if it's set we'll have half the Group round here in two minutes flat.'

'Yeah, right, do it.' Franklin turned to the driver. 'What d'you think?'

'No good trying to 'loid it, sir, not with that lock. I suggest we smash the glass panel and try that way. But if the bolts are on, or it's mortised, we've had it.'

'If the bolts are on, it means someone's at home.' Franklin

studied the door absently. 'Could you get through that glass?'

The PC driver moved closer and examined the door. 'Looks like it's laminated, sir. Take a bit of doing, but I reckon so.'

'She might be in bed asleep.' Franklin looked at his watch.

'Bit early, sir. It's only just gone ten.'

'I know.' Franklin should have been off duty five minutes ago.

'D'you want me to have a go then, sir?' asked the driver flatly. He didn't like Franklin and was glad that it was he who had to make the decision.

'Mmm!' Franklin dithered. At his former station, the police rarely worried about the social standing of their customers; here, on the DPG, every one of them was important. The Commissioner would hear about this – would have to be told in fact – and just about every one of Franklin's senior officers, all the way up. He had been a policeman for seventeen years, long enough to know that he was facing a situation where anything he did was certain to be wrong, and that to do nothing would be wrong too.

The driver walked to the car and returned with his truncheon.

'Go on, then,' said the Inspector.

The driver hammered at the panel, succeeding at first only in denting the laminated glass. It took three or four minutes of concentrated effort before he was able to stand back to reveal a hole large enough to get a hand through.

'Well, try it,' said Franklin.

The PC put his gloved hand through the opening and, with the help of some strained facial expressions, found the latch. 'Ah!' he said, and pushed the door open. 'Careless!'

Swiftly, Franklin pulled off his gloves and drew his revolver before stepping into the hallway. The lights appeared to be on all over the house. He pushed a door which swung open noiselessly on its oiled hinges; it was a sitting room, tastefully furnished with what appeared to be genuine antiques. Two or three table lamps cast relaxing little pools of light. But there was no one there.

'Deserted!'

The Inspector started and turned suddenly; he hadn't heard the PC enter the room. 'What?'

'There's no one downstairs, sir.' The PC smirked slightly at the revolver in the Inspector's hand.

'It's like the *Mary Celeste*,' said the radio operator, joining them from the hall.

'Someone had to say it,' said the driver.

'Well don't stand around. Search upstairs.' Franklin holstered his gun, and watched the two PCs as they went up the open pine staircase. He walked through to the kitchen and looked around, whistling softly at the luxury of it, and wondering what his wife would give for such a workshop.

'Mr Franklin!'

The Inspector walked quickly into the hallway again and looked up the flight of stairs. 'What is it?' He took the stairs two at a time to where the PC driver stood on the landing, and stopped in the doorway of what was obviously the master bedroom. His gaze swiftly surveyed the king-sized bed with its undisturbed counterpane, the built-in wardrobes, and the dressing table that ran the full length of the opposite wall. On the thick white fluffy carpet, between bed and wardrobes, lay the body of a woman attired in a full-length satin robe. Her arms were flung out above her head, and her long brown hair lay in a sweep across the carpet, almost as if it had been arranged.

'It's the Home Secretary's wife, sir,' said the PC driver, 'and she's dead.'

Detective Inspector Francis Wisley's tour as Special Branch duty officer was due to finish at eleven o'clock. At half-past ten, he walked into the reserve room and started to read the messages, putting his distinctive initials on each as he satisfied himself that the appropriate action had been taken.

He reached the message that recorded the information he had passed on to Inspector Franklin of the DPG about the Home Secretary. 'Did we get a result from the DPG about

Dudley Lavery's wife?' He glanced across at the Detective Sergeant sitting on the other side of the room.

'Nothing yet, sir.'

'Give them a ring, will you? This message looks untidy without a result.'

The Sergeant was about to tap out the number when a light came up on the panel. He listened for a second or two and then glanced at Wisley. 'Inspector Franklin's on now, sir. Wants a word – on line two.'

Wisley flicked down the switch and picked up the handset. 'Duty officer,' he said. He pulled a pad towards him and then snapped his fingers at the Detective Constable. 'Pen, quick,' he mouthed, and started writing rapidly.

The head of Special Branch, Deputy Assistant Commissioner Donald Logan, was the first to arrive at Scotland Yard, or at least that part of it occupied by Special Branch, having been on the fifth floor for the dining-out of one of his colleagues.

'Who have you told so far?' Logan stood elegantly in the doorway, one hand in the pocket of his dinner-jacket.

'The Commander Ops and Chief Superintendent Winter, sir,' said Wisley. 'Mr Scott is on leave apparently.'

Logan nodded. 'Yes, I know.' He smiled to himself. Trust Ted Scott to start his leave the day before something like this happened. It meant that poor old complaining George Winter would be the Acting Commander in charge of the personal protection officers, who to a man detested being called bodyguards but usually were, at least by the Press and the public. 'Who is on protection with the Home Secretary?' he asked.

'DCI Lisle—'

'Right now, at this minute, I meant.'

'DS Selway, sir.'

'Have you told either of them?'

'No, sir. As far as I know, the Home Secretary's still at the House.'

'Well, get on to Selway now, and tell him to bring the

8

Home Secretary here as soon as he can. I don't want him going to Cutler's Mews before we have a chance to talk to him. Can you get him on the air?'

'I'll try, sir.'

'Well, don't you do it.' He waved at the Sergeant. 'Let one of the others do it. And don't tell him why; just say that it's imperative that the Home Secretary comes here before he goes home. Right . . . ' He swung back to face Wisley. 'Now get the Commissioner for me – I'll speak to him – and you'd better get hold of ACSO. . . . ' He paused to get out his wallet; the DAC always knew the exact whereabouts of the Assistant Commissioner Specialist Operations who was his boss, and head of the CID. He scribbled a number on a piece of paper and handed it to Wisley. 'Then ring Commander Campbell and tell him to stand by.' Logan had already decided that the Anti-Terrorist Branch would be involved in this, come what may. 'In fact, I'll speak to him, too.'

'The Commissioner, sir,' said Wisley, handing the receiver over and standing up to allow the DAC to sit down.

It took the Commissioner twenty minutes to get from his official residence in Barnes to New Scotland Yard. Having sharply overcome the initial doubt in the mind of the operator at the Central Command Complex that it actually was the Commissioner on the phone, Sir James Gilmore was none the less surprised that a traffic car had arrived at his house within ninety seconds of his replacing the receiver; this miracle was not explained by the traffic division driver who had been fortunate enough to be patrolling less than a mile away when the call came through.

The constable on duty in the Back Hall of New Scotland Yard was not so lucky. Although he had heard the squeak of the revolving door, he failed immediately to look up from doing the crossword in the following day's *Daily Telegraph* which had just arrived, and was not aware of the Commissioner's arrival until Sir James was passing him. 'Good evening,' said Gilmore icily.

The constable tried to rise quickly to his feet, only to find that his stool was too close to the counter and he was trapped. 'All correct, sir,' he said hurriedly.

'Good.' The Commissioner made his way to the lift and rode to the eighteenth floor.

Wisley held open the swing door leading from the lift lobby. 'Mr Logan's in his office, sir.'

'Thank you.' The Commissioner nodded, and made his way down the corridor to the DAC's large corner room.

Logan and his two colleagues rose as Gilmore entered. 'You know Frank Hussey, my Commander Operations, sir,' said Logan, 'and this is Detective Chief Superintendent George Winter who's acting Commander Protection.' He smiled. 'Ted Scott picked a good week to go on leave.'

Gilmore smiled too. 'I don't think we'll be having an early night tonight somehow, gentlemen,' he said.

Logan glanced at the clock. 'I'd offer you a drink, sir,' he said, 'but I'm expecting the Home Secretary at any moment, and in the circumstances it might seem a trifle impolitic.'

'Yes, of course. Peter Frobisher not arrived yet?'

'Not yet, sir. He was at a CID dinner at the Novotel in Hammersmith.'

The Commissioner laughed. 'Pity I didn't think of that; I passed it on the way.'

Logan thought it unwise to tell Gilmore that the Assistant Commissioner was going to get to the Yard as soon as he could, but, as Frobisher had succinctly put it: 'If the bloody woman's dead, there's no rush'; consequently he had taken his wife home in his official car first before making his way back into Central London.

'What's the background to this business, Donald?' asked the Commissioner.

'In brief, sir, the Home Secretary tried to telephone his wife from the House at around six-thirty, I think it was, but got no reply. Apparently she should have been at home. He tried again, twice from his club, and then again from the House at about nine-thirty or so, but still got no reply. He expressed his concern to Detective Sergeant Selway, his protection officer, who arranged for the DPG to check. The rest I told you on the phone, sir.'

The Commissioner nodded. 'If I remember correctly, you had quite a fight to get him to have a protection officer, didn't you?'

'Yes. But we couldn't persuade him to have a man on the door. It's beginning to look like a case of "I told you so".'

DI Wisley appeared in the doorway. 'The Home Secretary, sir.'

Although Dudley Lavery was in his mid-fifties, he still retained his youthful looks, helped by a full head of dark hair, with only a trace of grey, and a loose lock that fell persistently across his forehead. He looked around at the small assembly and smiled the ready smile that had captivated hundreds of women voters. His left hand was in his jacket pocket and he seemed to be leaning forward slightly, an illusion that gave him an air of purpose. 'James,' he said, pushing out a hand in the Commissioner's direction. 'An august gathering, if I may say so. This must be something terribly serious.'

'I think you know Donald Logan, the head of my Special Branch,' said Gilmore, 'and probably Frank Hussey and Mr Winter too?'

'Indeed, indeed,' murmured Lavery. He beamed at Logan. 'A most enjoyable luncheon, I recall.'

'The Home Secretary was a guest at our senior officers' luncheon club a month or two back, sir,' said Logan to the Commissioner, and turning to Lavery, said: 'Do sit down, sir.'

'If you'll excuse us, sir,' said Commander Hussey, 'Mr Winter and I have things to do.' They hadn't – at least not immediately – but Logan and the Commissioner had decided that they didn't want a crowd when they broke the news to Lavery of his wife's death.

'I'm afraid we have some bad news for you concerning your wife, sir,' said the Commissioner without preamble. A lifetime of policing had taught him that there was never much profit in skirting round the subject of bad news and he had had time to reflect that it was something like thirty-five years since he had delivered his first death message, as a very

11

young constable in Paddington. 'I'm sorry to have to tell you that she was found dead at your house earlier this evening.'

Slowly the Home Secretary's smile ebbed from his face, and he stared at the Commissioner, transfixed and unbelieving. There was a silence in the room, as though activity everywhere had been suspended. Slowly, Lavery leaned forward, supporting his head in his hands, staring at Logan's plain green carpet. After some time he looked up. 'Good God!' he said. 'But how – I mean, was it a heart attack, or did she fall . . . ? What in hell's name happened?'

'It would appear,' said Gilmore in measured tones, 'that she was murdered.'

'Murdered . . . ?' Lavery repeated the word in a whisper, and slowly shook his head. 'But what . . . how . . . who would do such a thing?'

'A preliminary examination of the scene' – the Commissioner struggled on pedantically – 'indicates that she was strangled by an intruder.' He paused, wondering, as he always did, why there was no easy way of telling the bereaved that their loved ones had met a violent death, and realising, yet again, that there never could be an easy way. 'Although I have to say,' he continued, 'that there was no sign of a forced entry.' He glanced at Logan for confirmation; the DAC nodded.

Lavery looked up sharply. 'What d'you mean by that?'

'In our experience,' said Gilmore, 'it could mean that the killer was known to your wife, or, conversely, she opened the door to a complete stranger . . . .'

'She would never have done that. Good God, I've told her never to do that.' He looked at Logan. 'Your people have told her that: Tony Lisle gave her a long lecture when I was appointed.'

'I must emphasise though,' continued Gilmore, 'that those are only our first thoughts. We may be wrong.'

Lavery stood up suddenly. 'I must go there,' he said.

'I don't think that that would be a very good idea, Home Secretary. The Anti-Terrorist people are there at the moment, examining the scene. There are forensic scientists, fingerprint people, and photographers. And of course they are waiting for the pathologist to arrive.' Gilmore glanced at his watch. 'In fact, she should be there now.'

Lavery looked up wearily. 'Who is it?'

'Pamela Hatcher. She's very good.'

The Home Secretary nodded. 'Yes,' he said. 'I know of her work.'

'I should sit down, sir,' said the Commissioner. 'There's nothing you could do if you went there.'

'Except get in everybody's way, James, that's what you're really saying, isn't it?' He smiled.

'In the nicest possible way – yes.' Gilmore glanced at Logan before looking at Lavery again. 'I have reason to believe, Home Secretary, that Donald has some very good brandy in his cupboard. I think we might be able to persuade him . . . '

Logan crossed the room to his cocktail cabinet and poured three stiff measures of Courvoisier XO.

'Thank you, that's most kind,' said Lavery, gently swirling the brandy in his glass. 'Well, James, what happens now?' The winsome television smile crept slowly back to his face.

'I have ordered the Anti-Terrorist Branch to take charge of the inquiry, sir, and they—'

'D'you think it's a terrorist matter then?' asked Lavery sharply. Gilmore's first mention of SO13 Branch obviously hadn't registered.

The Commissioner gestured briefly with his free hand. 'We have no idea, at least not at this stage.'

Lavery took a mouthful of brandy and rested the glass on the arm of his chair, steadying it with his hand. He gazed at it briefly as the politician in him reasserted itself. 'I'm not very keen on that, James.'

'But, sir—'

'I would much prefer it if Special Branch were to conduct the investigation. I know them and they know me.' He glanced at Logan before speaking again. 'The political ramifications could be enormous. I have to accept, of course, that there is no way that this will remain out of the media, but there will be some delicate enquiries, and . . . well, Special Branch are political people, aren't they? Discreet, and they understand the political scene.'

'They are not accustomed to investigating murders, Home Secretary,' said Logan. The last thing he wanted was to be stuck with an inquiry into the death of Lavery's wife, one that could be protracted, or worse, insoluble.

Lavery dismissed the DAC's excuse with a wave of the hand. 'You undersell your Branch, Mr Logan. In my experience, they are very accomplished detectives. You wouldn't argue with that, surely?'

'Of course not, but my detectives are specialists in a very specialised field.' He was about to add that they were also very busy, but realised in time that it would be impolitic to imply that the murder of Lavery's wife did not have a very high priority.

Lavery sighed. 'I appreciate, James, that as police authority I must not interfere with matters of operational policing,' he said to the Commissioner. 'Even if it is my wife who is the subject of your inquiries,' he added.

Gilmore capitulated. Lavery had just said what he had been thinking, and wondering how to put into words. As usual, the acumen of the politician had defeated the staidness of the administrator. Lavery was absolutely right, of course, but it would not be clever for a Commissioner to make an enemy of a Home Secretary, particularly over what, to the politician, seemed a comparatively unimportant point of police procedure. Gilmore gave in gracefully: 'Very well, if that is what you wish, Home Secretary, I shall arrange for Donald to assign one of his senior detectives to the case.'

'Thank you, James, I am most appreciative.' He glanced at the clock. 'And now I must go.'

'Where, Home Secretary? Where do you propose going?'

Lavery pondered on the question. 'Well, my club, I suppose.'

Gilmore pursed his lips. 'Have you nowhere else you could go?' Lavery raised his eyebrows. 'I was thinking that it might be prudent to have you under guard,' continued the

Commissioner. 'Under closer guard than you have permitted us to provide hitherto.' The comment was barbed, but Gilmore was sufficient of a tactician to realise that sooner or later someone was going to ask what the police had been doing if the Home Secretary's wife could be murdered in her own home while her husband was occupied with affairs of state. Already he could visualise the editorials with their 'What hope for the rest of us' themes, and wanted to remind Lavery that it was he who had categorically refused to have a policeman stationed outside his door at Cutler's Mews. It was not the first time that Gilmore – nor indeed Logan – had had to deal with such naïvety among Cabinet Ministers who could not understand that their lives might be in danger simply because of the office they held, but it was the first time that it had had such dire consequences.

Lavery raised his hand. 'Point taken, James, but do you seriously think that someone was hoping to kill me and killed Elizabeth instead?'

Gilmore shrugged. 'I don't know, Home Secretary, but I have no intention of risking it.'

'All right, then. I have a friend – we were in chambers together – who I'm sure would put me up for a day or two, at least until I can get back into Cutler's Mews. I shall be in the country at the weekend anyway. I wonder if I might use your telephone?'

'Of course.' Logan stood up and the Commissioner made to move.

Lavery waved them down. 'There's no need to go,' he said, and walked towards Logan's huge desk. 'I dial nine for an outside line, I presume,' he said, taking out his pocket book.

'It's a little more complicated than that,' said Logan. 'What's the number? I'll get it for you.'

# Chapter Two

Detective Chief Superintendent John Gaffney drove from his Richmond flat in his own car. It took him about twenty-five minutes to reach Scotland Yard, and after a brief and acrimonious exchange with a security guard who disputed his right to leave his car in the underground car park – an exchange in which the security guard came second – he made his way to the eighteenth floor.

'Mr Gaffney,' said the Commissioner, 'I have agreed, somewhat reluctantly I may say, to have this matter investigated by Special Branch.' Gaffney nodded. 'But that is purely cosmetic. It will really be an SO13 inquiry in the sense that you will use all their resources, and incidentally, as many more as you need. I don't have to say that this matter has to be resolved and resolved quickly. I'm sure you understand that?'

'Yes, I do, sir.' Gaffney realised only too well that if it went wrong he would get the blame, but if it turned out successfully, the Anti-Terrorist Branch would get the credit. 'Where is the Home Secretary now, sir?'

'Staying with a friend of his, another barrister. But you needn't worry about him: the place is surrounded by police.'

'I'm not worried about him, sir,' said Gaffney, 'but I shall need to interview him.'

'Oh? What for?'

This Commissioner had never been a detective and at times it showed. Gaffney shot a glance at his DAC, standing behind Gilmore, but Logan's face remained impassive. 'Well, sir, the assumption seems to have been made that this is a terrorist killing, but from what little I've heard there is nothing to support that theory so far.'

16

'Mmm!' The Commissioner fingered his moustache. 'Yes, well, go carefully, Gaffney. It is the Home Secretary you're dealing with.'

'Yes, sir,' said Gaffney patiently, 'I know.' He was mildly amused by the awe in which Cabinet Ministers were held by certain senior officers, the more so as politicians seemed on the whole to have little regard for them in return. Gaffney had spent the three years prior to his promotion guarding the Prime Minister, and had come to the conclusion that it was connected with the Honours Lists: who got awards and who didn't. At the top of this scale were the chief constables wanting knighthoods: Gaffney called it the 'K' factor.

Cutler's Mews resembled a police reunion. There were four police cars in the narrow cobbled alleyway, and two or three white vans, at least some of which had the justification of belonging to the technicians involved in the inquiry. There were uniformed policemen standing about chatting, and the front door of Number Seven was wide open, releasing a shaft of light on to the DPG vehicle that had been first on the scene...and was still there. On the doorstep were the local Divisional Chief Superintendent and a chief inspector in uniform clutching a clipboard.

'Hallo, John,' said the Chief Superintendent. 'Nice to see the Branch here eventually.'

'I have been getting my instructions from the Commissioner,' said Gaffney drily, 'who, incidentally, is about five minutes behind me. Almost his last words' – Gaffney broke off to look around at the widespread police presence – 'emphasised the need for discretion.' Engines were starting even before he reached the sitting room.

Dick Campbell, the Commander of SO13, the Anti-Terrorist Branch, levered himself out of an armchair as Gaffney entered the room. 'Hallo, John, good to see you. I've just been talking to the Commissioner on the phone. He told me – in very guarded language – that you've caught this one.' He laughed.

'Yes, sir,' said Gaffney, 'but you don't have to look so pleased about it.'

Campbell laughed. 'Oh, but I am, John, I am.' He became serious again. 'It's going to be a bastard; I've got that feeling in my bones. Frankly, John, I don't think that this is a terrorist job; it just hasn't got the feel about it. I've never known manual strangulation to be the terrorist's MO – not in circumstances like this.' He shrugged and thrust his hands into his trouser pockets. 'Needless to say, anything I can do to help, just say the word. You've got all the technical you need; keep it for as long as you want it. Pamela Hatcher's upstairs, taking temperatures and all that sort of thing. You'd better have a look at the body before it's shifted.'

Campbell led the way upstairs and into the main bedroom, now illuminated by floodlamps. On the floor, near the body, a brown-haired woman sat cross-legged. She wore jeans and a baggy sweater, and appeared oblivious to everyone else in the room, as she peered through her gold-rimmed spectacles at the clip-board on which she was making notes.

'Pamela, this is John Gaffney from Special Branch.'

'Oh, hallo.' The pathologist got nimbly to her feet, and, after juggling with her clip-board, stuck a hand awkwardly in Gaffney's direction. 'I'm just about finished here.'

Gaffney shook hands with her. He reckoned she was about forty-seven or forty-eight years old, older than he had expected, although, with the reputation she had acquired in the field of forensic medicine, she could hardly have been younger.

'John is the officer in the case,' said Campbell.

'Oh?' She took off her glasses and dropped them into her handbag, then she lifted her single pigtail away from her sweater and let it fall again. 'Unusual – Special Branch investigating murders, isn't it? Still, I suppose it makes a difference, being Lavery's wife.'

Gaffney smiled. 'To us, it seems it does,' he said. 'But not to you, of course.'

Pamela Hatcher laughed. 'Can't do really, can it? A corpse is a corpse, whoever it is. What can I tell you?'

18

'How, and how long? That'll do for a start.'

'The first one's easy – well easier. I'm almost sure it's manual strangulation. Look here.' Gaffney smiled at the assumption that everyone else had made, but he knew that pathologists needed more proof than what appeared, at first sight, to be the cause of death. Pamela Hatcher bent down and pointed with her pencil at the marks on the neck. There were four round bruises, each about half an inch across, evenly spaced on the left of the throat, while on the other side, under the jaw, was one larger impression, along with some contusions and scratches. 'Single-handed, by a right-handed assailant, almost certainly.' She stood up. 'Of course all of that is subject to the results of the post-mortem. As for how long –' She paused to tap her teeth with her pencil. 'Well, that's a bit more imprecise, as you know, but given that it's strangulation, that the heating's on and there are no windows open, probably between six this evening and ten o'clock. Sorry I can't do better than that.'

Gaffney smiled. 'That'll have to do,' he said. In common with all detectives, he was always mildly irritated by the occasional television pathologist who, after thirty seconds' examination, would stand up and give an exact time of death. 'Is that how the body was?' Gaffney gestured at the corpse.

'No. I had to turn it to get temperature readings, but your chaps got photographs before I started.' She began to put her things away in her case. 'Where will you take it – Horseferry Road, presumably?'

Campbell nodded. 'Yes, that's our local.' He saw the pathologist to the front door and then returned to the bedroom. 'Not a lot I can do for you now, John,' he said. 'These lads are better at it than we are.' He nodded towards the small group of photographers, fingerprint officers and scenes-of-crime men who were now waiting to get to work. 'If I were you, I'd just take a seat and let them get on with it. I'll see you tomorrow.' He glanced at his watch. 'Or later today, I should say.'

★ ★ ★

It was eight o'clock in the morning – some ten hours since the discovery of the body – before Gaffney was able to declare himself reasonably satisfied with the scientific examination of the Home Secretary's London home. It was gloomy daylight outside, but the slight drizzle did nothing to deter the gaggle of reporters who huddled at the entrance to Cutler's Mews, attracted there by some journalistic sixth sense. The steady hum of rush-hour traffic was a long way away, and there seemed to be a vacuum of silence around Gaffney and his team.

The photographers, having taken shots from every conceivable angle of everything that might be of the slightest value, had departed to start preparing their prints. The fingerprint officers – among the most senior at the Yard – had dusted everything with their powder, and lifted one or two of the more interesting impressions to be taken away and examined at leisure.

Then had come the liaison officers from the Forensic Science Laboratory who had searched for anything which a scientist might be able to connect with the killer: hairs, fibres, dust, urine, excreta, semen, saliva; over the years they had found them all, but on this occasion the only thing to excite their interest was a small deposit of mud on the stairs. They had carefully placed it in a plastic bag for analysis, but one of the detectives was prepared to put money on its having been left there by a policeman rather than by the killer.

It was with a certain amount of misgiving that Gaffney finally authorised the removal of Elizabeth Lavery's body to the Horseferry Road mortuary to await Pamela Hatcher's post-mortem examination later in the day. Then he set his small team of detectives to work.

Skilled at searching scenes of crime, the Anti-Terrorist Branch officers carefully carried out a visual examination of the house. Each room was visited in turn, but there was nothing for them to find. Everything was as it should be: no sign of a struggle; no sign of a forced entry; no sign of a hurried departure.

In the bedroom where Mrs Lavery's body had been found,

one astute searcher on hands and knees found a piece of paper under the bed.

'What's that?' asked Gaffney.

The detective sat back on his haunches and examined his find. 'It's a House of Commons order-paper, sir. A week old!'

'Huh!' Gaffney scoffed. 'His daily isn't very good at her job.'

'It's got a phone number on it, sir.'

'Okay,' said Gaffney wearily, 'stick it in a bag and take it back with you.' He sighed. 'Bloody marvellous, isn't it?' he said, addressing no one in particular. 'A murder, and all I've got is a teaspoonful of mud and a week-old order-paper – which isn't exactly a surprise in an MP's house.'

It was half-past eight. One of the two Special Branch officers whom Gaffney had had sent down to guard the house against sightseers – police as well as public – now appeared in the sitting room. 'Your car's here, sir,' he said.

'You rang, sir?' Detective Chief Inspector Harry Tipper grinned, closed Gaffney's door and, uninvited, dropped into one of the armchairs.

'Sorry about cancelling your leave, Harry.'

'I'm not,' said Tipper. 'I was only decorating. The missus reckons it's a set-up, and that I arranged a recall to get out of it.'

'I wish that's all it was,' said Gaffney. 'Last night, the Home Secretary's wife was found murdered at their London home, Cutler's Mews . . . '

'Yeah, I know. It's in the papers, and it was on the news . . . breakfast television.' Tipper gestured at the pile of daily newspapers that Gaffney had had brought in but had not had time to look at.

Gaffney nodded. 'The Home Secretary tried to ring his wife two or three times during the evening, and got no reply. He was trapped at the House apparently: a three-liner at ten o'clock; so he got Selway to—'

'Who's Selway?' asked Tipper, interrupting.

'DS Selway; he's on protection with the Home Sec.' Tipper

nodded. 'Anyway, he got Selway to try and find out if the phone was duff, or she'd gone out, or what. Selway got the Diplomatic Protection Group to pay a visit. They broke in . . . ' He paused to sift through some copy messages on his desk. 'Inspector Franklin to be precise – he was the DPG duty officer – and he found madam on the bedroom floor, apparently strangled. That's confirmed by the pathologist's preliminary examination. No sign of forcible entry, and a full examination of the scene has produced precisely sod-all in the way of evidence.'

Tipper shook his head slowly. 'There must be something. Any contact between two items and you've got a trace of each left on the other.' He smiled.

So did Gaffney. 'I know all about Locard's principle of exchange,' he said. 'It's finding the bloody things that's the problem. All we have is a trace of mud off the stairs, and a House of Commons order-paper.' He sucked through his teeth. 'Big deal.'

'Any sign of sexual interference?' asked Tipper.

'Pamela Hatcher says no.'

'Anything missing?'

'What are you thinking? Frustrated burglary?'

Tipper nodded. 'Something like that.'

'Not as far as we can tell. I'm going to try getting the Home Secretary round there this morning to have a look, but there was none of the usual signs of a break-in.'

'House-to-house?' Tipper examined his fingernails. He shared the view of many other policemen that house-to-house enquiries were cumbersome, used a lot of manpower and were rarely productive; in short, they were a last resort.

'Got a team out starting about now. Don't hold out much hope though, Harry. I suspect that most of Lavery's neighbours will be out during the day, and it's our luck that the au pairs, domestics and home helps won't have been there at the crucial time.'

'And what was the crucial time, guv'nor?'

'Pamela Hatcher puts it between six in the evening and ten o'clock last night.'

22

'And what time did the Home Secretary make his first call to his wife – the first one she didn't answer, that is?'

'Don't know, Harry. I haven't been able to see him yet, but that's one of several points to be cleared up.'

Tipper looked blankly out of the window. 'I thought I'd finished with murders when I got transferred to the rarefied atmosphere of Special Branch,' he said. 'Oh well!' He grinned and turned to face Gaffney. 'Here we go again. What have we got, sir?'

'Dudley Lavery's been Home Secretary since the last election. He's fifty-four according to *Who's Who*, and his wife, the late Elizabeth Lavery, was twenty years his junior. She was an actress by all accounts, and it was her first marriage: his second. Beyond that, we do not know a lot.'

'Twenty years younger...' Tipper looked thoughtful, but said nothing further. 'Any claims? Terrorists – anything of that sort?'

'No, not so far. I don't doubt that we'll have the usual run of duff stuff within the next few hours.'

'You say duff...' Gaffney nodded. 'But could it be a terrorist attack?' asked Tipper.

'It doesn't look like one – in my experience they use the bomb, the bullet, or, less frequently, the blade – but anything's possible. I've got a couple of lads beavering away in Records, just to see what there is there.'

'Right. What d'you want me to do then, sir?'

'Come with me to see the Home Secretary, Harry.'

'Aren't you going to get your head down, at least for a few hours?'

'No!' Gaffney laughed scornfully. 'Keep going for a bit yet; at least until we can see where we're going.'

Tipper laughed. 'Some hope of that. I've got a suspicion that this inquiry's going to be a bit like marking time in marshmallow.'

Dudley Lavery was a politician who believed that the show must go on; consequently Gaffney and Tipper had only to make the short walk through St James's Park Underground

23

station to Queen Anne's Gate in order to interview him.

'I am sorry to have to trouble you, sir,' said Gaffney when the two detectives were shown into Lavery's large office overlooking Petty France, 'but there are one or two questions I have to ask.'

Lavery led them towards the group of armchairs that occupied one corner of his office. 'Of course, of course,' he murmured. 'I quite understand; you have your job to do. I only hope that you're successful in bringing this fellow to book.' He looked wistfully across the room as he sat down facing Gaffney. 'Not that it'll bring my wife back, of course, but it may save some other poor woman.' He seemed already to have convinced himself that his wife had fallen victim to some itinerant strangler. He glanced at Tipper, appearing to notice him for the first time. 'Er – I don't think . . . '

'No, I'm sorry, sir. This is DCI Tipper; he'll be assisting me in this inquiry.'

'Good, good. Special Branch, of course?'

'Yes, sir,' said Tipper. He didn't think it necessary to tell Lavery he was a recent transfer and had spent the major part of his service investigating murder and other sordid crimes.

Lavery glanced at his watch. 'What can I do to assist you, Mr Gaffney?'

'Perhaps you can tell me about yesterday evening. I understand from Selway that you rang your wife several times.'

'Yes, that's so.'

'Why?'

'I'm sorry . . . ?' The Home Secretary looked vaguely mystified by Gaffney's question.

'I asked why you were ringing her, sir.' He gazed at Lavery, his face devoid of expression.

'Well I just wanted to make sure she was all right. I do get a bit concerned when she's in the house on her own, you know.'

'And yet you refused to have a police officer on duty there.'

Lavery leaned back with the sort of expansive expression he usually reserved for fatuous questions in the House. 'That's a different matter. It is in fact a pointless exercise, having a policeman standing on the front doorstep of a house like mine. There's a rear entrance, and windows on the back as well. You'd need a small regiment to protect it properly. Anyway, there's an alarm system—'

'Which wasn't set,' said Gaffney quietly.

'Wasn't set, but surely . . . ?'

Gaffney shook his head. 'It wasn't set.'

'But I thought it must have malfunctioned.' Lavery looked surprised. 'Elizabeth would never—'

'Would never have what, sir?'

'I've told her over and over again that she must keep the alarm set all the time, whether she's in or out. And what about the panic buttons? There's one in the bedroom.'

'I know, sir, but we have a detective inspector who does nothing else but technical protection – you've met him, I believe' – Lavery nodded – 'and he spent a couple of hours going over your system early this morning. The alarm was definitely not set, and the panic buttons had not been activated – not a single one of them.'

Lavery glanced at each of the detectives in turn. 'But what does that mean?'

'On the face of it, sir, it would appear that your wife knew who killed her, or admitted a total stranger to the house having first turned off the alarm, or having failed to set it. And at no time did she press a panic button.'

Lavery gently and silently clapped his hands together two or three times before bringing them to his lips in an attitude of supplication. 'I just don't understand; I don't understand at all.'

'Do you know of anyone who was a regular visitor to your house, or for that matter, who could have called without causing a surprise?'

'Well yes. There are two or three, maybe even more.'

'Such as?'

'Well there's my House of Commons secretary. She often pops in to collect mail – that sort of thing – and she helps out with Elizabeth's mail, too; the political stuff emanating from the constituency. You know the sort of thing: opening

25

fêtes, judging baby contests, all the sort of rubbish that seems inextricably linked to governing the country.' A brief smile of cynicism crossed his face. 'Then there's Edna. She's the daily help; comes in every morning about eight to do the housework . . . '

'Yes,' said Gaffney, 'we met her this morning. Had to send her away, I'm afraid.'

'Mmm, that won't have pleased her. Did you tell her why, incidentally?'

'She knew. Anyway, there was no point in not doing so; we're going to have to talk to her at some time or other.'

'Why?' Lavery looked up suddenly.

'I don't know, sir,' said Gaffney blandly, 'but with any inquiry you have to keep asking questions until you get the right answers.'

'Oh!' Lavery did not appear too impressed by that basic tenet of criminal investigation.

'Anyone else who might come and go?'

'Only your chaps.' Lavery was talking about the three Special Branch Officers, led by DCI Tony Lisle, whose task it was to guard the Home Secretary. Ironically they had no brief to guard his wife.

'How many of these people had keys to your house, sir?'

'Mary Diver – she's my House of Commons secretary that I mentioned – and Edna; oh, and of course, your chaps. I thought it was a good idea for them to have a key each.'

'And none of them has reported the loss of keys?'

'Not as far as I know. It's possible, I suppose.'

'Perhaps we can get back to yesterday afternoon, sir.' Gaffney glanced across at Tipper, busily making notes in his pocket book.

'Yes, of course,' murmured the Home Secretary.

'Do you recall the first time you telephoned your wife?'

Lavery reflected for a few moments. 'I suppose it must have been about half-past six, or thereabouts; I can't be absolutely certain.'

'And where did you phone from? The House presumably.'

'Yes.'

'And you rang again at intervals?'

'Yes, I did. A couple of times from my club, and then again from the House. Four times in all . . . ' He paused. 'Yes, four times would seem about right.'

'You mentioned your club.' Lavery nodded. 'You went to your club during the evening, then?'

'Yes, I did. That would have been at about seven o'clock, I suppose; perhaps a little later.' He smiled at Gaffney. 'I should think you'd do better asking John Selway. Don't your chaps have to write down all these times for their diaries or their expenses, or whatever? John told me all about it one day; I think he was trying to enlist my aid to get it stopped.'

'I dare say,' said Gaffney. It was a constant irritation to CID officers of chief inspector rank and below to have to keep a minute-by-minute account of their working day, and they were cynically unimpressed to be told by officialdom that it was for their own protection. 'May I ask why you went to your club?'

'To get a bite to eat – a decent bite to eat – and to do a bit of reading in quiet and uninterrupted surroundings.' Gaffney looked questioning. 'I'm trying to read through the new Prisons Bill,' continued Lavery, 'and it's so radical, so controversial, that we've got to get it right. In the House there's always some crisis, some back-bencher with some moan, that breaks into what you're doing. In the club it's peaceful, and I can sit down and get through something like that in half the time.'

'And so you telephoned your home twice from the club?'

'Yes, exactly so. Once before dinner and once after.'

'What time did you return to the House?'

'At about a quarter to ten, I suppose; in time for the ten o'clock division, anyway.'

'And in time to make one more call to your wife?'

'Yes.'

'If I can just go quickly through that again, sir,' said Gaffney. 'You telephoned your home four times during the course of the evening. The first call was made at about six-thirty from the House of Commons; then you went to

27

your club for dinner at about seven, made two more calls from there, and then another from the House just before the ten o'clock division.'

'That sounds about right.'

'But it was not until then that you got Selway to find out if there was anything wrong?'

'Yes.'

'Why not sooner, sir? You waited about three and a half hours after the first call before asking police to look into the matter.'

'It sounds deliberate when you put it like that, Mr Gaffney, but it wasn't really until I got to the House for the division that it dawned on me how long she'd been out – or not answering – when she was supposed to be at home—'

'Then why—?'

'But by ten o'clock I was getting a bit concerned.' Lavery spoke as though Gaffney hadn't interrupted.

'You were certain that your wife should have been at home?'

Lavery smiled benignly. 'As sure as one can ever be of one's wife,' he said. 'She may have gone out somewhere – that's what I thought. You never can tell. I imagined that she might have gone to the theatre – on a whim, you know – or maybe popped in to see one of her acting friends . . . ' He spread his hands, the honest politician turning away the wrath of the aggressive interviewer, much as he would do on television.

'Did she do that sort of thing often?' Gaffney didn't know why he'd asked that question; it wasn't relevant.

'Occasionally, yes, but she would normally leave a message with Mary, or with Charles Stanhope. He's my private secretary here at the Home Office,' he added, forestalling Gaffney's next question. 'It was he who showed you in when you arrived.'

'There is one other thing,' said Gaffney, changing tack once more. Lavery raised his eyebrows enquiringly. 'I should like you to check over the house to see if anything has been stolen.'

'You think this may have been a burglary then?'

28

'I really don't know at this stage,' said Gaffney. 'I don't want to put you to any great trouble, but I need either to pursue that theory, or eliminate it.'

'Quite so. Would, say, five o'clock do?' He walked to the door of his office and opened it wide. 'Charles, I've got nothing marked in for five o'clock, have I?'

'No, Home Secretary,' said a distant voice.

'I'll meet you at the house then – Cutler's Mews, that is.' He smiled. 'I presume you want to be there, Mr Gaffney?'

Gaffney nodded. 'Five o'clock, sir.'

# Chapter Three

The two detectives strolled back to Scotland Yard, deciding against lunch in one of the several nearby pubs, mainly because Fleet Street's finest were almost bound to be lying in wait, and it wouldn't look good for the man investigating the untimely death of the Home Secretary's wife to be seen drinking during the lunch-hour. Instead they bought sandwiches and cartons of soup and took them back to the office. The drizzle had now turned to sleet.

The head of the Yard's Press Bureau was talking to Detective Sergeant Claire Wentworth when Gaffney and Tipper entered the incident room. 'Ah, John,' he said, 'just the man I want to see.' He pushed his glasses back up to the bridge of his nose, something he did on average about once a minute. 'What the hell am I to tell these fellows?'

'There's nothing you can tell them,' said Gaffney, 'other than what they know already. Mrs Lavery was found dead at her home in Cutler's Mews at about ten o'clock last night. Enquiries are continuing.'

'Yeah, but they want to know what happened. How was she killed; was it a burglary; you know the sort of thing, John?'

'Oh yes, I know the sort of thing, but I'm not prepared to release that sort of information. If we tell them she was strangled, we'll have every nut in the world ringing up to confess that he did it. We've had a few already, claiming to have murdered her with anything between a tomahawk and a harpoon gun. No, I'm sorry, but that's all they're getting for the moment.'

The Press Bureau chief nodded. 'Okay, John, I'll do my best to keep them at bay.' He paused at the door. 'If you can spare a couple of minutes this afternoon, just to have a few words with them down in Press Bureau, I'd be grateful.'

'I bet you would.' Gaffney laughed. 'I'll see what I can do, but I'm making no promises.' Dismissing the Press from his mind, at least temporarily, he turned to Claire Wentworth. 'What have you got?'

He had entrusted Claire Wentworth with the onerous task of being office manager for the whole inquiry, and, looking round the incident room, it appeared that she had organised herself very rapidly. Extra telephones had been installed; filing cabinets of varying shapes and sizes acquired, and a huge whiteboard which had not been there yesterday already had messages scrawled on it. Her cool and unruffled glance of appraisal took in the orderly files of messages, the growing stack of statements, and finally the computer terminal: essential parts of any major investigation. 'There is one file, sir, which could be of interest.' She turned to the safe and spun the wheel of the combination lock. 'This is it. . . . ' She handed Gaffney a pink folder. 'Oh, there's one other thing, sir . . . ' She turned in her chair. 'Tom, that message about the mud . . . ' She held out a hand. A detective handed over a flimsy without comment, and she scanned it briefly. 'Yeah, that's the one.' She looked up at Gaffney enquiringly. 'Mud on the stairs matches the mud in the mews. That make sense, sir?'

Gaffney shrugged. 'Had to be really. I can see how this inquiry's beginning to shape up already.' He paused at the door. 'Put in an action, Claire, to check who had keys to the Home Secretary's house and whether anyone has lost them. Mr Lisle will be able to help you with that.'

Gaffney sat down behind his desk, stifled a yawn and took out a packet of cigars. For a few moments he read the file which Claire Wentworth had given him. Then he yawned again and stretched his arms above his head. 'Well, that's a start, I suppose.' He closed the file and pushed it in Tipper's direction.

With the skilled eye of the experienced detective, Tipper

31

skimmed through it, absorbing the essentials and skipping the unnecessary, before replacing it on the desk and looking up. 'What d'you reckon, guv'nor? Is this Drake bloke the usual nut-case, or is there something in it?' He tapped the file with his forefinger.

Gaffney shrugged. 'Bit of both probably, Harry. There's no doubt that his wife was arrested, and there's no doubt that she died in prison, on remand. I suppose that's enough to turn anyone's brain, but whether they're just empty threats, or whether he meant it, is something we're going to have to find out.'

'Who's this sergeant who interviewed him?' asked Tipper, 'and put the official frighteners on him, according to that . . . ?' He pointed at the file. 'Might be as well to have a chat with him first, before we go sailing in there.'

'He can go and see him again, at least before we waste our time.' Gaffney drew the file towards him and flicked it open. 'Jenkins . . . ' He looked thoughtful. 'I've got a niggling suspicion at the back of my mind . . . ' He pressed the switch on the intercom. 'Claire, find DS Jenkins if you can.'

Ten minutes later Claire Wentworth appeared in the doorway. 'DS Jenkins, sir,' she said, 'is on protection duty with the Foreign Secretary . . . '

'And?'

'And he's in Tokyo. From there he goes to Kuala Lumpur and then on to Singapore. Due back Tuesday week.' She smiled sweetly and closed the door behind her.

'She's got a lovely arse, that girl,' said Tipper distantly, and then, turning to Gaffney with a grin, added: 'I've come to the conclusion that today's not your day, sir.'

The houses in Sofia Road, Streatham, had all been built in the far-off days of the 1930s, when the threat of war was just a disconcerting blemish on the horizon, and property like Number Seventeen was being offered – if the advertisements were anything to go by – to clean-cut, smiling young families for a moderate deposit and reasonable monthly repayments. The reality was, in all probability, very different, but even so, it was fairly certain that the families of fifty years or more ago, would not have recognised the Sofia Road of today. Not an inch of kerb space was free of cars, most of which were at least ten years old, some much older, and the ethnic origins of the majority of the residents had little in common with those who had moved into the houses when they were new.

'Yes?' A shining black face, utterly devoid of expression, peered at Detective Sergeant Mackinnon round a door that had been opened a mere six inches, and immediately recognised him as a representative of white man's law.

'Mr Drake live here?'

'Upstairs.' The woman turned and walked away, leaving the front door ajar.

Mackinnon and Detective Constable Paul Bishop made their way up the uncarpeted staircase to the first floor. The first door they came to had half a postcard pinned to the middle of it. It bore the single name 'Drake'.

Mackinnon rapped on the wooden panel; there was no reply. He tried the handle and found that the door was unlocked. 'Hallo!' he said. 'Anyone there?' There was still no reply, and they moved slowly into the room, looking cautiously around; this was, after all, the residence of a man who had made written threats to murder the Home Secretary.

Mackinnon looked round the room, at the threadbare carpet, the dirty curtains against dirty windows, and at the settee and the armchairs that were worn and probably flea-ridden. On the far side of the room, there was a half-open door from which most of the paint had long since peeled; Mackinnon pushed it gently and peered in. It was the kitchen, littered with dirty crockery and greasy pans on every available surface, which included a board over the bath. 'Give me a hand with this, Bish,' said Mackinnon.

'What are you going to do, skip?'

'Have a look under it. We'd look a bit bloody silly if his body was eventually found in there, wouldn't we?'

Together they lifted the board and looked beneath it, but it was empty. The two detectives retreated to the sitting room.

33

'Christ!' said Mackinnon. 'What a bloody stench.' He waved a hand in front of his face.

'Is that it, then?' Bishop stood in the centre of the room, hands on hips, surveying an unmade divan in the corner.

'I reckon so, but where the hell's Drake?'

'He's certainly not here. Perhaps he's done a runner.'

'We'd better start with the friendly lady who let us in.' Mackinnon shrugged and made for the door.

The woman appeared in the doorway of her room, two children clinging to her skirts and staring up at the policemen with great wide white eyes and open mouths. 'Yes?' she asked flatly.

'We're police officers,' said Mackinnon. She nodded; she had known that. 'We're looking for Mr Drake. D'you know where he is?'

'No!'

And you wouldn't tell us if you did, thought Mackinnon. 'When did you last see him, then?'

The woman appeared to give the question some thought. 'I don't know,' she said. 'A week, maybe two.' She shrugged again and started to close the door.

'Thanks for your help,' said Mackinnon as the door was shut firmly in his face. 'I'll get the Commissioner to send you one of his special letters of commendation for your valuable assistance.'

'What now, skip?' asked Bishop.

'We try all those other doors, mate, and see if anyone has any idea where he might be. Then we take his room apart, bit by bit.'

'Don't we need a warrant for that?'

'Yes.' Mackinnon banged on another door.

The face of an Indian peered furtively out at the detectives. He proved to be the only other occupant of the house in residence at the time. 'Yes?'

'Police,' said Mackinnon in a tired voice. 'We're looking for Mr Drake.'

'Not here. Across there.' The Indian pointed to the door of Drake's room.

'Yes, I know.' Mackinnon nodded wearily. 'He's not there.'

'Ah! Gone out perhaps.'

'When did you last see him?' There were times when Mackinnon wondered how he put up with the monotony of a detective's job.

'Yesterday morning.' The Indian paused. 'I think . . . ' Then he nodded. 'That's right. It was yesterday morning.'

'What was he doing? Going to work?'

'Oh no. Captain Drake does not work—'

'*Captain* Drake?'

'Yes. He is Captain Drake.'

'What's he a captain of?' asked Mackinnon.

'I don't know, but he's always called "the captain".'

Bishop touched Mackinnon's elbow. 'It's all right,' he whispered. 'It's on the file. He was an army officer; got the boot for dipping into the mess funds.'

Mackinnon laughed and turned back to the Indian. 'He doesn't work, you say?'

'UB40 business – unemployed.' The Indian raised his eyes to the ceiling.

'What was he doing – yesterday morning – when you saw him?'

'Going out. He had his overcoat on.'

'Did he speak?'

'He just said "Good morning".'

Mackinnon slipped a photograph out of his pocket and showed it to the Indian, but said nothing.

'That's him,' said the man, 'but he's older. That must have been taken a long time ago.'

Mackinnon turned the print over and looked at the date on the back. 'Ten years ago,' he said, 'but at least you recognised him.' It meant that others might recognise him from the only photograph the police had, if they had to start searching for him. Mackinnon had an open mind; it was just possible that a man who had several times threatened to kill the Home Secretary might have killed his wife instead.

'Thanks,' said Mackinnon. 'Come on Bish, let's go and have a poke about in his room.'

'What about the warrant?'

Mackinnon pushed the door of Drake's room open. 'I'm the Sergeant,' he said, as he walked in. 'If it all goes pear-shaped, it's down to me. Anyway, who ever heard of a warrant to do Drake's drum?' He laughed at his own joke, but Bishop couldn't see the funny side of it.

They spent a desultory half-hour examining Drake's meagre belongings without furthering their knowledge of the man or his whereabouts.

'You've read the file, Bish. What's it all about?' Mackinnon made no excuses for not having researched what he saw as a mundane job. Hundreds of people wrote threatening letters to the Queen, the Prime Minister and the Cabinet, and to members of both Houses of Parliament. Most of those letters finished up in Special Branch where they were filed. Occasionally the more persistent writers would be seen and warned, but for the most part there was no real harm in any of them. In most cases the spidery handwriting extended the full width of the paper, leaving no margins and in the experience of the police this was usually indicative of some mental instability. Often the rambling narratives rehearsed some real or imagined grievance, or claimed some kinship, legitimate or otherwise, with the Royal Family, and were for the most part incomprehensible. But once in a while, the writer would enclose a bullet, or make a half-hearted attempt at constructing a letter-bomb; then the police would act with great urgency, as they would with cases like Drake who had simply written, about three times a week, 'You killed my wife – I will kill you.' He had signed the letters and put his full address at the top. Consequently he was seen and warned. For a while they stopped, but recently they had begun again, albeit from a different address – Sofia Road – and Mackinnon had supposed that, in Drake's view, that made it all right; gave him a fresh start, so to speak. Now with the murder of the Home Secretary's wife, Drake became of sudden interest. Perhaps he had decided to exact an eye for an eye . . . or a wife for a wife.

'Drake's wife killed their ten-year-old son. It was a mercy

killing really; he was suffering from some incurable wasting disease. One night she couldn't take any more and smothered him with a pillow. The doctor called the police simply because Mrs Drake told him what she'd done.'

'What happened to her?' Mackinnon was opening and closing drawers in a varnished chest. 'Broadmoor?'

'Didn't get that far. Remanded in custody. Application for bail to High Court judge in chambers, refused. Plea to Home Secretary—'

'Refused, *sub judice*?'

'Didn't get a chance. She hanged herself in Brixton. Drake's twisted mind has blamed Lavery ever since.'

'How long ago was all this, Bish?'

'Three years, skip.'

'But Lavery wasn't Home Secretary then.'

'I know. Does it matter?'

'Not a lot.' Mackinnon removed a large envelope from the drawer he was searching and opened it. 'Hallo . . . and what have we got here?' He emptied the envelope's contents on to the top of the chest of drawers. 'Newspaper cuttings.' He started to sort through them with his forefinger. 'Well, well, well! Would you look at that. This bloke's been doing some research.' The cuttings were about Lavery and dated from his appointment as Home Secretary, but more interesting to the two detectives, were cuttings about Elizabeth Lavery's acting career when she had been known as Elizabeth Fairfax, which clearly Drake had had to obtain from the back-numbers departments of newspaper offices.

'Now what do we do?' asked Bishop.

'Find him,' said Mackinnon, 'with a little help from our friends.'

It was about half a mile to the police station in Streatham High Road, and the station officer, whose single medal riband indicated that he had at least twenty-two years' service, smiled as Mackinnon mentioned Drake. 'Well, well, our friend Captain Drake,' he said. 'And what has he been up to?'

'That's what we're anxious to find out,' said Mackinnon.

The station officer grinned. 'You don't think he's got anything to do with the murder of the Home Secretary's wife, surely?'

'Why should you ask that?' Mackinnon's eyes narrowed.

'Because he's always in here, demanding that we arrest the Home Secretary for murder. He's got some bee in his bonnet about Lavery having been responsible for the death of Mrs Drake. There's no harm in him, though; I reckon his brain's gone after that business with his son and his wife.'

'I wish I had your confidence,' said Mackinnon.

The Sergeant shook his head and made a sucking noise through his teeth. 'I can't see him killing anyone, not old Ernie Drake.'

'Thank you for your expert advice,' said Mackinnon with a sarcasm that was lost on his uniformed colleague, 'but do you have any idea where we might find him? Where does he usually get to?'

'As far as I know, he spends most nights in the Sofia Arms – top of his road – and then goes home to bed. I reckon if you have a word with the landlord up there, he'll put old Drake in the clear. Might save yourself a lot of bother.' He pushed his thumbs under the buttoned flaps of his breast pockets and nodded confidently. He was clearly a man who placed a high priority on saving himself a lot of bother.

# Chapter Four

A coterie of pressmen still waited despairingly at the entrance to Cutler's Mews, their shoulders hunched against the cold, and their inadequate anoraks providing little protection against the biting sleet. They stamped their feet and chain-smoked. They were waiting for the Home Secretary to return to his house because their picture editors wanted it on the front page. But so far there had been no sign of Lavery.

The arrival of Gaffney and Tipper at a quarter to five had caused a flurry of interest which waned immediately the photographers recognised them. Gaffney was unhappy that only one policeman had been stationed at the entrance to the mews, and knew that he would be swept aside in the rush the moment the Home Secretary drove in at five o'clock.

'Get on the phone to the DPG,' said Gaffney to the DC who opened the door of Lavery's house. 'Better still, the local nick. I want two or three PCs down here to prevent that lot running amok.' He indicated the group of miserable photographers. 'If it's left to one PC they'll be all over the house, given half a chance.'

'Wouldn't it be better if I gave Central Command Complex a call, sir, then they could send the nearest unit?'

'And broadcast it to the world in the process,' said Gaffney caustically. 'Get hold of someone at the nick, like the duty officer . . . ' He walked into the sitting room, continuing to issue instructions over his shoulder. 'Tell him to get somebody to report to me here urgently, but don't tell them why. And tell them to use personal radio, not main force, or we'll have the rest of bloody Fleet Street down here.'

Tipper was standing in the centre of the room, his hands in his pockets, and doing what he always did at a murder scene: getting the flavour, he called it. 'The bedroom's immediately over this room, sir, is it?'

'Yes.' Gaffney dropped wearily into one of the armchairs. 'Of course, I was forgetting, you've not been here before, have you? We'll have a look round when the great man's been and gone. And after that, Harry, I'm going home to bed. I'm sure it'll all look much easier tomorrow.'

'Maybe,' said Tipper without enthusiasm. 'But you know what they say, guv'nor: every day further away from a murder, the harder it gets to solve.'

Gaffney snorted. 'A great help you are, Harry,' he said.

Blue light suddenly reflected on the wall opposite where Gaffney was sitting, and he leaped from his chair. 'What the bloody hell . . . ?'

'Looks like the feet have arrived,' said Tipper laconically. 'The feet' was the term he always used to describe the Uniform Branch.

An inspector appeared in the doorway of the sitting room and saluted. 'Mr Gaffney, sir?' He looked enquiringly at the two detectives. 'One territorial support group, sir. That's one inspector, two sergeants and twenty. Where d'you want them, sir?'

'For Christ's sake,' said Gaffney. 'Don't you know there's a bloody war on?'

'War, sir?' The Inspector looked mystified.

'Yes, against crime. I want two or three men to make sure that that bedraggled and pathetic group of pressmen at the entrance to the mews behaves itself, that's all. It's not a bloody riot, unless you're thinking of starting one.' He looked out of the window. The mews was filled with three transit vans, each with its blue light spinning aimlessly. 'It might interest you to know that in about five minutes from now, the Home Secretary will be attempting to get in here, and given that the Metropolitan Police have already allowed his wife to be murdered, he's probably going to look on your little effort as a classic example of closing the stable door after the bloody

40

horse has bolted. So I suggest that you do something about it. Now!'

The Inspector left rapidly, and shortly afterwards the transit vans started reversing into the main road, captured on film by a team of photographers with nothing better to do.

The Home Secretary was late in arriving, by some twenty minutes or so, which was no more than Gaffney had expected. The Press, duly restrained by the four policemen who had been placed at the entrance to the mews by the chastened Inspector, were galvanised into action. They took as many photographs as possible, feverishly wiping their lenses clear of sleet between exposures, except for one unfortunate whose camera was trapped by the unyielding zip-fastener of the anorak beneath which it had been placed for protection against the inclement weather. The foul language which this provoked would, under normal circumstances, have warranted proceedings for the use of obscene language likely to occasion a breach of the peace, but as the speaker was a woman the PC nearest to her decided not to bother; it was what his instructor at the police training school used to call inverted sexism.

Dudley Lavery seemed more strained than when Gaffney had seen him that morning, as though the reality of his wife's death was at last beginning to register.

'I don't wish to detain you any longer than necessary, sir, but I should be grateful if you would look round, just to satisfy yourself – and indeed me – that nothing has been taken.'

Lavery nodded absently, and peered around the sitting room as though in the house of a stranger. He wandered back into the hall and then slowly, like a man labouring up a steep path, made his way upstairs.

At the door of his bedroom he paused, staring round reflectively. He remained like that for some time, and then turned. 'Where exactly?' he asked.

'Just there, sir.' Gaffney pointed to where Elizabeth Lavery's body had been found by Inspector Franklin.

The Home Secretary gazed at the spot for some time,

as if trying to visualise the sight of his dead wife's body. Eventually he looked up with a sigh, like a man who has broken off praying. 'Everything seems to be in order, Mr Gaffney. Perhaps I should just have a look in the dressing table; it was where my wife kept most of her jewellery.' He walked across the room and started to open and close drawers. 'I told her not to; told her to put it all in a safety deposit box, but she wouldn't listen.' He took out a leather jewel case and opened it. He poked around among the pearl necklaces and the ear-rings and the brooches as though searching for something. He tutted. 'Careless,' he said, half to himself. He closed the box and put it back in the drawer; then he shrugged. 'I don't know,' he said. 'I suppose it's all there; I don't really know what she had and didn't have.' He opened another drawer, vaguely moving the contents about, and pulled out an ornate chain. 'I've not seen that before,' he said. It was about thirty inches in length, with a medallion at one end. 'Looks like one of her theatre props.'

'May I have a look, sir?' asked Tipper. He took it from Lavery and turned it over in his hands, examining the medallion. 'I think you're probably right.' He returned it to Lavery who dropped it back into the drawer.

It was a painful process, and it took over an hour, following Lavery from room to room as he reminisced rather than searched, until they found themselves, once more, at the front door. 'I'm pretty sure there's nothing missing, Mr Gaffney.' Lavery appeared to come out of his reverie, ready to face the outside world again.

'Thank you for your assistance, sir.'

'Not at all,' said Lavery. He paused, his hand on the banisters. 'I was thinking about the funeral. When do you suppose that she . . . that the body will be released?'

'It's a matter for the coroner, of course, but—'

'I know that,' Lavery snapped. Then he sighed and shrugged his shoulders. 'I'm sorry, I . . . It does rather depend on when you chaps have no further need of it, doesn't it?' The television smile came into play again.

'Difficult to say at the moment, sir. As soon as possible, is the best I can do.'

Lavery nodded and walked through the doorway, allowing himself to be ushered quickly into the back of his car by Tony Lisle, his protection officer. Within seconds, the car was pulling out of Cutler's Mews, the traffic held up for it by a PC, and illuminated by the sudden floodlights of a television crew which had just arrived; they had missed the early evening news, but were making sure of the later one.

The landlord of the Sofia Arms just nodded when Mackinnon produced his warrant card; he was accustomed to regular visits from the Old Bill in his part of the world. 'Ernie Drake? Yeah, I know Ernie Drake. What's he been up to, poor old bugger?'

'Was he in here last night?'

'No, not last night. Unusual that.' The landlord wiped the section of the bar he was leaning on, and dropped the cloth out of sight. 'What's your pleasure, gents?' He was a firm believer in keeping on the right side of the law.

They each settled for a pint of bitter. 'Are you sure about that?' asked Mackinnon.

'Absolutely, guv'nor. It's because he's so bloody predictable. Seven o'clock every night he comes through them doors, orders a pint of Guinness and sits there' – he pointed to a chair in the corner, near the dartboard – 'and just stares into space. About quarter past nine he has another pint and goes back to the corner again, and he'll just sit there then until eleven o'clock.'

'You mean he just has the two drinks?'

'He might have a third, if someone takes pity on him and buys him one – bought him one myself occasionally – otherwise it's just the two,' said the landlord. 'I don't mind; he doesn't do any harm to anyone. Most of the regulars in here know what happened and they feel sorry for him. He's not all there, I don't reckon, but he wouldn't do no one any harm.' He paused. 'What's he been up to then?'

'He's missing from home,' said Mackinnon.

* * *

It was gone seven o'clock by the time Gaffney and Tipper got back to Scotland Yard, and Gaffney was ready to cave in. 'I'll just have a quick look through the messages, Harry, and then I'm going to call it a day.'

Mackinnon tapped on the open door and waited until Gaffney looked up.

'Yes, Ian, what is it?'

'I went to see Ernest Drake, sir. . . . '

'Drake? Who's Drake?' It was nigh-on ten hours since Gaffney had handed Mackinnon the file on Drake, and he was beginning to slow up.

'The bloke who writes to the Home Secretary, threatening to kill him.'

Gaffney nodded. 'Yes, what about him?'

Mackinnon advanced towards Gaffney's desk. 'He's disappeared, sir. He's always in his local boozer from about seven until chucking-out time. Didn't show last night, and he's not been seen since.'

Gaffney sat down and signalled Mackinnon to do the same. 'Harry!' Tipper looked up from the file he was examining. 'You'd better listen to this.' He turned back to Mackinnon. 'Go on, Ian.'

Mackinnon outlined what he had learned – little though it was – and finished by telling Gaffney about the press-cuttings. 'I brought those away with me, sir,' he said, and placed the envelope on the desk in front of his chief superintendent.

'Mmm!' Gaffney leaned back in his chair and gazed reflectively at Tipper, a half-smile on his face. 'Well, Harry, what d'you reckon? It can't be that easy, can it?'

Tipper grinned. 'It's too bloody easy, guv'nor. There's got to be a catch somewhere. Bloke writes threatening letters to the Home Secretary on account of he thinks that Lavery's responsible for his wife's death. The night Mrs Lavery's murdered, Drake does a runner . . . ' He shook his head.

'So what do we do? Nothing?' said Gaffney with a smile.

Tipper laughed and stood up. 'You know we can't do nothing, sir, you're just winding me up. We circulate Ernest

44

Drake to all forces and to all ports, and when we find him we talk to him about the murder of Mrs Lavery. And what's more to the point, it's just possible that it's down to him.'

'It's more than just possible, Harry.' Gaffney ran a hand through his hair. 'See that it gets done, will you?'

'Yes, sir,' said Tipper, and turning to Mackinnon, said: 'You heard the guv'nor. Get cracking.'

Mackinnon looked at Tipper, his face expressionless. 'Yes, sir,' he said.

Gaffney waited until the door had closed behind Mackinnon before speaking again. 'All in all, Harry, it's been a pretty frustrating day,' he said. 'We've got precisely nowhere.'

'Not entirely, sir. The thing that interested me was that chain.'

'The theatre prop, you mean?'

Tipper nodded. 'Except that it wasn't a theatre prop.' He put his hand in his jacket pocket and withdrew the chain, examining it briefly before laying it on the desk in front of Gaffney. 'I took the liberty of taking possession of it after the Home Secretary had left. It's gold. I reckon about two grandsworth. There's a hallmark on the reverse of the medallion, and another on the clip.'

Gaffney whistled. 'Two thousand. And Lavery said he hadn't seen it before.'

'Which begs the question: who gave it to her?'

'He may have seen it before, Harry. He's still in shock, don't forget. On the other hand, I wouldn't have thought that he'd ever have forgotten seeing her with that round her neck.'

'I don't think it's meant to be worn round the neck,' said Tipper. 'Unless I'm mistaken, it's a waist chain, and it's worn next to the skin.'

Gaffney smiled. 'Gift from an admirer, then?'

'More likely from a close friend,' said Tipper. 'One who'd want to admire it in place.'

Gaffney examined the medallion. It was about two inches in diameter, and parts of the gold had been cut away to leave two intertwined letters in a circle. 'I don't know what that means,' he said. 'The letters M and C.' He looked thoughtful. 'Could be someone's initials – not hers certainly – or Roman numerals for nine hundred or eleven hundred, I suppose.'

Tipper laughed. 'If it had been M and S, I might have been able to help you, guv. I reckon it's the initials of the bloke who gave it to her.'

'Or woman,' said Gaffney with a smile.

Tipper shook his head slowly. 'Don't want another job like that one,' he said. He was thinking of the Penny Lambert case that he and Gaffney had been involved in some years previously.

Gaffney leaned back in his chair and lit a cigar. Then he gazed reflectively through the smoke. 'I think we need to know where that came from,' he said. 'Get hold of DI Wisley – he's a fairly discreet sort of bloke – get him to do the rounds of the better end of the trade and see if he can get a trace on it. But tell him to go easy, and tell him not to breathe a word about the connection with Elizabeth Lavery, or it'll be all over the Press in no time at all.'

Tipper leaned over and took the chain. 'Recovered stolen property which we're anxious to restore to the rightful owner,' he said.

Gaffney scoffed. 'Yes,' he said, 'and that might be nearer the truth than we know.'

Gaffney was in his office by 8.30. He had eventually got home to Richmond at a quarter to nine the previous evening, and offset the emptiness of his flat by downing two large Scotches. It was at times like that that he tended to pity himself, and to recall with regret that his wife Vanessa – or ex-wife as she now was – would not be coming back.

Claire Wentworth was in the office before he even had his coat off. 'Results are coming in, sir, but there's only one you might want to know about.'

'Yes?' Gaffney put his overcoat on a hanger and put it into his office wardrobe.

'D'you remember the Commons order-paper found under the bed, sir?'

'What, that week-old thing?' Gaffney sat down at his desk and pulled out his packet of cigars.

'Yes, sir. It had a telephone number scrawled on it.'

'Yeah. What about it?'

'The phone number goes out to Mr Walter Croft; he's an MP.'

'Hardly surprising,' said Gaffney. 'Okay, Claire, thanks. Leave me a note of it, and I'll have a chat with him. Put it down as an action for me.' He grinned up at her. 'And keep nagging me about it, because I'm sure to forget.'

She smiled. 'And the DAC would like a word with you, sir.'

Gaffney glanced up at the clock over the door. 'Is he in already?'

'Been here a good half-hour, sir.'

Gaffney quickly drank his coffee, put his cigars back in his pocket, and walked down the corridor to the DAC's big corner office.

Logan was sitting in an armchair reading *The Times*. 'Help yourself to coffee, John, and come and tell me how you're getting on.'

'I've just had coffee, sir, thank you, and the answer to your question is not very well.'

Logan laughed and folded the newspaper. 'How much are the Anti-Terrorist Branch helping?'

'As much as they can, sir. They're masterminding all the scientific stuff, fingerprints, photographs; all that sort of thing, but not much of it's helping right now. The simple fact is that someone entered Number Seven Cutler's Mews the night before last, either by invitation or stealth, and strangled Elizabeth Lavery. Beyond that we don't know a great deal.'

'Is the Home Secretary being helpful?'

'Co-operative, sir, but not very helpful. Not that that's his fault; what he doesn't know, he can't tell us. We went through the place last night – took over an hour; much bigger than it looks from the outside – and he eventually came to the conclusion that nothing had been stolen.' Gaffney paused in thought for a second or two. 'Funnily enough, having said that, he actually found something he claimed not to have seen before.'

'Oh?' Logan frowned.

'A gold waist chain – at least that's what we think it is – that Harry Tipper reckons must be worth about two thousand pounds.'

'And Lavery hadn't seen it before?'

'No, sir, so he says.'

Logan smiled. 'A gentleman friend?'

'Possibly. And frankly I wouldn't be surprised. She was a good-looking girl, and twenty years younger than her husband. There's a lot of temptation about for a woman like her. . . . '

'What are you doing about it?'

'I've set Wisley to find out where it came from – discreetly, of course – which shouldn't be too difficult; it has a distinctive medallion on it with what looks like someone's initials.' Gaffney paused for a moment to separate what he had been saying from his next piece of information. 'There's also a man called Drake – Ernest Drake – who is an habitual writer of threatening letters to Lavery.'

Logan looked doubtful. 'Not the only one though, surely?'

'No, sir, but this one's different. Blames Lavery for the suicide of Mrs Drake while on remand for unlawful killing, and he's gone missing from his flat in Streatham. In fact, he went missing just before the estimated time of the murder, and hasn't been seen since.'

Logan smiled, but he didn't bother to ask Gaffney what he had done about it: he knew. He stood up and walked across to his desk. 'That's the number that Lavery called the night before last,' he said, tearing a page off his scribbling pad. 'It's the chap he stayed with. Said he was a close friend. Might be worth having a chat with him. He could shed some light on Mrs Lavery's activities. If there's anything out of the ordinary that is.'

Before retiring from the Metropolitan Police three years ago, Fred Hutchings had specialised in the sort of burglaries that

48

resulted in the theft of valuable jewellery. Although only a detective inspector, he had developed an expertise that caused detectives throughout the country – and even from abroad – to consult him on a regular basis whenever they wanted to know anything about specialist jewel robbers. Even after taking up his present post as chief security officer with a bullion firm in the City of London, he continued to advise his former colleagues, a situation to which his new employers had no objection; it was a useful two-way flow of intelligence.

Hutchings examined the chain briefly before taking out a jeweller's glass and peered closely at the hallmarks. Then he leaned back in his chair. 'Nice piece of work, that,' he said, 'very nice indeed.' He scribbled a name and address on a piece of paper and pushed it across the desk to Francis Wisley. 'And that's who made it,' he said. He paused. 'And it'll cost you a pint,' he added with a smile.

It was one of the better-known firms of West End jewellers; discreetly opulent and clearly patronised by those to whom quality was the only criterion. There was a quietness about it when Wisley entered that reminded him of a Harley Street waiting room.

'May I assist you, sir?'

'I'm a police officer,' said Wisley. 'May I see the manager, please.'

'One moment, sir.' The assistant sniffed slightly and turned away.

The manager was tall, grey-haired, and probably in his late fifties. 'Perhaps you'd like to come into my office,' he said.

Wisley hoped that it was an acknowledgement of the sensitivity of his enquiry rather than a dread of having policemen sullying the atmosphere of his expensive shop. 'Thank you.' He followed the stately figure, feeling as though he had become part of a procession.

The manager gave the chain a cursory examination and nodded. 'Oh yes,' he said, 'I remember this piece. We made it about . . . ' He pondered briefly. 'Seven or eight months ago, I should think. Is there a problem, Inspector?'

'It's the proceeds of a robbery,' said Wisley blandly. 'We're anxious to restore it to its rightful owner.'

The manager took out a glass and examined the maker's mark before turning to a large ledger that rested on top of a safe. Quickly he skimmed through the pages until he found the corresponding reference. 'Yes,' he said thoughtfully, 'we made it for a Mr Colin Masters. He has an address in Wimbledon. Here, I'll jot it down for you.'

'What kept you?' Gaffney smiled as he spoke.

'The fog, sir,' said DI Wisley, and grinned. Secretly he was pleased with himself at having solved Gaffney's enquiry so quickly.

'Well, who is he, this Masters bloke?'

Wisley looked smug. 'I spoke to the collator at Wimbledon, sir, and he says that he's got a bit of form – way back – and that he's an SO11 Main-Index man.'

Gaffney looked up sharply. 'You're joking,' he said. It was rhetorical; he knew fine that Wisley was not. 'Christ, that's all we need.'

'That's a print-out of his CRO microfiche,' said Wisley helpfully. He passed a buff folder across the desk. 'Only one: robbery with violence, about seventeen years ago.'

Gaffney skimmed through it and handed it back. 'Well done, Francis. You can book that into the Incident Room, not that I think we'll need it again.'

# Chapter Five

'I thought you'd be beating a path to my door.' Commander Murdo McGregor dropped a match into the ashtray and brushed pipe ash from his waistcoat. 'And I think you'll be wanting to talk to me about a certain Main-Index man called Colin Masters.'

Gaffney smiled. 'Now, how did you know that, sir?'

McGregor had been in charge of the Yard's Criminal Intelligence Branch for four years and it was doubtful whether any criminal of substance could move in London without his knowledge. Some of the criminals in whom he took an interest did not have previous convictions for crime, but in most cases that was not for want of trying, and although knowledge was not always evidence, it often went a long way towards helping.

'Well now,' said McGregor, 'you Special Branch chaps aren't the only ones to know about intelligence-gathering, you know. My man at Wimbledon—'

'Your man?'

McGregor nodded. 'Collators work for SO11 Branch, John, or had you forgotten? The moment someone takes an interest in one of my collection, I get to hear about it. As soon as your man Wisley put the phone down, the message came through.' McGregor smiled knowingly. 'What's your interest, John?'

Gaffney outlined what he knew so far, explaining the apparent connection between the murder of Elizabeth Lavery, the gold chain, and now Masters.

'Interesting,' said McGregor mildly; he was not a man given to demonstrative reactions. 'It sounds as though Mr Masters is overreaching himself somewhat. D'you reckon he

51

was having it off with the Home Secretary's wife, then?'

Gaffney shrugged. 'Looks very much like it. It doesn't really matter, of course. The fact that there is an association of some sort could provide us with a lead.'

McGregor nodded. 'Actress, did you say she was?'

'Yes, sir. At least up until her marriage to Lavery.'

McGregor laid his pipe gently in the ashtray and chuckled. 'Shady lot, the acting profession,' he said.

'What sort of villain is Masters?' asked Gaffney.

By way of an answer, McGregor stood up and walked across to his safe. 'Seeing it's you, John, you can have a look,' he said, laying a thickish docket on the desk in front of Gaffney. 'He's a lucky man. He's only got one previous to talk of, and that was seventeen years ago: armed robbery and he got a handful at the Bailey.' He picked up his pipe again and looked around for his matches. 'That was before they went soft; probably get a pound out of the poor box today.'

'But he's gone straight since then?' Gaffney smiled.

'Aye, and pigs might fly. As a matter of fact we thought we had him about a year back,' said McGregor. He pointed with his pipe stem. 'It's on there: conspiracy to rob, GBH, breathing – all that – but the bastard managed to duck out of it.'

Gaffney looked up from the file. 'Yes,' he said, 'and I've just seen who his brief was.'

'Oh?'

'Dudley Lavery, QC, MP, who is now her Majesty's Secretary of State for the Home Department.'

Those who did not know Tommy Fox were tempted to describe him as dandified. It was a mistake. Although a slender six feet tall and a snappy dresser – today, for instance, he wore an immaculately cut suit in Prince of Wales check – he was also the Detective Chief Superintendent in charge of the Flying Squad. Furthermore, some years previously, he had been awarded the Queen's Gallantry Medal for disarming a robber who had made the terrible mistake of pointing a loaded pistol at him. It is said that Tommy Fox walked swiftly across the room, seized the gun with his left hand, and felled the robber with a single blow to the jaw with his right; the villain was not to know that Fox was a southpaw. Witnesses testified to the Honours Committee that he then stood on the gunman's hand, bent down and said, 'You're nicked, you saucy bastard'. It may be, though, that the last part was apocryphal; such stories tend to be embellished in the Metropolitan Police, and particularly in the Flying Squad. However, it is fair to say that only fools trifled with Tommy Fox.

'I am reliably informed that you're interested in one of my favourite villains.' Fox stood framed in Gaffney's doorway, his hand resting lightly on the handle, and grinned. Unlike some of his colleagues, Fox had not bothered with elocution lessons; his East End patter, spoken in a rich Cockney accent was, he said, the language that his clientele understood.

Gaffney laughed. 'Colin Masters, you mean?'

Fox advanced into the room. 'I'm sorry to have to say, John, that it was me who arrested him the last time he was up. And he got away with it.'

'So I saw from the file. Any idea where he is now?'

'He's got a place in Wimbledon. And he's got one in Spain.'

'Yes, I saw that too.'

'I won't ask why you're interested in him,' said Fox with a disarming smile, 'because you Special Branch buggers never tell anybody anything, but I wouldn't mind having a little money riding on the fact that he was defended by a brief called Lavery, who later became Home Secretary, and whose missus got topped the night before last.'

Gaffney nodded. 'As a matter of fact, Tommy, there's a bit more to it than that. We found some jewellery in Lavery's house that we've traced back to Masters.'

'Have you now? Well, well.' Fox grinned. 'Not poking her, was he?'

Gaffney wrinkled his nose in mock distaste. 'Please, Tommy, we're not accustomed to that sort of full frontal approach up here in Special Branch.'

Fox laughed. 'If I know Masters, there's no other construction you can put on it.'

'This place in Spain – is it his?' asked Gaffney.

'Oh yes! And paid for out of the proceeds of crime, if I'm any judge. It's about twenty miles outside Seville; where the oranges come from—'

'And the hairdressers,' said Gaffney quietly.

'It's quite a set-up. Typical Spanish villa built round a swimming pool. Cost a few grand, I should think, even over there.'

'Have you seen it, then?'

'No,' said Fox, laying a forefinger alongside his nose, 'but I've got some good informants. He has weekends there from time to time. Usually takes a few of his cronies across, together with their women. Sometimes they'll stay there for up to a fortnight or more.'

'When's that?' asked Gaffney. 'After they've pulled off a job?'

Fox laughed derisively. 'Unfortunately, it's not that easy. If it was, we'd have nailed the bastard years ago.'

'Oh?'

'Masters calls himself a company director; to be more precise, a director of companies, saucy sod. He is too. He buys and sells things, so he claims, but I've a shrewd suspicion that he sells more than he buys, if you see what I mean. He takes in laundry too, but we've never caught him at it.'

'Through Spain, you mean?' There were several high-grade criminals who were in the business of exchanging stolen money for untraceable and legitimate money . . . at a price: 'laundering' is what both policemen and criminals called it.

'Bloody sure of it, John. And there's been more than a hint that he's into drugs in some way. Trouble is, he's got a bloody good accountant; bent as arseholes, of course.' He sighed a sigh of resignation. 'Never mind; he'll come one day. They always do.' He leaned forward. 'Reckon him for this Lavery job, do you?'

'I don't think it's that simple,' said Gaffney, 'but let me

54

say that there are reasons why it might be profitable for me to have a little chat with him.'

'Well, good luck. You'll get sod-all out of him.' He relapsed into silence for a moment or two. 'The only redeeming feature is that basically he's still a villain, and he'll never get out of the habit of occasionally doing things himself. And another thing: like most of his type, he always bears a grudge, and if he reckons someone owes him he'll work it off one way or another.' Fox looked thoughtful. 'I'll tell you what, though, John. There's a geezer called Waldo Conway, used to run with Masters; in fact, he went down when Masters got off: that job I was telling you about. Waldo's doing a five-stretch in the Scrubs . . . ' He paused. 'Or it might be in Wandsworth. Anyhow, a chat with him might be helpful. Non-attributable, as they say in Fleet Street.'

'What can you tell me about Masters himself?'

Fox laughed. 'Flash bastard, he is. They call him Mr Gold.' He adjusted his pocket handkerchief. 'Gold watch, gold bracelet, gold cuff-links, gold chain round his neck. He's even got a gold-coloured Rolls-Royce; I always thought that was a bit over the top.' Fox regarded himself as an arbiter of good taste.

'All of which, I presume, can be shown to be the proceeds of legitimate business?' asked Gaffney. Fox nodded sadly. 'Isn't that thumbing his nose a bit? Putting himself on offer like that, I mean.'

'Yeah! But that's him; reckons he's too fly for the likes of us, with his clever accountant and his clever lawyers. But there are a few villains who don't want to know about Masters. It's natural enough; they reckon he's pushing his luck with the Old Bill, just taunting us to find the evidence. We will, of course; it's only a matter of time, and they all come in the end.'

'Where's he come from?'

'Oh, he's a local boy. Born in Wandsworth and went to a comprehensive school thereabouts. Didn't get any O-levels though.' Fox smiled benignly. 'There isn't an O-level for screwing – safes or women. He was caught bang to rights

55

when he was about twenty-one – that'd be about eighteen years ago – and he went down for five for armed robbery. His dear old mum, Gawd bless 'er, came trotting along to the Bailey to tell his lordship that young Colin had been mixing with the wrong sort of lads, and he was always such a good boy at home. As a matter of fact, it was the other way round: he was the ringleader. She couldn't understand it, what with him bringing in the coal and chopping the firewood.' Fox scoffed. 'He had to; his old man was doing two years in the 'Ville, for housebreaking. He learned a few tricks while he was in stir, and when he came out he swore he'd never do time again.' Fox sighed and glanced at his watch. 'And he never has, the bastard . . . but he will.'

'What's his method, then?'

'Nothing simple, believe me. We're pretty convinced that he sets up jobs; and they're good jobs too. He's a very bright lad, make no mistake about that. He seems to have the nose to suss out something big, and can assemble the right team for it. What's more, he takes care of them; looks after their birds if they get nicked, particularly if they've got kids. He doesn't care that much, of course, but it's a form of insurance against them grassing. That's always the danger when you get a clever bastard like Masters working it all out. When the foot-soldiers get nicked and he doesn't, they sometimes get vindictive. That's why he got pulled last time: someone spoke out of turn.' Fox yawned. 'And that particular villain's disappeared off the face of the earth; almost certain to be part of a motorway now, but we've no way of proving it. The mistake Masters made, of course, was to get involved in the job himself, but that's what I was saying earlier on, you see; he reckoned someone owed him, and he was going to take it out of his hide . . . personally. They never learn, even the big-time villains, and frankly that's our only hope of catching them.' Fox stood up. 'If there's anything else I can help you with, give me a shout. And if you're in danger of nicking Masters, let me know, will you, just so I can come and watch.' He paused and smiled maliciously. 'Have you still got Harry Tipper up here?' he asked.

Gaffney nodded. 'Yes . . . and I'm keeping him.'

'He knows Conway. As a matter of fact, I think he nicked him once . . . when he was a proper policeman. Be lucky!' With a wink and a grin he left the office, slamming the door behind him.

You asked me to arrange an appointment for you to see Mr Croft, sir,' said Claire Wentworth.

'Croft? Who the hell's Croft?' asked Gaffney.

'He's the MP whose telephone number was on the order-paper that was found in the Home Secretary's house, sir.'

'Ah! So I did.'

'He's in Ankara; an Inter-Parliamentary Union meeting, I think it was.' She consulted a note on her desk and nodded. 'Apparently he's combining it with a bit of a holiday, and won't be back for about a fortnight. His secretary's promised to ring the moment he returns. I emphasised the urgency.'

Gaffney laughed. 'Urgent is the one thing it isn't, but thanks anyway.'

'I'm so sorry to have kept you waiting; I'm Desmond Marshall.' He was tall, and slightly stooped as though he had spent a lifetime ducking through doorways and had eventually got stuck like it. 'Do come in, Chief Superintendent.' Gaffney's rank rolled off his tongue with the practised ease of a man who had spent years at the criminal bar, examining police witnesses.

Gaffney returned the secretary's newspaper with a smile and a brief word of thanks, and followed the barrister into his office.

'The Temple is becoming impossibly overcrowded, you know,' said Marshall, shifting a pile of pink-taped briefs off a leather armchair which had definitely seen better days. 'There, do sit down. I expect you could do with a cup of tea; I certainly could. Hang on a moment.' He walked through to the outer office again and Gaffney heard him asking the secretary for two cups of tea.

'Absolute bugger of a case today,' continued Marshall,

returning. 'Excuse me doing this; didn't want to keep you waiting any longer than necessary.' He pulled off his bands and replaced them with a collar and an Old Harrovian tie; it was the only one Gaffney could readily identify because of its similarity to that of the Criminal Investigation Department: something which did not please all Old Harrovians.

The secretary appeared in the doorway, balancing two cups of tea and a sugar-bowl on a small tray. Marshall smiled at her and looked at Gaffney. 'There are still some things in the legal profession that can be done with astonishing speed.' He glanced back at the girl. 'That was very quick of you, my dear,' he said.

The secretary blushed and put the tray down; she obviously fancied Marshall. 'I made it as soon as you came in,' she said. 'I thought you'd be needing one.'

'Splendid.' Marshall seated himself, jacketless, behind the large partners desk and sipped his tea sadly. 'I've given up sugar,' he said. 'My wife says it's poison.' He looked up and smiled wearily. 'Well now, Chief Superintendent, what can I do for you?'

'As I said on the phone, Mr Marshall, I am investigating the death of Elizabeth Lavery.'

Marshall nodded gravely. 'Yes, what a bloody tragedy, absolutely awful. Strange thing really, we're dealing with it in the courts all day long, but it doesn't touch you until it happens to someone you know. Any leads yet?'

'Nothing to talk of.' He had no intention of telling Lavery's friend what he had learned about Masters, but there would be some profit in getting Marshall to talk about him, if that was possible. 'I was going to suggest that it might be helpful if you could tell me a bit about the Home Secretary. We know the public persona, so to speak, but not much about Dudley Lavery the man.' Gaffney leaned forward and stirred his tea.

'Mmm! Difficult to know where to start really.' He smiled the smile he usually reserved for juries when trying to convince them that the pack of lies his client had just told was the gospel truth. 'At the beginning, I suppose. Dudley had the best of everything: public school, Oxford, commission in the navy. The only thing he couldn't seem to do was to pick a wife . . . ' He broke off, apparently alarmed at what he had just said. 'I take it this conversation is in confidence, Chief Superintendent?'

Gaffney nodded. 'Of course. I'm merely trying to discover something of Mr Lavery's background; or, more particularly, Mrs Lavery's.'

'Yes.' Marshall seemed reassured. 'I suppose it was because Dudley was a workaholic that his first marriage was a disaster; an absolute wash-out.'

'When was that?'

Marshall pursed his lips, thinking. 'I knew you were going to ask that.' He paused again. 'I'm working it out backwards,' he said. 'Let me see; Dudley must have been called when he was about twenty-three, straight after he came out of the navy.' Seeing Gaffney's raised eyebrows, Marshall added: 'National Service, two years. I think he was about thirty when he married.' He nodded, as if confirming his own statement. 'He was working damned hard then to establish his practice. He was adamant that he was going to take silk bang on ten years; I think we all say that when we start. Never do though.' He smiled at the folly of his own youthful naïvety. 'Some of us don't do it at all,' he said ruefully. 'I think Dudley did it in thirteen, after all; it's not bad. I seem to recall he got his seat in the same year; yes, I'm sure he did; we always seemed to be opening champagne in chambers that year.' He held up a packet of cigarettes. 'Do you do this?' he asked.

'No thank you, not cigarettes anyway.'

'Very wise; wish I didn't.' Marshall stood up and walked to a cupboard in the huge old-fashioned bookcase. He took out a bottle of whisky and turned to face Gaffney. 'I've yet to meet a detective who doesn't do this, though,' he said.

'Nor have I, but just a small one, please.'

'Right,' said Marshall, spinning the top off the bottle and immediately demonstrating that his concept of a 'small one' was somewhat different from Gaffney's. 'I suppose Dudley must have been about thirty-six then,' he continued, settling himself behind his desk once more, 'and he'd been married for five years probably. Very ordinary sort of girl, Dorothy, and if that sounds disparaging it's not meant to; she'd have made him a damned good wife if he'd let her. But he was never at home; always in court or in the House. To be a lawyer-MP is a recipe for a disastrous marriage, believe me.'

The door opened and a head appeared round it. 'Oh, sorry, Marshall.' The door closed again.

'Poor sod,' said Marshall. 'Probably finish up holding a conference on the stairs.' He looked as though he didn't much care. 'It was an amicable divorce, although some said that Dudley had been playing around with his secretary for a while . . . ' He shrugged. 'Frankly, I think it was malicious gossip. You've no idea what a bitchy lot they can be in the the Temple . . . particularly about someone who's success-ful. Anyway it got to the point where Dorothy had had enough . . . of being neglected, I should think. She's married to a doctor in the States now, I believe.'

'How did he meet Elizabeth?'

Marshall chuckled. 'Clark turned up with this brief—'

'Clark?'

'Yes, he's one of the solicitors we deal with. It was a defamation. Well, Dudley doesn't do much in the way of civil – not that sort, anyway – but Clark imposed on him to see the plaintiff, one Elizabeth Fairfax. And that was that. She was an actress, as you probably know, and once he'd met her, he was lost. Very attractive girl . . . . Must have been about twenty-nine at that time, I should think.'

'About five years ago, that would have been then?' asked Gaffney.

'Be about it,' said Marshall. 'If I remember correctly, some gossip columnist had written a piece about her suggesting that she'd only got a part in a television play because she'd been to bed with the producer. Probably had too, but the truth is no defence to libel, as you know.' He paused briefly and looked slightly guilty at what he had just said. 'Anyway, Dudley took the case and settled out of court. Got a substantial settlement, as I recall.' His hand played a silent tattoo on the desk-top. 'Six months later they were married.'

'Bit sudden, wasn't it?'

Marshall sniffed. 'I think Dudley thought he was running out of time. Nearly fifty then, he must have been; bit late for getting married. Of course the cynics said that he was hoping for a Cabinet post come the election, and he wouldn't get one without a wife. As for Elizabeth, I think she saw great benefit in having a husband who appeared destined for Government, whether she continued her acting career or not.'

'Had she been married before?' Gaffney was having to be patient; much of what the lawyer was saying was of little interest, but he didn't want to shut him up.

For a moment or two Marshall stared reflectively at the ceiling. 'There was a wonderful expression that my mother used to use when she thought that we children weren't listening: married but not churched. That, I think, would fairly accurately have been Elizabeth's previous state.' He anticipated Gaffney's next question. 'An actor, I think he was; she was living with him for quite some time, I believe. I don't know what this attraction is in the acting business, but it seems fairly prevalent.'

Gaffney winced inwardly; his wife had left him in favour of an actor. 'And that lasted until something better came along; like a Member of Parliament who was also a high-earning lawyer?' he asked savagely.

Marshall laughed. 'I can see that it's not only the law that your profession and mine have in common, Chief Superintendent,' he said. 'It's also congenital cynicism.'

'D'you know the name of this actor?'

'No, I don't recall it. Come to think of it, I don't know that I ever knew it.'

'Would Mr Lavery know, d'you think?'

Marshall looked up sharply. 'I'm not sure he even knew of his existence, or if he did, probably preferred to pretend he didn't.'

'How did you know then?' asked Gaffney quietly.

Marshall smiled. 'As I said just now, the Temple is a hotbed of gossip, my dear fellow, but as is always the case

with these things, the husband would be the last to hear. But why does this actor interest you?'

'To eliminate him from the inquiry . . . or not, as the case may be.'

'Yes,' said Marshall, 'I suppose so. I'm sorry I can't help you.' He paused. 'I suppose you could ask Dudley . . . .'

'I could,' said Gaffney, 'but I'd prefer not to.'

Marshall nodded. 'Yes,' he said, 'I think you're right.'

'I understand that Mr Lavery once defended a man called Masters?'

Marshall's eyes narrowed slightly. 'Why should you ask that?'

Gaffney shrugged. 'No particular reason. I just happened to come across it on a file recently.'

'What a strange coincidence.' Marshall looked as though he didn't believe that, but then he was a criminal lawyer; questioning statements was his business. 'As a matter of fact, we were both involved in that case; Dudley led me. Masters and three of his cohorts were up at the Bailey. Conspiracy to rob, if I remember correctly, plus malicious wounding, GBH, and one or two other odds-and-sods; the Crown Prosecution Service had really gone to town for a change. Didn't do 'em much good, mind you.' He smirked at the recollection. 'It was a complex tale – good one to defend – and absolutely ideal for Dudley. Masters had apparently sold some merchandise to another – so the story went – but the said purchaser had failed to pay. Masters and his co-conspirators had repossessed the goods, so it was said, but in the process had repossessed slightly more than they were entitled to. In addition, there was damage to property, like the breaking down of doors, and sundry employees of the welshing purchaser appear to have suffered actual bodily harm – or worse – during the incident. I'm sure you visualise the scene, Chief Superintendent?' Marshall spoke airily and waved a hand vaguely above his head.

Gaffney smiled. 'Indeed I do.'

'Dudley did well. He blew the conspiracy indictment apart, and a couple of them went down for robbery, but friend

Masters got off.' Marshall paused and put his head on one side. 'Do you ski at all, Chief Superintendent?'

Gaffney looked puzzled. 'No,' he said. 'I do sometimes skate on thin ice, though,' he added drily.

Marshall laughed. 'It's just that the way Dudley cut through the indictments against Masters reminded me of a downhill slalom champion. Apparently it couldn't be proved that he had actually taken part, even though he was there. Fickle things, juries.'

'You can say that again,' said Gaffney with feeling.

'Anyway, on the day the trial ended, Dudley had arranged to take Elizabeth to lunch – he'd obviously learned from having neglected his previous wife – and she met him at court. Masters was there, in the entrance hall, having just been acquitted, of course, and was vigorously pumping our hands, when Liz turned up. So Masters offered to take us all out to lunch . . . oh! and he offered us all the free use of his villa in Spain. Well, I say all of us; it was obviously directed more at Dudley than at me. For two reasons, I think: Dudley was the silk, and he'd got a very attractive wife.'

'You're not suggesting—'

'I'm not suggesting anything, Chief Superintendent, but as a general rule, villains are insensitive to social barriers, other than those which they themselves erect. But then I don't have to tell you that, do I?'

'A villain? Is that how you saw him?' asked Gaffney.

Marshall smiled owlishly. 'Oh, come now, Chief Superintendent. I know he describes himself as a company director, but he has got a previous for armed robbery, albeit years ago, and he'd just got off another, similar count.' Gaffney smiled and shook his head, and Marshall laughed. 'Don't tell me that you're one of those policemen who believe all that crap about innocent until proved guilty, surely?' He smoothed a hand across the top of his desk. 'He might have a Rolls-Royce and a lot of money, but he's basically a crook.' He smiled. 'And if you repeat that, I'll sue you. However, I digress. Dudley refused, naturally. It's not a good thing to mix business with pleasure – in our trade any more than in

yours – and if anything was guaranteed to put the lid on his becoming Attorney-General, it would have been keeping that sort of company.'

'When did all this happen?' Gaffney knew the answer to that, but it was in his nature constantly to cross-check information that came to him in the course of an inquiry.

'Just before the election; six months before, I suppose.' Marshall looked sharply at Gaffney. 'I must say you seem very interested in Masters . . . .'

Gaffney chose to ignore the implied question. 'You said he had hopes of becoming Attorney?'

'Yes, but that was all changed when Purdy died; on election night, you'll probably recall. Dudley was due to be made Attorney, so he told me, but was offered Purdy's job at the Home Office instead, which was a tremendous bit of luck for him. Apparently the PM didn't want to shuffle his new front bench around too much, not right at the start of the administration. It's a very senior appointment, of course, and one or two noses were put out of joint. Made Dudley a few enemies in the party—'

'Enemies?'

Marshall laughed. 'Only political ones,' he said. 'Not the sort you're looking for. Funnily enough, it didn't please Liz too much, either.'

'Really?'

'She rather fancied being Lady Lavery, which she would have been if Dudley had been made a law officer, but of course Home Secretaries don't get automatic knighthoods.'

'Did that cause a rift between them?' asked Gaffney.

Marshall laughed outright. 'A rift? My dear fellow, he worshipped the very ground she walked on, and she, in turn, deferred to him in everything. That marriage was as solid as a rock. That's why it's such a bloody tragedy.'

# Chapter Six

'I understand you wanted to see me, sir?' asked DCI Lisle.

Gaffney nodded. 'Where's the Home Secretary at the moment?'

'He's at the House, sir. John Selway's with him.'

'Sit down, Tony.' Gaffney was not very impressed with Tony Lisle. He was young for a chief inspector, and was said – by others – to be a rising star. Gaffney had to admit that he was prejudiced against the Special Course scheme which projected some talented youngsters into the higher ranks when they weren't always ready for it, and Gaffney knew of one such case which had had disastrous and tragic results. He sighed. 'How's the Home Secretary taking it?'

'Well, he's a typical politician, sir. Remarkably resilient; but I dare say it'll hit him eventually.'

'What d'you mean? That it hasn't really sunk in yet?'

'Oh, I think it's sunk in all right, but I don't think he's come to terms with the fact that it's permanent, and what's more, just what effect it'll have on his political career.'

'Tony,' said Gaffney, leaning back in his chair and linking his hands loosely behind his head, 'what the bloody hell are you talking about?'

Lisle sat up a little. 'Well . . . He seems to be carrying on more or less as though nothing's happened. He's submerged himself in work, and the only reminder is when someone comes up to him and murmurs something sympathetic about his loss. Then he looks all sort of funereal and thanks them, then he carries on again. It's almost as if he's trying to pretend it hasn't happened. I think it'll come home to roost during the recess when he hasn't got the Commons to go to.'

65

'What'll he do then?'

'Difficult to say, really, sir. I suppose he'll spend some time in the country – his place in Shropshire – but I don't know if he'll have a holiday abroad this year.'

'Where does he usually go?'

'South of France. Stays with Earl Barclay – or at least at Earl Barclay's place – at Le Trayas.'

'Who's Earl Barclay? I've never heard of him.'

Lisle smiled. 'Oh, he's not a real earl, sir, it's his name; he's an American banker, I think.'

'Mmm. Tell me, Tony, was Elizabeth Lavery over the side?'

Lisle's eyes opened in astonishment. 'I'm not sure I know what you mean, sir . . .'

'Yes you do. And don't come that old loyalty crap with me. You work for Special Branch, not the Home Secretary, and one day, when you've finished the assignment you're on, you'll come back and work here again. So don't forget who your guv'nors are.'

'No, sir, well I don't—'

'Right, then. Was she over the side? Was she having it off? In short, was she having an affair with another man? That plain enough for you?'

'I don't think so, sir.'

'Which? Don't think it's plain enough; or no, she wasn't at it?'

'I don't think she was having an affair, sir.' Lisle spoke flatly; he was unaccustomed to the type of onslaught that Gaffney had just unleashed on him.

'Right. Now, I've had their marriage described to me as rock solid. Would you go along with that?'

For a moment or two, Lisle remained silent while his conscience sorted itself out. He glanced at Gaffney's expression of mounting impatience, and decided rapidly which way to play it. 'I got the impression they weren't very close, sir,' he said hesitantly.

'Why? Did they fight, argue, what?'

'Well no . . . It's just a feeling I got.'

'Good. Thanks very much for dropping in. And now I want to see Selway. And I mean now.'

'Yes, sir, but he's at the House with the Home Secretary—'

'I know,' said Gaffney tersely. 'You told me. So go and relieve him.' He had decided that Lisle was probably not the best man to be guarding the Home Secretary, and determined to talk to Commander Scott about it when the latter returned from leave.

'What time did you take the Home Secretary from the House to his club, John? I presume that's what happened?'

'Yes, sir.' Selway dropped into Gaffney's armchair and crossed his legs. 'We were at the House in time for prayers and stayed there until six-fifty.' Selway had got his pocket book out now. 'We arrived at his club just before seven, minutes before, in fact; traffic wasn't too bad.'

'Where is his club, John?'

'It's the Chesterfield, sir, in South Molton Street.'

'Right, yes, I know it. Now then, he told me that he'd rung his wife before he left the House. Did you know about that?'

'Not at the time, sir. He told me that later, much later; when we got back to the House for the ten o'clock division.'

'So you didn't know about these phone calls he'd been making until then?'

'No, sir.'

'Did this often happen? This business of getting worried about his wife, and phoning up to see if she was all right?'

Selway shrugged. 'I don't know, sir. If he did, it'd be more a case of checking up on her, I should have thought.'

'Oh? Was she two-timing him, then?'

Again Selway shrugged. 'I don't know for sure, sir, but let me say that I wouldn't have been surprised.'

'Why d'you say that?'

'Don't know exactly, but I always got the impression that she didn't care for him as much as he cared for her. She seemed to do whatever she wanted to do; always got her own way. He's a fool in my opinion.' Selway leaned forward

67

slightly. 'D'you know, guv'nor, he bought her a new car for a birthday present and she cribbed about the colour, so he had it changed.'

Gaffney laughed. 'You'd do that for your missus, wouldn't you?'

Selway scoffed. 'She'd be lucky if she got a bicycle . . . and she'd have what she was given.' He leaned back in his chair again. 'The farmhouse is another bone of contention . . . .'

'In what way?'

'They've got this old farmhouse in Shropshire, miles from anywhere. And madam was not very keen on that at all. Apart from the bloody awful journey up there, there was nothing to do when they arrived; well, nothing for her to do, that is. I got the impression she liked the bright lights, and there's not a lot of them up there.'

'And they rowed about it?'

Selway shook his head. 'They never rowed about anything. I don't think I've ever heard him raise his voice to her, but I've heard her complaining about having to spend weekends up there, more than once, and on one occasion she refused point-blank to go, right at the last minute.'

'What happened?'

'She stayed in London . . . at Cutler's Mews, I suppose.'

'And he went.'

'Had to. It was a civic dinner in the constituency, if I remember correctly. Quite frankly, I think the main problem was the disparity in ages: there's something like twenty years between them.' Selway laughed. 'For her it must have been like trying to get her father to go to a disco.'

Gaffney nodded. 'Yes, I know. He's fifty-four; she was thirty-four.'

'I think they were just on different wavelengths,' said Selway. 'A generation gap, I suppose you'd call it. But in public, of course, they were brilliant – a really devoted couple as far as the rest of the world was concerned – not a sign that she was bored out of her mind. Still, she was an actress . . . and I've yet to meet a politician who isn't an actor.' Selway paused. 'Not that he had to act. He absolutely adored her, and it showed: he'd have given her anything.'

'You said that she didn't like going to Shropshire. What did she do when she stayed in London?'

'Occupied herself with her film work, I suppose.'

'Work?'

'Only very conventional stuff, as befits the wife of a Home Secretary.'

Gaffney smiled inwardly at the perversity of that. A liaison with a main-index villain, if it turned out to be true, certainly didn't befit the wife of a Home Secretary. 'What was this work? Any idea?'

'Acted as a consultant of some sort, sir . . . to a film company, I believe. At least, that's what they said; to tell you the truth, I never knew for certain.' Selway stretched out his legs. 'D'you mind if I smoke, guv'nor?' He had been a policeman for twenty-five years – twenty of them in Special Branch – and had known Gaffney when he too had been a sergeant.

'Go ahead, John.' Gaffney pushed an ashtray across his desk.

'There was one occasion when he had a gentle go at her – more in sorrow than anger, I suspect – about not going up to the constituency with him very often.' Selway paused thoughtfully. 'It was at Cutler's Mews, in the sitting room, about a year ago now, I suppose; can't be sure. There had been some talk of a change in the programme. It was the usual thing: no one knew for certain, and no one had the guts to ask him, so I went to have a quick word.'

Gaffney laughed. 'I've had some of that,' he said.

'Anyhow,' continued Selway, 'I'd got as far as the sitting room door, when I heard him saying that he wished she'd go up to Shropshire more often. Well that didn't please madam at all. She gave him a right bollocking – four-letter words and all – about having her own career and not having time to waste on pudding-faced voters.' Selway blew a cloud of smoke into the air. 'They obviously didn't know I was there, so I thought it was better to retreat, and wait until later to see him.'

'Very wise.' Gaffney smiled, thinking back to his days at Downing Street. 'Did you ever hear anything about another man?'

Selway looked thoughtful for a moment or two. 'No, sir,' he said firmly, 'but as I said just now, I wouldn't have been surprised. She was a bloody attractive woman, and friendly, too.'

Gaffney raised an eyebrow. 'Friendly?'

Selway grinned. 'Not that friendly,' he said. 'I meant towards the likes of us. There was nothing stuck-up about her. Always ready to share a joke with the lads, which is more than I can say for some. To be perfectly honest, I liked her: she was a nice girl.'

'About the night before last, John. You say you took him to the Chesterfield at seven o'clock?' Selway nodded. 'And he stayed there until when?'

Selway's gaze dropped to his pocket book. 'Left there at nine-twenty, sir, and got to the House at half-past.'

'Mmm, that more or less accords with what he said; I think he put the time of return at a quarter to ten. Then he made another phone call, he said –' Gaffney looked up. 'Where would that have been from? His office?'

'No idea, sir. I suppose so. Things haven't changed much since you were on with the PM. I was in Speaker's Court, waiting . . . been there about ten minutes, I suppose, when the PC on Ladies' Gallery Entrance came across and said the old man wanted to see me, urgently.'

'So that would have been about quarter to ten?'

Selway consulted his pocket book again. 'A quarter to ten exactly, sir. I went up to his office and he told me that he had tried several times that evening to get in touch with his wife. He said that she was supposed to be at home, but wasn't answering the phone; he asked me if I could get someone to check.'

'And that's when you rang the Diplomatic Protection Group?'

'No, sir. I rang the Special Branch duty officer, Mr Wisley. I presume that he rang the DPG.'

Gaffney nodded. 'Yes, of course,' he said, 'I've got that written down somewhere. Did the Home Secretary mention that he'd phoned his home as early as six-thirty?' He looked down at his notes.

'No, sir, he just said several times. Why? Is it important?'

'Only in that it might help to fix the time of death perhaps more accurately than the pathologist was able to. On the other hand, Mrs Lavery could have been out until say nine, come in and been murdered by someone who followed her through the front door. There are all sorts of permutations. However, that's my problem, not yours. So you didn't actually see him making any of these phone calls?'

'No, sir.'

'Not even at the club?'

'No. We leave him to his own devices there – it's the usual practice. He said that there was no record of a Home Secretary ever being assassinated in a gentlemen's club.'

Gaffney laughed. 'What did you say to that?'

'I said that there wasn't a record of a Prime Minister being assassinated in the Palace of Westminster ... until it happened.' Selway paused. 'There's no great risk, mind you, leaving him on his own ... ' Gaffney raised an eyebrow. 'Well I suppose there's always the chance that the ancient club retainer who's been there for fifty years, will suddenly go raving mad and decide that tonight's the night he's going to murder the Home Secretary.' Selway shrugged. He knew as well as Gaffney, and anybody else who had done the job of protecting VIPs, that you only reduced the risk, never eliminated it. 'We normally wait in the secretary's office. We can see the main lobby from there, and there's always Sid – he's the hall porter – to keep an eye out for any movement. Usually the upstairs steward will give him a ring to say that the old man's on the move.'

Gaffney finished writing his notes and looked up. 'And then you brought him here to see the Commissioner, after the ten o'clock division?'

'Yes, sir.'

Gaffney leaned back and yawned. 'What sort of character is he, John?'

Selway thought for a moment or two. 'Clever ... ' he said eventually, 'and he would like to be Prime Minister ... like a lot of other politicians. In some cases you can see the naked

71

ambition, but he's not like that. I reckon he could make it without really trying.' Selway reached across and stubbed out his cigarette. 'I remember that there was one occasion when he got bloody shirty about a television programme he did, up at their place in Shropshire. I don't know if you saw it: some major comment on law and order.'

'I vaguely recollect something of the sort. Why? What was special about it?'

'Well when it came out on television, you got some footage of him playing a hard game of tennis with his missus. Then there was the interviewer talking to him beside the tennis court . . . '

'So?'

'It was taken the other way round.'

'Other way.'

'Yeah. The interview was shot first, then they filmed him playing tennis, but when it came out they'd put it the other way round. He was absolutely furious. He was straight on the phone to the public relations people at party HQ, ranting and raving about this "deception" as he called it; then he found out that it was their idea.'

'What was the point of that?'

Selway smiled. 'Apparently it was so that your average punter would see him playing a hard game of tennis and then being interviewed, and would you believe, he wasn't even out of breath. And him fifty-four years old and all.'

'Christ Almighty!' said Gaffney.

'Well, sir, that's the political world for you, and I dare say that most ambitious politicians would have been delighted.'

Gaffney laughed. 'One other thing, John – actually, there are two other things – but first, how's he taking it: the death of his wife?'

'Badly, I think. He's not a demonstrative sort of bloke –' Selway broke off. 'No, that's not quite what I mean. He's well able to disguise his feelings – all politicians can do that to a greater or lesser degree – but you can see occasionally, when no one's looking, a sort of intense sadness creeping over him, as though he's regretting not having done more for her when

72

she was alive.' He shook his head. 'God knows he's nothing to reproach himself for on that score, though.'

'Thanks, John, that's all been a great help.' He stood up. 'I'll let you get back now.'

Selway paused at the door. 'You said there were two things, sir. What was the other?'

'Ah yes!' Gaffney grinned. 'Leave a written statement of all you've told me, will you?'

'I knew there'd be a catch,' said Selway. 'I don't wonder people aren't keen to help the police.'

Mackinnon hovered in the doorway. 'You wanted me, sir?'

Gaffney waved a beckoning hand, and finished the sentence he was writing. 'Yes,' he said. 'Actors!'

'Actors, sir?' Mackinnon approached Gaffney's desk apprehensively, almost stealthily.

'Elizabeth Lavery – as Elizabeth Fairfax – was living with an actor before she married the Home Secretary.'

'Yes, sir?' Mackinnon knew what was coming next.

'Find him.'

Mackinnon smiled a sickly smile. 'Is there any more than that, sir?'

Gaffney smiled too. 'No!' He relented. 'We took her address and telephone books from the house,' he said. 'She's almost bound to have the name of her agent there somewhere. Get hold of him, and see what you can find out. If he doesn't know, he'll know someone who does, if I know the acting business.' And Gaffney did know; his ex-wife had been a theatrical agent.

Detective Inspector Henry Findlater was in charge of the Criminal Intelligence Branch surveillance team. He was barely five feet eight inches tall – the statutory minimum, as policemen call it – and with his owl-like spectacles had the appearance of a rather dim-witted and youthful student. He was not dim-witted however; on the contrary, he was very astute, an astute and Calvinistic Scot.

'Mr Masters is not at home, sir,' he said to Gaffney. 'There

73

is no answer to repeated knockings. Information is that he is in Spain. He was last seen the day before yesterday.'

'The day of the murder, in other words.' Findlater nodded. 'How the hell did you find that out, Henry? I hope you haven't alerted the neighbourhood.'

Findlater looked pained, and, had it not been for the disparity in rank, would probably have made a caustic remark. 'Certainly not, sir. I had some market research done.'

'Market research?'

'Yes,' said Findlater. 'We were conducting a survey into two-car families on this occasion.' He took off his glasses and wiped them. 'And that necessitates enquiring about next-door neighbours who are out. So that we can get an accurate survey, you'll understand.'

Gaffney smiled. 'Of course.'

'In short, he was seen the day before yesterday, has not been seen since, and our obo all day has revealed no sign of him either.' He smiled. 'I took the liberty, therefore, of speaking to your chaps at the airport, who were able to turn up a report about the departure of Masters—'

Gaffney sat up sharply. 'What?'

'They always report his movements, sir. He's a main-index villain.'

'I know that, but why in hell's name didn't they let me know? And straight away.'

'Probably because they didn't think that you had any interest in anyone as sordid as an SO11 main-index man, guv'nor,' said Tipper drily from the corner of the room. 'They don't know you've got Masters in the frame, do they?'

Gaffney relaxed, smiling. 'No, Harry, you're quite right, they don't.' He looked across at Findlater. 'When did he go, Henry?'

Findlater glanced from Gaffney to Tipper and back to Gaffney. 'Yesterday afternoon, sir.' He flicked open his pocket book. 'Left Heathrow at fifteen-fifty on Iberia Airways flight 617 for Seville.' He paused. 'That was the first available flight to Seville after the murder, sir.'

'Thank you, Henry,' said Gaffney. 'Thank you very much

indeed.' He waited until the door had closed behind the diminutive Inspector and turned his chair to face Tipper. 'What the hell do we do now, Harry?'

Tipper leaned back in his chair, crossed his legs at the ankles and smiled. 'There's not a lot you can do except wait. We haven't got a shred of evidence; certainly nothing that would warrant extradition.'

'What d'you suggest then?'

'I think that we should go and have a chat with Waldo Conway who is in the Scrubs – I've checked – and also see what Enrico can do to assist.'

Enrico Perez was a Spanish policeman attached to his country's embassy in London where he occupied some vaguely defined diplomatic post. He spoke faultless English, bought his suits in Savile Row, and was an anglophile. Within five minutes of receiving Gaffney's telephone call, he had seized a bottle of duty-free Spanish brandy and leaped into a taxi outside his embassy in Belgrave Square.

'Why are you working late on a Friday, John?' He opened his arms expansively.

'Go easy, Enry,' said Tipper, relieving Perez of the bottle which he was waving about. He always called Enrico 'Enry' in exchange for Enrico's contraction of his name to 'Arry'.

'I am working late on a Friday, Enrico, because someone took it into his head to murder the wife of the Home Secretary.'

Perez flopped into an armchair and allowed his arms to fall on either side until his hands were almost touching the floor. 'Yes, I heard about it. Of course, it was just around the corner from the embassy.'

'Did you hear anything?' asked Tipper, foraging in Gaffney's cupboard for some glasses.

'You think I am in the embassy at that time of night?' Perez laughed. 'It was the Spanish who invented the phrase *mañana*, you know, Arry.' He poured a measure of brandy into each of the glasses and slid the bottle across the desk towards Gaffney. 'Keep it,' he said. 'Cheers!' He raised his glass, took a sip and stood it on the floor beside his chair. 'Now, what can I do for you?'

'We have an interest in a man called Colin Masters, Enrico. He has a villa in Seville – well, actually about thirty kilometres outside Seville – and we want to talk to him in connection with Mrs Lavery's murder.'

'Aha!' said Perez. 'Extradition?'

'Not a hope; there's no evidence.'

Perez laughed and touched his nose. 'Just this, eh?'

'As you say, just that,' said Gaffney. 'D'you think that you can help?'

Perez felt about on the floor for his brandy and took another sip. 'You know that he's there, John?'

'We know that he left Heathrow on the day following the murder, on an Iberian flight for Seville. It's almost certain that that's where he went, but we'd like it confirmed.'

'Okay!' Perez withdrew an expensive leather-bound notebook from his pocket, and a gold pencil. 'What is the address?' He noted it down at Gaffney's dictation. 'I can certainly have someone find out if he's there, but presumably you don't want him alerted?'

Gaffney shook his head. 'Not at the moment. He's probably unaware of our interest in him, so I don't want him to feel threatened.'

'But if he's committed the murder, he won't come back. And if there's no evidence, you can't extradite him. I suppose that his papers are in order?'

'I imagine so. Anyway, you're in the Common Market now, so that makes it much more difficult.'

Perez shrugged. 'Sometimes there are ways. He's not a Basque separatist, is he?' he asked hopefully, and they all laughed. 'Okay, John, I'll do what I can, but beyond confirming that he's there, and perhaps letting you know if he makes a move, there's not much more we can do.'

'Well, even that will be a help, Enrico.'

'Glad to be of assistance. Now it's poets' day, yes? So let's have some more brandy.'

# Chapter Seven

Once a convicted person has been sentenced to a period of imprisonment, he is handed into the custody of the governor of the prison in which he is to be incarcerated. Once this has happened, the police, despite having in all probability arrested the prisoner and assembled most of the evidence which sent him down, cannot just wander into one of Her Majesty's prisons for a quick chat. There is a form for it; there is a form for most things in the Metropolitan Police. This particular form has to be signed by a senior officer, and is then served by the interviewing officer on the governor, requesting him to produce the named prisoner for interview, unaccompanied by a prison officer.

Despite all that, a prisoner may refuse to be interviewed by the police; that is his right. It is one of an ever-increasing number of rights campaigned for by influential people who usually live in elegant parts of London and who have rarely, if ever, met a villain – much less a victim – in their sheltered little lives. This does not, however, prevent them from pontificating on crime and punishment, as well as on a whole variety of other subjects of which, similarly, they know little or nothing. As far as crime and punishment go, the views of those with a direct responsibility for maintaining law and order, and discipline in prisons, are much more interesting . . . and valid.

Fortunately for policemen investigating crime with which it is thought that an inmate of a prison may assist, the said inmate is usually curious to know what it is the police want to talk to him about. He is, after all, more aware than most that he is under no obligation to say anything, but that anything he does say, et cetera, et cetera . . .

The huge outer doors of Wormwood Scrubs prison closed behind the police car containing Gaffney and Tipper before the equally huge doors in front of them were opened. This cunning airlock system, as it is called, is designed to prevent the escape of prisoners. It doesn't, of course, as the escape of the spy George Blake from that very prison had proved . . . but he had cheated by going over the wall.

'Leave your car over there,' said the gate officer to Tipper. 'It'll be all right – no one'll nick it.' He cackled at his own joke, and Tipper grinned a sickly grin; he had heard it every time he had entered a prison.

After the usual amount of in-house administration, telephone calls and elaborate key work, Gaffney and Tipper came face-to-face with Waldo Conway, serving five years for robbery and other related offences, in one of the interview rooms in D Block.

'This is Mr Gaffney, Waldo,' said Tipper. 'He's all right, he's from Special Branch.'

Conway relaxed slightly. Whatever it was they wanted to talk to him about, it was unlikely that they wanted to charge him with anything. Conway would be the first to admit – not to the police, of course; he never admitted anything to the police – that he'd pulled some strokes in his life, but nothing in which the Special Branch would be obliged to take any action. Nevertheless, he still retained the foxy expression which was a permanent feature of his countenance. 'Oh yeah!' he said.

'I want to talk to you about Colin Masters, Waldo.'

Conway stood up. 'Goodbye, Mr Tipper.'

'Sit down,' said Tipper, with no trace of a smile. 'It won't hurt.'

'Huh! You don't know Colin Masters, then.' Reluctantly he resumed his seat. 'And I ain't grassin',' he added as an afterthought.

'Tell me about Seville, Waldo,' said Tipper. He took a packet of cigarettes out of his pocket and slid it across the table. 'I suppose you're short of snout, as usual.'

Conway pocketed the cigarettes without comment, and without a word of thanks. 'What about Seville?'

'How many times have you been there?'

'What makes you think I've been at all?'

'Stop sodding around, Waldo. I know you've been there. Now what sort of set-up is it?'

Conway ran a hand round his mouth. 'I hope this is confidential, Mr Tipper.'

Tipper nodded. 'Of course it is. You don't think I'm going to advertise who I've been talking to, do you?'

'It's a villa that Colin owns. Out of the town about twenty miles, I suppose, on the Cadiz road.' He pronounced the name of the city as though describing people who carry golf clubs round a course. 'It's off the road, as a matter of fact; it's miles from anywhere.'

'Yeah? And what's there?'

'It's like I said, just a villa. It's a smashing place, mind. Big. There's sort of three sides to it, round the swimming pool.'

'And what goes down there?'

Conway shrugged. He was very reluctant to talk about Masters to the police. Masters was a powerful man, physically and in terms of the influence he wielded, and had been known to turn very nasty when someone talked out of turn. 'Nothing much.'

Tipper also knew of Masters' reputation, and knew also that Conway would need to be persuaded that he was unlikely to come to any harm as a result of talking to the police. 'Look, Waldo, it's not Colin we're interested in, so much as one of his lady-friends.'

A look of naked fear crossed Conway's face. He ran his tongue round his lips, then glanced rapidly at each of the detectives in turn before centring once more on Tipper. 'You've got to be bloody joking.' His voice was a hoarse whisper, and Tipper noticed little beads of sweat on his forehead. 'I'm saying sod-all about her.'

Tipper was in his element, practising the craft he knew. This political stuff was all very well, but jousting with a villain was his *métier*. 'When I came in this nick this morning,' said Tipper softly, 'I handed over a form signed by Mr Gaffney here. That form will find its way to the office, where one of the clerks is a trustie . . . yes?' He looked enquiringly at Conway. 'And in no time at all, my son, the entire prison population is going to know that the Old Bill popped in this morning to have a quiet word with Waldo Conway.' He smiled nastily. 'And not any Old Bill, either, but two heavyweights from the Bladder o' Lard, no less.'

Gaffney, sitting to one side, smiled. It was a long time since he had heard anyone using the rhyming slang for Scotland Yard.

'I'm not saying anything, Mr Tipper. It's more than my life's worth.'

'To continue, Waldo,' said Tipper conversationally, as though Conway hadn't spoken, 'word will be about that you've been very helpful. On the other hand, if you have a little chat with me and my guv'nor, I shall let it be known that you wouldn't say a word. And I shall start by complaining bitterly to that screw outside that I've had a wasted journey; you know what they're like for a gossip. However, if you see fit not to assist the police in their hour of need, I shall put it about that you spent the morning singing like a corrupt canary.' He paused to give his statement effect. 'So if I was you, Waldo, I'd have my money's-worth.'

Conway looked round desperately. It was too late. If only he hadn't let his curiosity get the better of him; if only he'd refused to see the police at all; if only . . . He opened his mouth, but no sound came. He tried again. 'Could I have a drink of water, Mr Tipper?'

'I think we might do even better than that; I'll see if we can persuade the authorities to produce a cup of coffee.'

'I s'pose you haven't got a light, Mr Tipper, have you?' asked Conway when they were settled once more.

Silently, Gaffney passed his lighter across the table, and Conway took a deep lungful of smoke. He returned the lighter and sat back, partially recovered.

80

'You know, of course, that this bird got topped on Wednesday evening,' said Tipper. Conway nodded miserably. 'Well, my job is to find out who topped her. Now, you can start by telling me how often you saw her at Colin's place in Seville.'

Conway swallowed, a movement made more noticeable by his accentuated Adam's apple. 'Only the once, Mr Tipper.' Tipper's eyes narrowed. 'God's honest truth, Mr Tipper.'

'Yeah, all right, Waldo. Go on.'

'I reckon it was the first time she'd come down there. Well, I know it was because Colin said so.'

'Did you know who she was?'

'No. Well, not then, like; not straight away. He told me after.'

'After what?'

'After she'd been there for a bit.'

'How long was she there for?'

''Bout a week, I s'pose; bit longer maybe.'

Tipper shot a glance at Gaffney who shrugged. They were both wondering how she had got away with a week's absence from her husband, and what sort of tale she'd spun him.

'What were you doing down there, anyway? What were you celebrating?'

'Nothing. It was Colin; he just fancied having a week in the sun. That's all. Nothing wrong with that, is there?' he asked defensively.

'Depends who's paying for it—'

'Colin did.'

'And where did the money come from?' Tipper stared intently at Conway until his gaze dropped.

'I don't know nothing about that.'

'And right now I don't care,' said Tipper. 'But I might.' The implied threat registered. 'Did you travel down together?'

Conway looked horrified. 'Christ no! If we'd done that we'd have spent a couple of hours getting turned over by your blokes at the airport. Do be reasonable, Mr Tipper.' He paused. 'No, we travelled down separate like.'

'And what about Mrs Lavery?'

'Who?' For a moment or two Conway looked genuinely puzzled. 'Oh, Liz, you mean?'

Tipper nodded patiently. 'Yes, Liz.'

'She come down on her own, after the rest of us got there. I remember that, because it was very hot—'

'Would be,' said Tipper quietly.

'And we was round the pool, and Colin was swearing a bit because he had to drive out to pick her up from . . .'

'Seville?' Tipper prompted him sarcastically.

'Yeah, but I was trying to think of the name of the airport. Got it: San Pablo. Well the plane never got in till nine o'clock in the evening, and it was a bleedin' long drive. I reckon it was gone ten before he got back.'

'Yes?'

'Never saw her that night; never saw her until the next morning.' He laughed. 'Well, you know what it's like—'

'No!' said Tipper pointedly.

The subtlety was lost on Conway. 'The three of us was sitting round the pool, getting pissed on cheap Spanish plonk. My bird was some brass I'd picked up with, and she was flaunting herself about the place, flashing her tits at Colin, cheeky little cow. If there's one thing a brass can sniff out it's the old readies; they don't care who's got it so long as some of it rubs off on them. And they don't care what they have to do to get it, neither.' He sniffed: an eloquent comment on the archness of women. 'Then this Liz bird comes out of the house. She had to be different, didn't she? We was drinking plonk, but she wanted gin and tonic. Got it an' all. Mind you, I reckon she was chancing her arm with Colin. I've seen birds come and go before, we all have, lots of them. Still, she soon learned.'

'Learned what?' Tipper was getting a little weary of this tedious recital, but let Conway go on, amazed that he had got him to talk at all. He knew the power of Masters: he didn't take kindly to people telling tales behind his back.

'Well, she was parading around in a bikini that must have cost about two sous a square inch; nothing to it, there wasn't: three little bits of cloth and a lot of string. The rest of us was

82

a bit pissy by then, and my bird, Sharon, was starting to have a go at her. She was topless see, Sharon was. Then she takes the bottom half off an' all, still flashing herself at Colin, but now there was a bit of needle like, with this other bird coming in the frame.' He laughed. 'She chucked the bottom half at Colin, like she was a stripper.' He paused thoughtfully. 'S'matter of fact, I think she was. Anyway, like I said, Shar was having a go at this Liz bird, telling her to get hers off an' all. Well she wasn't having none of that.'

'Was this just your bird having a go, or were you at it, too?' asked Tipper. He wasn't really interested, but didn't want Conway to think he was wasting his time in case he stopped talking.

'You'd better believe it, Mr Tipper. I mean, blokes don't take the piss out of another bloke's bird, not if he's a mate, and specially if it's Colin's bird. No, it was just Shar. Well, Colin never took to that, like, and he shouts across to Liz and tells her to get her bikini off, same as Shar.'

'And did she?'

Conway laughed. 'She gets all arsy about that and sticks her hands on her hips and says something about not being one of his tarts and not being a stripper neither.'

'I should think he enjoyed that,' said Tipper mildly.

'Yeah! Well, it all went sort of quiet. Colin puts his glass down, and lays his lardi in the ashtray. Then he gets up off his sun-lounger, dead slow like, and walks across to where she was standing. Oh, he says, you can do a strip on the telly, but you can't do it here, is that it, like.'

'What was that about?'

'Well, it seems she done a nude scene on telly, years ago when she was an actress. I didn't know what he was talking about. I never knew she'd been on no telly.'

'Yeah, all right,' said Tipper impatiently. 'Then what?'

'Well, this Liz bird says something about it having been part of the play, or part of the plot, or something. It's what all them acting birds say, ain't it? Anyway, my Shar has a giggle at that, but Colin gives her a bit of a hard look and she shut up. Anyhow, to cut a long story short' – Tipper

83

looked up at the ceiling – 'he says, well it's part of the play here, he says. Then he puts one hand down her bra and the other down her briefs and just rips 'em off. Like I said, there wasn't hardly nothing to 'em anyway. Then he slaps her face, real hard, and chucks her in the pool. There, you high and mighty cow, he says, now you're the same as her. Then he goes and sits down again, smiling, and smoking his lardi.'

'And was that it? What did she do, walk out?'

'Couldn't, could she? We was miles from anywhere, like I said. Colin had picked her up from the airport in his motor. If she'd wanted to piss off, she'd have had to walk, 'bout twenty miles. No. She was stuck. I wasn't going to give her no lift, not without the nod from Colin. Anyhow, she crawled out the pool, and walked across to where I was and took my glass of plonk off me. Then she walked across to where Colin was sitting, dead cool like, and chucked it all over him. Put his lardi out, that did,' he added mournfully.

Tipper laughed. 'What did he do then?'

'He grabs hold of her by the wrist, hard, and he tells her to go and wait for him in the bedroom.'

'Well?'

'Well, she stands there, just staring at him for a bit, then she turned round and went straight indoors. Colin sits around for another ten minutes, smiling and finishing his drink, then he goes indoors an' all. Never saw 'em again for about two hours.' He looked wistful. ''Eard 'em, though; noisy little cow, she was.'

'And she stayed for a week, you said?'

Conway put his head on one side for a moment or two. 'Yeah, about that.'

'And what?'

'Nothing really. They got on all right after that. I mean, me and Shar knew Colin was giving her a seeing-to – no point in him bringing her otherwise – so she couldn't be too toffee-nosed, could she? I mean, we was at it, an' all.'

'She must have been mad,' said Tipper, as much to himself as to Conway. 'You knew by then who she was, didn't you?'

'Oh yeah.' Conway nodded. 'We knew all right, but we wasn't going to grass. Why should we? Colin's right hard, and if Shar had let on, she'd have got striped, and a tom who's had a face job's out of business. Anyway, we thought it was insurance.'

'Insurance, Waldo? What are you talking about?'

'Yeah, well it don't seem so funny now, but it was a big laugh at the time. Colin screwing the Home Secretary's missus. I reckoned she'd square things up if any of us got in bother.' He laughed cynically. 'Some bleedin' hope. If that'd been true, I wouldn't be sitting here now, would I?'

'What about the Press?'

'What about 'em?'

'Surely they'd have got hold of it. Let's face it, Waldo, there's a lot of villains in Spain and the Press are always sniffing around.'

Conway looked at Tipper as if despairing for his reason. 'Mr Tipper,' he said patiently, 'they only write about the ones who's finished, washed up, on the trot; got no muscle left, see. They don't put nothing in the paper about the blokes who's still at it. Too risky, see. Colin let them know. Anyone who wrote anything about him or any of his mates was down for a good smacking.' He laughed. 'I tell you what, Mr Tipper, they'd never have played the violin again. Nor a bleeding typewriter, and they knew it.'

'Was that the only time she went to Spain?'

'I don't think so. I heard she went a few times, but it was the only time she was there when I was there. I don't . . . ' He paused. 'No, I tell a lie . . . '

'How unusual,' murmured Tipper.

'No, I did see her there again, about four months later. That's when she started wearing the chain. That was—'

'What chain?' Tipper's voice did not change; there was no variation to indicate that Conway had mentioned something which suddenly interested him.

'It was a gold chain that Colin give her, with a big medal thing on the end. She used to walk around with sod-all on except that bleeding chain round her waist, with the medal hanging down in front of her fanny. Called it her badge of office. Colin said, when she wore that, she was his. I reckon it must've cost a bomb; solid gold it was. Gold chain for a gold lady, that's what Colin used to say. Pushover for a good-looking bird is Colin.'

'Was marriage ever mentioned?' Tipper asked.

Conway scoffed. 'What, Colin? No chance. Didn't fancy getting tied up with no bird, not Colin. Screw anything that come along, but he never wanted to marry any of them. Mind you, he never told her that; never told none of them that. I reckon she thought she was there for good; started lording it a bit, so I heard; you know, being the boss's bird: all that.' He held fingers and thumb up, and opened and closed them like a duck's beak. 'She fancied that villa in Spain bit; go over there any time. And of course, Colin seemed to have more gelt than her old man. I don't s'pose he had. If I know nobs like Lavery, he'll have it all salted away in stocks and shares and all that crap. Colin's used to be in bundles. Always seemed to have a roll of fifties as thick as your arm.'

'What was the attraction? It wasn't her sort of world.'

'Colin was the pull. There's a lot of society birds like her who like a bit of rough. And Colin's rough. Let's face it, Mr Tipper, he's just a South London boy. I know he's got all the gear, but that's him, ain't it? I suppose she liked living two lives. You know, the one in London with everyone bowing and scraping because of who her old man was, and then out in Spain with Colin, with no one giving a sod who she was. Colin treated her like any other tart. He'd slap her around an' all. I've seen him give her a good belting across the arse, and he never give a toss who was there. He even had her in the pool once – with us watching.' He laughed at the memory and then coughed, remembering who he was talking about and who he was talking to. 'I asked her once why she stood it. She said she loved him, silly little cow.' He paused to light another cigarette. 'Mind you, I think Colin was getting a bit brassed off with her; think he was about ready to give her the elbow.'

'Oh? What did she think about that?'

'Dunno. Never see her again, after that last time.'

'Did Colin ever see her in London?'

Conway frowned. 'Bloody hell, no. I know Colin'll push his luck, but he said once that that'd really be chancing his arm. He ain't daft, Mr Tipper. And I'll tell you what – he wouldn't have topped her, neither, if that's what you're thinking.'

'How can you be so sure? He's a violent man. You said yourself that no one would cross him, and you say he wasn't above giving Liz a hiding.'

'That's the way we are, Mr Tipper; you know that. We'll do a blagging and if any bastard's daft enough to put up a fight, he'll get a smacking. I don't know why they do it. It ain't usually their money anyhow, and if it is, it's insured, so why all the aggro?' He shrugged, baffled by the unreasonable attitude of the average victim. 'Why should he do her in? Don't make no sense. He'd've just told her to piss off. What could she have done, sued him? No, he wouldn't have topped her, Mr Tipper, not Colin. Where's the profit in that?'

# Chapter Eight

José Galeciras turned the Land Rover on to the earth road that joined Masters' villa at Puente Alcazaba to the main highway. It was a warm day but an earlier light drizzle had dampened the dust and prevented it from rising; a dust that in the summer would cover them from head to foot, and would penetrate their olive-green uniforms and leave a film on their patent leather tricorn hats: the *tricornio* that distinguished the *Guardia Civil*. Galeciras spat over the side of the Land Rover and glanced briefly at his colleague. He shrugged and then swore as the vehicle hit a large stone. It made no sense to either of them. The telephone call from their *Teniente* in *Sevilla* had told them to find out if Señor Masters was at his villa. When they asked why, they were told to mind their own business, but to be discreet. Pah!

They knew the villa, of course; had visited it before. They were usually given a beer if Masters was there and spotted them. He had told them that it was good that the police were looking after his property; he didn't want *bandidos* stealing from him when he was not there. He was a nice man and such a statement tended to negate the rumours that they had heard in some quarters that Señor Masters was a criminal himself. If this were so, thought Galeciras, then why would he be able to travel between Spain and England so often without being arrested. Galeciras had read about the British police and their famous Scotland Yard; they would not have let Masters go free if he was a criminal. Maybe. He had also heard of British policemen coming to Spain to arrest people, but going back without them. Perhaps they weren't so clever; and perhaps Señor Masters was a criminal after all.

He shrugged. But the *Teniente* in *Sevilla* need not have been so rude.

Masters' villa had been built on a hill, and he could see in all directions from it; and there were no near neighbours. Consequently he saw the approaching *Guardia Civil* Land Rover when it was still some way away. On this occasion he was staying at Puente Alcazaba on his own. There was a very good reason for that, but it was unlikely that the approaching *pareja* as they called them – the pair, because they always travelled in twos – were concerned about that. If the British police really were interested in him, Interpol would have been alerted, and he would have been visited by some nasty bastard from Seville, or even Madrid; not the local fuzz.

He walked across the broad patio and leaned over the gate. '*Buenas tardes,*' he said as the Land Rover came to a stop.

The two policemen alighted and stamped their feet to straighten their trousers; then they tugged at the hems of their tunics. '*Buenas tardes,* Señor Masters.' Galeciras flicked at his tricorn with his gloves by way of a salute.

'*Muchas* hot today, *si*?' Masters' joke-Spanish was his way of covering the apprehension that was second nature to him whenever he had dealings with the police, whatever their nationality. In his book, the approach of the police never meant anything but trouble. The only difference was that some foreign police forces were susceptible to occasional bribery, and you usually got value for money; the sodding British would take your money and nick you as well.

Galeciras nodded. 'Yes, it is.' He was proud of his English. His wife had encouraged him to take English classes in Utrera, near where they lived, but there were few Englishmen on whom to practise in that part of Spain – even in summer – and a conversation with Señor Masters was a rare chance to try out what he had learned.

Masters pulled open the gate. 'You'd better come in and have a beer.'

For a moment the two policemen hesitated. It was not

89

a question of the proprieties of having a drink while on duty: it was a case of whether they should leave the Land Rover where it was or drive it through the gateway. Galeciras shrugged once more, and reached into the vehicle, pulling out two machine-carbines. Then he and his colleague followed Masters.

'Expecting trouble?' Masters gave a tight laugh and pointed at the guns.

Galeciras laughed too. 'We don't want anyone to steal them,' he said.

Masters strode across to the bar at the edge of the swimming pool and took three cans of beer out of the refrigerator. He poured them into ornate glasses and handed them round. Then he raised his glass. 'Good luck.' He took a sip and grinned. 'How d'you say that in Spanish?'

'*Buena sombra.*'

Masters nodded. 'Yeah. Must try and remember that. Well, how's crime, lads?'

'How is it?' Galeciras looked puzzled.

Masters laughed nervously. 'English expression,' he said. 'Means er – what?' He tried desperately to think of some suitable phrase that the Spaniard would understand. 'How's business?'

'Ah! Business is very good.' Galeciras took another swig of his beer. 'My comrade –' He indicated his partner with a jerk of the head. 'My comrade, he shot a *bandido* last week.' He pointed at the two machine-guns resting incongruously on one of the poolside tables and made a noise like gunfire. It wasn't true, but Galeciras felt that he had to justify his existence.

'Oh, very good,' said Masters unconvincingly. 'Always nice to know you lads are looking after my *hacienda*.' He laughed again. He knew that he shouldn't be worried that the two policemen were standing on the very flagstones that he had sweated over replacing a few weeks ago, so that they looked as if they'd been there for years, but it made him feel uneasy nevertheless. 'Why don't you lads take the weight off your plates?' he asked, pointing at the poolside chairs.

90

'I'm sorry, I don't—'

'My fault,' said Masters. 'That's London English: means sit down.'

'Ah!' Galeciras grinned. 'No thank you, *señor*.'

'Another beer, then?'

Galeciras held up a hand. 'No thank you, *señor*. We have other places to go. We just come to see you are okay, yes?'

'Oh yes, very good. Drop in any time, lads. Always welcome. Liberty Hall, this is.'

They drove slowly down the track, watched thoughtfully by Masters from the gate. 'What is this Liberty Hall?' asked Galeciras' partner. 'I thought it was Puente Alcazaba.'

John Gaffney looked out of the window of his office on the eighteenth floor of New Scotland Yard, absently watching the depressing flurries of snow which swept sideways across his line of vision. He turned to face Harry Tipper, reclining in an armchair and slowly stirring a cup of coffee. 'Five bloody days, Harry,' he said, 'and no further forward than we were on day one.'

'What did Enrico have to say, guv'nor?'

'Just that the local Old Bill had confirmed that Masters was at his place in Seville – or just outside it – and was apparently on his own.' He threw his packet of cigars on to the desk and sat down in his swivel chair. 'Which is some help and no help, if you see what I mean.'

'Sort of,' said Tipper. 'I think we're just going to have to be patient.'

'That's a bit difficult when we've got the team we've got breathing down our necks.' He ticked them off on his fingers. 'Apart from the Home Secretary, of course, there's the PM, the Commissioner, and I've no doubt that Her Majesty is quite interested in the result.' He spun on his chair and peered out of the window towards the Mall, as if seeking inspiration from a Buckingham Palace that was all but invisible through the snow. He turned back and saw for the first time a neat pile of papers on a side-table. 'What's that lot?'

'Result of the house-to-house, sir.'

'Any good?'

'Nope!' Tipper sniffed forlornly. 'Only one thing . . . '

'Yes?'

'One of the neighbours . . . ' He leaned forward and took the top sheet off the pile. 'Number Nine said she heard a taxi pull into the mews at about eight o'clock – give or take half an hour – and leave again almost immediately.'

'Give or take half an hour?' Gaffney looked puzzled.

'Yeah! She knows it was during a commercial break on television, but can't remember which break it was.'

'Smashing!' said Gaffney sarcastically. 'As a matter of fact, I didn't think that cultured people like that lot ever watched commercial television.'

'Neither did I,' said Tipper. 'Bit too ordinary for them.'

'So what results have we got from that?'

Tipper shook his head. 'Nothing yet, sir. I've been in touch with Cabs Office but it usually takes one hell of a time, and frankly they don't hold out a lot of hope. In the meantime what the hell do we do next . . . sir?' He relaxed again and grinned.

'Consider what we've got, Harry, that's what we do. Now,' he continued, 'in five days there has been no claim from any terrorist organisation. Why's that?'

Tipper shook his head. 'Because it's not down to terrorists, that's why . . . '

'But it might have been a mistake.'

'So? They'd still claim it; but there's been nothing, and I reckon it's too late now. Secondly, there appears to be nothing missing from the house, so burglary's out.' He reflected on that. 'But I reckon it was never in. Strangulation's not a usual method for a housebreaker to use. Cosh, maybe; gun more likely, these days. But strangulation? I doubt it, somehow.'

Tipper nodded. 'I'd go along with that, sir . . . if he'd bother at all. There's no sign that she put up a fight.' That was true. There was no sign of resistance from what they had seen, nor from the scientific examination of the body:

her fingernails had not been found to be secreting blood or skin that might have indicated a desperate effort to thwart her attacker. 'In most cases a breaker, surprised by a woman, would cut and run.'

'So we're left with Masters,' said Gaffney. 'But I find that story of Conway's hard to swallow. Are we seriously expected to believe that the Home Secretary's wife is cavorting around naked in a swimming pool with an SO11 main-index villain, and that her old man appears neither to know nor care?'

'And don't forget, guv'nor, that Colin Masters took it on his dancers on the first available flight out of Heathrow after the murder.'

Gaffney nodded. 'And then there's the chain. Asking for trouble, leaving that at Cutler's Mews where her old man might find it. Why not leave it in Seville, at Masters' villa?'

'What, with all those criminals? Someone might have nicked it,' said Tipper with a smile. 'Hold on though, guv, that might just be it.' Tipper leaned forward, resting his elbows on his knees and linking his fingers loosely together.

'Might just be what?'

'D'you remember what Conway said about Masters giving Liz Lavery the push? Or at least thinking about it.' Gaffney nodded. 'Suppose that is what happened. He kicked her arse out of it and she takes the chain back home as a keepsake – or something she can hock come a rainy day – and bungs it in the drawer of her dressing table and forgets it. Masters knows it's adrift, and tops her to get it back—'

'No! He didn't get it back, did he?'

'Well, maybe he couldn't find it,' said Tipper.

'Oh come on, Harry, it was in just about the most obvious place.'

'Okay, try this one, then.' Tipper smiled ruefully. 'Heard she'd been topped; knew that the chain had gone from Spain and guessed where it was. Thinks he's going to be our front-runner and has it on the toes until we nick someone else.'

Gaffney nodded slowly. 'Sounds better. Maybe someone's working one off on Masters by murdering her.'

'That's an interesting theory. Could have been one of his former lady-friends, you mean?'

'Possible, but strangulation is not usually a female crime.'

'Hired assassin?' Tipper grinned. 'On her behalf?'

Gaffney smiled. 'I think we're drifting off into the realms of fantasy here, Harry. What d'you reckon your chances of pulling that off would be? Just suppose for one moment that you put yourself about in the market place offering a contract. So you get a taker and he says, "Who is it?" Quite casually you mention that it's the Home Secretary's wife; he's going to run a mile, yes?'

Tipper nodded gravely. In his years of experience in criminal investigation, which was considerably more than Gaffney's, he had dealt with one or two so-called gangland killings. But that's what they were: villains taking out villains, because they'd got too big, or crossed into someone else's territory, or cheated, or taken more than they were entitled to. Or they'd grassed. He couldn't think of a single occasion when a killing of that sort had gone outside the victim's own circle of acquaintances. 'And what about Drake?'

'Yes,' said Gaffney. 'What indeed? Any news on him?'

'Nothing, guv.' Tipper shook his head. 'I've put an obo on his drum, but I think we're wasting our time. I've had a word with the DSS, but he's not been in for his benefit. I've asked to be alerted if he shows up anywhere else to claim it; at least it'll narrow the field, but I haven't got much hope. I reckon Thames Division's our best bet.'

'Thames?'

'Yeah!' Tipper grinned. 'It's a racing certainty they'll find him floating down past Tower Bridge.' He became serious again. 'So what do we do now?'

'I think we probe backgrounds a little more. But I don't want the anodyne statements of people like Desmond Marshall who'll tell you that their marriage was idyllic – there's no such thing – or information that you have to drag out of people like Waldo Conway, who I still reckon's lying through his teeth – '

'I don't,' said Tipper.

'He's terrified of Masters, Harry. I reckon he made that whole story up, so that if it got back to Masters he'd just laugh, and even bask in the sort of reputation that screwing the Home Secretary's wife would give him in the criminal fraternity, and Waldo couldn't be accused of grassing; in fact, he'd be congratulated for having the Old Bill over.'

Tipper pouted. 'Maybe. But don't forget the chain. Anyway who's left?'

'His agent.'

'His agent? What agent?'

'Lavery's constituency agent. One of the things the Special Branch has taught me is that, with politicians, their constituency agent is the one person who knows them better than anyone else.' He turned and reached for the telephone. 'But first, I think we'd better go and talk to the other side, just to put them in the picture. You never know,' he added, 'we might learn something.'

Hector Toogood was a senior Security Service officer with whom both Gaffney and Tipper had worked in the past. He sat behind his metal government desk and gazed at them bleakly. 'And what d'you expect me to do with a piece of information like that, John?' he asked. 'It's utterly incredible.'

Gaffney nodded amiably. 'Yes, it is, isn't it?'

'But if it's true, it represents a major security scandal. The Prime Minister will have to be told . . . '

Gaffney raised a hand. 'Now hold on, Hector, before you go running along to Downing Street – and possibly getting your fingers burned – let me just remind you that all we have is a piece of jewellery that was purchased by a known villain and was found in the Home Secretary's house. That's all. We have no idea how it got there, and nor, for that matter, has the Home Secretary. Added to that is the word of an extremely unreliable criminal who claims to have seen her – the late Elizabeth Lavery, that is – cavorting naked in a swimming pool with the said Colin Masters.' Gaffney had deliberately not revealed the source of his information – few policemen did – but in this case there was sound reasoning behind it. It was only with difficulty that Conway had been persuaded to talk at all. Any attempts by the Security Service to see him would be disastrous, and Gaffney might just need to see him again.

Toogood looked miserable. 'D'you know anything about the set-up in . . . ' He paused to consult the notes he had made during Gaffney's initial explanation. 'Puente Alcazaba?'

'It's about thirty kilometres or so south of Seville on the Cadiz road. It's at the end of a turning up a long dirt-track, and an approach can be seen for miles around. So if you've got any clever thoughts about surveillance, it'd better be bloody sophisticated.'

'This is terrible,' said Toogood. 'What are we going to do?'

Gaffney laughed. 'It's history, Hector. The woman's dead, strangled, and quite frankly I don't care what you do with that particular piece of information. My only interest is to see if you know, or can discover, anything which might help me to solve a murder. A murder I shouldn't bloody well have been investigating in the first place,' he added bitterly.

Toogood still looked unhappy. 'Cavorting naked in a swimming pool, you say?' He shook his head as though unable to visualise anyone doing that, let alone the wife of his political boss. 'I'm going to have to take this to the DG, John. I see no alternative.'

'He'll probably tell you it's a load of uncorroborated crap, Hector,' said Gaffney, smiling.

Toogood nodded. 'He probably will, but for God's sake, John, I can't sit on it.'

Gaffney stood up. 'I didn't think you would, Hector,' he said. 'Not for one moment.'

Sir Raymond Grierson, the newly appointed Director-General of the Security Service, looked up as Toogood entered, accompanied now by David Meaker, Toogood's own departmental boss.

'I have just received some rather disturbing information from Special Branch, sir,' he said. He had only just related it to Meaker who had reinforced Toogood's view that the DG

96

should be told without delay, despite the apparent tenuousness of Gaffney's tale.

'Sit down, gentlemen,' said Grierson, and listened dispassionately to Toogood's account. Then he leaned back in his chair and smiled in a way that made both Meaker and Toogood feel as though they had just been accused of making a noise during morning assembly. 'It seems to me, Hector,' he said at length, 'that what we have here is a whisper of unconfirmed scuttle-butt.' And that was more or less what Gaffney had said he would say. 'However, I suppose we had better set the wheels in motion . . . .' He nodded his dismissal and waited until the door had closed. Then he lifted the receiver of his special telephone. 'Richard?'

'Yes, Ray,' said the Chief of the Secret Intelligence Service.

The man behind the desk was a theatrical agent called Pearson. He was middle-aged and had the ascetic expression of one who suffered permanently from constipation. There was a sign on his desk which forbade smoking, and he looked like a candidate for an imminent heart attack. 'Can't you read?' he asked testily. 'There's a sign out there that—'

'I'm not looking for a part, I've got one,' said Detective Sergeant Ian Mackinnon. 'I'm a police officer from New Scotland Yard.' And he held his warrant card about six inches from the theatrical agent's nose. 'Are you Mr Pearson?'

'Great!' The man threw down his pen. 'I've been trying for three days now to get these bloody contracts sorted out.' He leaned back with an exasperated sigh. 'Well?'

Mackinnon retraced his steps and closed the door. Then he sat down uninvited. 'Elizabeth Fairfax,' he said. 'I understand that you were her agent.'

'So?'

'You know she's been murdered?'

'Yeah. I saw.' He leaned forward confidentially. 'I've had nothing to do with her for years. She switched agents. Said she'd found a guy who could get her a better deal.' He sniffed reproachfully. 'I know the kind of deal he'd got in mind.' He laughed cynically. 'Now, if you don't mind—'

"She had a boy-friend – a live-in boy-friend, as you might say – before she got married.'

Pearson nodded. 'I know. Don't they all?'

'Who was he?'

'Now you're asking . . . .'

'Indeed I am, Mr Pearson.' Mackinnon held the agent's gaze for a brief second.

Reluctantly, Pearson got out of his chair and walked across the office to a filing cabinet. For a minute or two he rummaged in the mass of paper before turning back to the detective. 'Paul Cody,' he said.

'D'you have an address for him?'

'Sure, except that he's not there anymore.'

'How d'you know?'

'Because he came storming in here one day, read my fortune for me, and told me he was going back to the States.'

'Going *back* to the States? He was an American?'

'Yes. He was a funny sort of American, though . . . .' Pearson looked thoughtful. 'I seem to remember he said he was born in Scotland. His father was a sergeant with the American Air Force, or some damn' thing. He didn't go to America until he was about seven. When he was eighteen or twenty, he came back here again. I think he thought he'd make a go of it more easily over here.' He paused to chuckle throatily. 'Didn't though. Trouble was, he thought it was my fault.' He sat down behind his desk again. 'There's no point in having these guys on your books if you can't place them,' he said. 'There's no percentage in that. Truth of the matter was that he was no bloody good. I got him one or two walk-ons. Even got him a four-week bit part in a soap. But after that, nothing.'

'How long ago was all this?'

'About five years, I suppose.'

'Was this before or after Elizabeth Fairfax married Dudley Lavery?'

'Just after, I think. Yes, it was. He was well pissed-off about that. I think that was half the trouble.'

'Where did he go in America? Any idea?'

'Nope! He said he was going to New York, to find fame and fortune on Broadway. Some hope. He's probably working in a fast-food takeaway now; that's where most of them seem to finish up. I'd be very surprised if he ever made a go of it.'

'How old would this Cody have been?'

Pearson thought for a moment or two. 'Early thirties; at the time that is. Probably about thirty-seven, thirty-eight now.'

'Thanks, Mr Pearson, you've been a great help.'

'It's in my nature, officer,' said Pearson. 'Is there a reward?'

'If there was,' said Mackinnon, 'you'd only get fifteen percent of it.'

# Chapter Nine

Jimmy Glover was rotund, short, and bald with just a monk's fringe round the back of his head from one ear to the other. His sports jacket had seen better days and there was not the vestige of a crease in his trousers. He lit a fresh cigarette with the stub of the old one and listened as Gaffney told him the purpose of their visit.

'Aye, I heard.' He moved papers about and reorganised the furniture so that the detectives could sit down. 'You'll never find a political agent with an office that's either big enough or decently decorated,' he said, looking round, 'even in this constituency where the Member is Home Secretary. What can I do for you?' He had a North-country accent and a brusque manner.

'Tell me about Dudley Lavery . . . and his wife.'

'Which one?'

'You knew the first wife?'

'Aye. I knew him when he were bugger-all, lad. I know all about our Dudley.' He leaned forward and Gaffney thought that he was about to impart a confidence, but he merely wanted to empty the ashtray into the waste-paper basket. 'I've been agent here for thirty year or more. Had twelve year of the last bugger afore he were packed off upstairs to make room for our rising star. Still, you'd know all about that sort of chicanery being from Special Branch . . . .' He paused. 'You are, aren't you?'

'Yes, that's right.'

'Thought as much. Course, we see a lot of Tony Lisle and John Selway, and t'other chap . . . what's his name?'

'Lenny Silvester – he's the inspector.'

'Aye, that's the fellow. Don't seem to see so much of him.'

'Probably the way the roster falls,' said Gaffney.

'Aye, happen. Well now, let me see. It were 1970 election. They packed last fellow off to the Lords like I said. Mind, he were getting a bit past it. Still, he weren't fussed. What do they get for signing the book – twenty-five quid a day?'

Gaffney nodded. 'Something like that.'

'And the best free car-park in London, too. Any road, along comes young Dudley . . .' Glover shook his head and cackled. 'He never knew whether he were punched, bored or countersunk then. Full of hisself now he is. He must have been . . . ' He looked at the ceiling reflectively. ''Bout thirty-five, I wouldn't wonder. He'd been a barrister for about twelve years but he knew bugger-all about politics, and that's a fact. Wet behind the ears weren't in it. Used to hang on to me then like I was a bloody lifebelt: "What do I do now?" or "What do I say?" and "Where do I go?". Bloody helpless, he were.'

'Did he have a fight on his hands?'

Glover smiled tolerantly. 'Nay, lad. This constituency's been ours since they invented democracy.' He cackled again. 'Or what passes for it. Be a bit different next time, mind, wi' boundary changes.' He sniffed. 'Any road, it were party decided they wanted to make room for our Dudley. Happens all the time in politics. Along comes this bright young chap—'

'Thirty-five, you said?'

'Aye, well, that's young in politics.' He lit another cigarette. 'There's not too many younger than that. Oh, I know you get these whizz-kids coming in straight from university at the age of twenty-one, but there's not that many. Mid-thirties is a good age to start in politics. Not that age makes a great deal of difference. We've got back-benchers of over sixty, been in the House twenty years, and still as daft as the day they arrived.'

'What was he like – in 1970?'

'More like 1969. He were nursing constituency for a year or more.'

'All right, then; 1969.'

'Very keen to learn. Bundle of energy. Nose into everything. Rushing about.' Glover rattled off a staccato description of the Member. 'Wi' about as much finesse as a man pushing a door marked "Pull".' He sighed resignedly. 'Still, that's what political agents are for: teaching them the trade. Bit like a nursemaid or a cross between a guardian angel and an awful spectre. It don't do to forget that your agent knew you when you were bugger-all. Some do, but most don't. It's as well that agents don't make a habit of writing their memoirs. I can't think why they don't, mind you; the bloody pittance they pay us.' He sniffed, loudly. 'D'you want a cup of tea?' he asked suddenly, as if daring them to accept.

'If it's no trouble,' said Gaffney.

'Everything's trouble in this place,' grumbled Glover. He walked across to a metal filing-cabinet, took out a teapot and three chipped china mugs, and carried them to the window-sill where an electric kettle stood on a tea-stained tin tray. Then he left the room to fill up the kettle.

'Happy soul, isn't he?' Tipper grinned.

'We're likely to get more from him than all the others put together,' said Gaffney.

Glover returned, kicking the office door shut with his foot. 'Still, it's his wife you're interested in, isn't it?'

Gaffney smiled. 'Yes, his late wife.'

'I don't know why he got shot of first,' said Glover. 'Bonny lass, she were. Dorothy she were called. Take sugar and milk?' He busied himself with what he called mashing the tea and then sat down behind his desk again. 'Fitted in very well up here, did Dorothy. More 'an can be said for next one.' He opened a drawer in his desk and produced a tin of biscuits. 'Help yourselves.' He pushed it towards them. 'This is a strange sort of constituency. You've got a bit of everything. Can't just confine yourself to the bit you like, the bit you feel at home in. There's factories as well, and council estates, and farms, and if you want their votes – and you want to keep them – you've not to be afraid of getting your hands dirty. Metaphorically speaking, of course. Now our Dorothy

102

was good at that. I've seen her in her wellingtons and an old anorak out all over the constituency, in all weathers too. All things to all people, she were. And I don't mean that in a derogatory way, neither.' He frowned at them. 'But as for the last one . . . ' He shook his head sadly, more because of her failure as a Member's wife, than her premature and violent death.

'Did that cause a rift, then?' asked Gaffney.

'Happen. Don't rightly know, lad. I know what caused a rift between him and Dorothy, though.'

'Oh?'

'Aye, from what I heard, it were a fancy bit of secretary at the House of Commons called Shirley . . . ' He screwed his face up and washed his hands silently. 'Don't know nowt else about it. Probably a load of gossip.'

'When was this?' asked Gaffney.

Glover's chin sunk on to his chest as he gave that some thought. 'More than ten years back,' he said finally. 'That were last straw for Dorothy, I reckon. She'd done her best, but she were nowt more'an a skivvy really. If he weren't in House he were in court somewhere. I think he only wanted a wife for decoration. Good thing to have, a wife. If you don't have one, they reckon you're queer, and that's a few more votes gone. More than you'd pick up because of it.' His face retained its lugubrious look; everything that Jimmy Glover had done for the past thirty years had been assessed in terms of votes: votes won or votes lost. For him there was no other yardstick. 'It wasn't as if I didn't warn him.'

'What about?'

'Splitting up in election year. That were daft.'

'Who left who?'

'Oh, she did, but it were his fault. I told him to go after her, patch it up, at least till after election.'

'And did he?'

'Nay, lad. Too busy.' He laughed scornfully. 'But at least they kept it quiet until after it was over – the election, I mean. Decent to the last, Dorothy. God knows why; right neglected, she were.'

'And then Elizabeth appeared on the scene?'

'Bless you no, not immediately. That were years on. Funnily enough that were an election year an'all. I reckon that's what got him going. They were starting to ask questions, see; particularly committee.' He ran his hand round his chin. 'Must have been two year after they split up that divorce came through.' He nodded in confirmation. 'Aye, that were it, and she wed a doctor from America; lives there now. And good luck to her; no more'an she deserves, poor lass.'

'Are you saying that the constituency party persuaded him to get married again, Mr Glover?'

Glover grinned a lopsided grin. 'Almost, aye. Told him he'd no hope of getting to Number Ten without a wife. I told him an'all.' For a second or two he stared at an out-of-date calendar on the opposite wall. 'Any road,' he continued, 'he got wed, like I said, to this Elizabeth.' It was obvious that he had not been much impressed with Lavery's second wife. 'Actress, she were; supposed to be, any road. Never saw her in owt on the telly, and that's fact. London stage perhaps.' He dismissed Elizabeth Lavery's acting career with a contemptuous sniff. 'Now, you'd never see her in boots and anorak; oh no, that'd not be to her ladyship's liking at all. I reckon she never minded the London part of it all. The cocktail parties and that sort of toffee-nosed carry-on. I heard her once, saying to Dudley: "They're not our kind of people". Huh! I don't know who she were talking about, but I can bloody guess.' He paused to push his hand inside his shirt and scratch his chest. 'Mind you, there's not a great deal of pomp and circumstance at a bring-and-buy in the church hall up at Crabtree. A right madam she were. All very fine at the Lord-Lieutenant's reception, dressed up in her best, but nowt so good looking-in on the bingo in aid of the party funds.'

'What did Mr Lavery think? Did he say anything to her?'

Glover pondered on that. 'I don't rightly know, lad,' he said slowly, and sniffed loudly. 'Never heard 'em bandying words, like, but there were occasions when the silence were a bit frigid.'

'Did she always come to the constituency with him?'

Glover thought about that for a bit, too. 'Aye, at first she did, but then not so often. It's a bit difficult trying to remember for sure. See, after the party got into office and he became the Home Secretary, he never come up hisself so often. I suppose then he must have had a surgery about once every three weeks. If we saw her up here four times a year, I reckon we'd count ourselves lucky.' He sucked through his teeth. 'Mind you, that depends on your point of view.'

'What was she doing while he was up here? Any ideas?'

Glover's eyes narrowed. 'Nay, lad, I don't rightly know. Perhaps you ought to ask t'Member.'

The clinical atmosphere of the entrance hall of the American Embassy in Grosvenor Square always reminded Gaffney of an operating theatre. He exchanged a few words of banter with the security guard who nevertheless insisted on his going through the metal-detector archway to prove that he was unarmed and did not, therefore, pose a threat to the stability of the United States Government.

Eventually he was shown into Joe Daly's office. Daly was the Legal Attaché, a euphemism for the senior FBI agent-in-residence.

'John!' Daly advanced across the office and shook hands vigorously. 'How ya doin'?' He was a huge bear of a man with a thick thatch of iron-grey hair, and a twinkle in grey eyes that peered out at the world from behind rimless spectacles, inviting it to see the funny side of life.

'I need some help, Joe.'

'Right, right.' Daly moved some newspapers off a small table to make room for the coffee that seemed to arrive automatically whenever a visitor appeared in his office. 'So what's new?'

Gaffney stirred his coffee. 'You've heard about the murder of the Home Secretary's wife . . . ?'

Daly nodded. 'Some job you've got on your hands there, John.' He was genuinely sympathetic; detectives the world

105

over appreciated the difficulty of crime with a political involvement.

'I need to trace an American citizen called Cody, Paul Cody.'

Daly pulled a pad of paper from his desk and rested it on his knee. 'Shoot!'

'There's not much.'

'Was there ever?' murmured Daly.

'He's an actor – or was – and left here to go back to the States about five years ago. He was going to New York; the bright lights of Broadway. He's now about thirty-seven years of age.'

'Is that it?'

'I'm afraid so.'

'Jeez, John, you want a miracle?'

Gaffney smiled. 'I have been told that the FBI is the finest investigative agency in the world.'

Daly snorted. 'Who told you that crap?'

'An FBI agent,' said Gaffney.

'Is that really all you've got?'

'There's one other thing which might help. I've been told that he was born in Scotland while his father was serving there as a sergeant in the US Air Force.' He paused. 'But I can't guarantee the reliability of that information.'

Daly sighed. 'I'll do my best, John. What d'you want to know about this guy . . . if we find him?'

'Anything he can tell us about Elizabeth Lavery – or Fairfax as she was known then – and where he was on the night she was killed.'

Daly looked up from his notes. 'You think he might have been responsible?'

'I don't know, Joe, but funnier things have happened.'

'Jesus Christ, I hope not,' said Daly. 'The President would go bananas if it was an American citizen who murdered your Home Secretary's wife.' He shook his head at the enormity of it all.

Gaffney laughed. 'You shouldn't have left the Empire,' he said.

★ ★ ★

The Home Secretary placed the tips of his fingers together and gazed out at the two detectives from beneath lowered eyebrows. 'Well, Mr Gaffney, you have some progress to report?'

'To be perfectly honest, sir, no. That is to say that our progress has been of a negative sort.'

Lavery smiled bleakly. 'Have you ever thought of becoming a politician?' he asked.

Gaffney smiled too, for the sake of politeness. 'What I mean, sir, is that we have effectively closed certain lines of enquiry.'

'Such as?'

'Such as the possibility that the murderer was a burglar whom your wife disturbed.'

'You are certain of that?'

Gaffney nodded slowly. 'As certain as one can be in any criminal investigation, yes. There was no sign of forcible entry. No sign of anything having been stolen . . . ' He glanced enquiringly at Lavery who nodded. 'In fact, no sign of anything untoward at all.'

'What are you suggesting, Mr Gaffney?'

'I'm not suggesting anything, but the line I am pursuing is that your late wife may have admitted the killer quite innocently and then—'

'Out of the question,' said Lavery heatedly. 'Your people – Tony Lisle – gave her specific—'

'I'm not suggesting a total stranger, sir; I'm suggesting someone that your wife perhaps knew, maybe only casually, or had met somewhere . . . '

'Mmm . . . ' Lavery stared down at his desk reflectively. 'Well that, of course, would encompass literally thousands; with me in politics and her in the acting profession.'

'Was she still in the acting profession?'

'In a way, but no longer on stage.' He smiled. 'No, she was an adviser. Costume, mainly, I think. It seemed to take up a lot of her time, I know. There were occasions when we didn't see each other for a week or more at a time.'

'What form did this job of hers take, sir?'

'Well, I don't know a great deal about the acting business, but her task apparently, was to be present when they were planning a play or a film, to make sure that the costumes were correct. It seems that mistakes can be made, particularly in period pieces, that could ruin the whole thing, so they tell me . . . .' He looked vacantly around the large office. 'So you see she could have run across all sorts of people in the film business.' He smiled benignly. 'And there are some scallywags in it, as I'm sure you know, Mr Gaffney.'

'Did your wife ever go to Spain, sir?'

'Spain . . . ?' The Home Secretary looked thoughtful. 'Yes, I believe she did. Something to do with India, I think it was.'

'India? In Spain?'

Lavery smiled tolerantly. 'It was a film that offended the susceptibilities of the Indian Government, something to do with the last days of the Raj – you know the sort of thing – and the Indians wouldn't grant permission for it to be filmed there. So it had to be made in Spain.'

'What was it called, the film?'

Lavery shook his head slowly. 'D'you know, I haven't the faintest idea.' He looked up with the incisive stare that he usually reserved for television interviewers who had asked a hypothetical question. 'Why? Does it matter?' He spoke impatiently as if to imply that he was very busy and hadn't the time to answer what he probably saw as banal questions, even if they did come from the police officer who was investigating his wife's murder.

'Not really, sir. It might just have saved me a little time,' said Gaffney and shrugged. One of the things he had discovered over years of close association with politicians was that those whose public image was disagreeable were usually very pleasant people in private, whereas the unctuously smooth individual with the beguiling interview smile was, so often, in private thoroughly objectionable. It made a pleasant change to meet a politician who appeared to be agreeable both in public and private. Gaffney could forgive him his impatience;

it must be gruelling to be reminded constantly of his wife's violent death. 'When would that have been, when your wife went to Spain?'

Lavery sighed gently. 'I hope you don't think I'm being unco-operative, Mr Gaffney' – he smiled the dental smile again that some public relations expert had told him carried conviction – 'but I really don't know.' He leaned back in his leather-upholstered chair and laid his hands flat on the arms in an attitude almost of despair. 'This is a terribly onerous job, and I'm afraid that I left my wife very much to her own devices, more perhaps than I should have done. If only I'd known.' His voice dropped to a whisper, and for a moment he stared blankly at the opposite wall before looking at Gaffney again. 'It might be a good idea if you spoke to Mary Diver; she's my secretary – for the constituency – and she works from the House. She used to do an awful lot for Elizabeth; I think you'll find she may be able to help.' He flipped over a page of his desk diary and glanced at the clock.

Gaffney took the hint and stood up. 'Thank you for your time, sir. I'm sorry to have to say, however, that I may have to trouble you again.'

Lavery stood up too, and walked to the door with Gaffney. 'Of course, of course. It's absolutely essential that this creature is brought to book; I'm sure I don't have to emphasise that. It's not only for my sake, but for the very reputation of law enforcement as a whole. If it can be seen that someone can escape with murdering the Home Secretary's wife, there is no hope . . . .'

# Chapter Ten

'I always like coming here,' said Tommy Fox, looking admiringly round Gaffney's office. 'It's so quiet and peaceful.'

'It's because we don't panic like the Flying Squad,' said Gaffney with a straight face. 'Why don't you sit down and tell me what's on your mind?'

'You're very kind, doctor,' said Fox, and relaxed into one of Gaffney's armchairs, carefully pulling the cloth of his trousers over his knees to prevent it bagging. Today he was wearing a dark grey suit with just the hint of a pin-stripe running through it, a pink tie and a matching handkerchief that cascaded out of his top pocket. 'I understand that you took my advice and had a little chat with friend Conway in the Scrubs; you and that scoundrel Tipper.'

Gaffney nodded. 'That's right.'

Fox examined his fingernails with care. 'Thought so, because Waldo Conway inexplicably fell down a staircase on Sunday morning whereby both his legs got broken.'

'Inexplicably?'

'Yes. Strange, isn't it? Even Waldo can't explain it. I suppose that being in stir you get careless; don't have to think for yourself, you see. Shame that. On his way to church, too.'

'Waldo – going to church?'

'Mmm!' Fox nodded seriously. 'He's on the parole kick.'

'Oh?'

'Oh yes. He got five years for armed robbery, right? So the minute he arrives in the nick he makes a bee-line for the prison chaplain, confesses all, promises he's a reformed character, and how sorry he is, and can the reverend help him find

110

God. All that bit. Now, if he can keep that up for . . . ' Fox broke off and looked at the ceiling, calculating, ' . . . twenty months, then he's up the Parole Board with a bloody good reference. Bingo! Out he comes and gets at it again.'

'What makes you so certain that his falling down stairs had anything to do with Harry Tipper and me paying him a visit?'

'Stands to reason. Your arrival in the nick was no secret, neither was the identity of the prisoner you went to see.'

'You're not suggesting that Masters could have got to hear of it that quickly, surely? He's in Spain. We only went to the nick on Saturday – the day before this unfortunate accident.'

'No. They're not that clever. But Conway spoke to the law, didn't he? That was enough. Anyhow, d'you know for sure that Masters is in Spain?'

'Yes, we got the local Old Bill to check for us. What's more he flew over there the day following the murder of Elizabeth Lavery.'

Fox took a slim cigarette case from his inside pocket and slowly tapped a cigarette on it. 'What have you got to connect Masters with that job?' He held the cigarette up in the air. 'D'you mind?'

Gaffney shook his head. 'A snippet of information, and something that Conway told me.'

'About Masters?' Fox's eyes narrowed. 'Anything to interest me?'

'Not really. You wouldn't believe it anyway. I'm not sure I do.'

'Well, that could account for him getting his legs done.'

'But no one could have known that, and he wouldn't have told anyone,' said Gaffney. 'Is he in solitary now?'

Fox laughed. 'You'd better believe it. He's tucked up in the prison hospital with his legs dangling from the ceiling. They said he was comfortable – whatever that means. But if he's been talking to you about Masters and the Lavery murder, I should think he's in grave danger of getting topped himself – when he gets better. Unless what he told you was a load of cobblers.'

'Meaning?'

'Well, he could have told you a load of bloody fanny, just so's you'd go away thinking you'd got something. Then he could tell Masters what he'd done. Probably get a pat on the back.'

'That's what I suggested to Harry Tipper might have been the case, but how d'you account for the great staircase tragedy?'

'Over-zealousness by locally employed personnel, or . . .' Fox drew the word out pensively. 'Or they may have thought he was talking about something else.'

'Such as?'

'Such as a heavy screwing on Tuesday night last week.'

'The night that Mrs Lavery was strangled?'

Fox nodded slowly. 'Yes. Up Boreham Wood way, damn them. Another mile or two and they'd have been on Hertfordshire's patch.'

'Why should they have thought that Conway knew anything about that? He's been inside too long.'

'Because my information is that it's down to Masters. Conway runs with Masters, and just because he's banged up for a while doesn't cut him off from the outside world. You know that, and I know that.'

'What was taken?'

'That's the strange thing, John. It's not been reported to police.'

Gaffney pursed his lips. 'Then how d'you know it happened?'

Fox looked offended. 'John, please. I haven't spent twenty-five years cultivating snouts for nothing, you know.'

Gaffney spread his hands and smiled. 'But why wouldn't it get reported? What was it, anyway?'

'Big house,' said Fox shortly. 'As for why it wasn't reported, well there could be several reasons.'

'Like?'

'Like the loser doesn't want police to know what was stolen. Or he wasn't insured, so there's no point – bit lame that, I must admit. But I suspect that the real reason is that

112

the loser is himself a villain, so he doesn't want the law sniffing around his drum . . . and he intends to take retribution in his own inimitable way – and that could be very nasty indeed.' Fox grinned horribly.

'And what do your snouts tell you about it?'

'I was afraid you'd ask me that. The word is that the house belongs to a villain called Bernie Farrell.'

'Perhaps he's been away. Will report it when he gets back from the South of France . . . or wherever.'

Fox shook his head. 'He's discovered it all right. For the very simple reason that this was one of the most sophisticated jobs that's been pulled for a long time. This little team obviously knew what they were about; they were in and out like a dose of salts. And they fixed the alarms which are wired into the Yard. But more to the point, word is that they put surveillance on the man so that they knew exactly where he and his missus were the whole time they were out of the house.' He sniffed. 'Went up West by all accounts. But there was a little team following them complete with bloody radios, if you please.' He chuckled. 'Murdo McGregor reckons he's going to recruit them for his surveillance team if he ever finds out who they are.'

'Seems all you're short of are the names.'

'I've got those, too.'

'What are you waiting for, then?' asked Gaffney.

'A complainant,' said Fox. 'If Farrell denies having been broken into – and he will – I'm going to get precisely nowhere.'

'What sort of villain is this Farrell?'

'Villain?' Fox looked startled.

'You said he was a villain. . . . '

'My dear chap,' said Fox with mock severity, ''tis but a rumour.'

Gaffney laughed. 'Come on, Tommy, or do I have to go traipsing down to Murdo McGregor again?'

Fox smiled. 'He's got no form at all, but he's bloody entitled to have. Everything points to him being well at it. He's got fingers in several pies in the West End. Like night-clubs, strip-joints, call-girls – escort agencies, he calls them – and a few minicab operations. Oh, and I think he's taken a recent interest in betting shops. But it's all beautifully wrapped up – legit; he's got several companies that neatly mask his operation. We've had a go at him, so have the Fraud Squad, and the Inland Revenue. All drawn a blank.'

'Another Masters, then?'

Fox scoffed. 'No way. He's a bloody sight shrewder, this finger.' He laughed humourlessly. 'His latest bit of nose-thumbing is his charity work—'

'Charity!'

'Yes, saucy bastard. He's trying to get all manner of persons of probity interested in some scheme he's got for the welfare and rehabilitation of ex-prisoners. Could be enlightened self-interest, I suppose . . . or it will be if I catch him.' He sniffed. 'As a matter of fact, we had to warn the Commissioner off recently. Farrell invited him to dinner to discuss his plans, cheeky sod. Murdo McGregor had a word in the Commissioner's shell-like and he went sick.'

'All very interesting, Tommy, and frustrating, too, but what has it got to do with my job?'

'Like I said, the whole thing was organised by Colin Masters, who promptly took it on the toes out to his gaff in Spain the very next day, so you tell me. Where did that come from, incidentally?'

'From Special Branch at Heathrow.'

'The saucy sod. Cool as you like. What are you going to do now?'

'He's got a place in Wimbledon,' said Gaffney. Fox nodded. 'I was thinking of getting a brief and giving it a spin. What d'you think? Or will that upset your job?'

Fox shrugged. 'There's bugger-all to upset, but it might do your job a load of harm.'

'How so?'

'Well,' said Fox. 'As I see it, Masters is sitting out there in Seville, waiting to see if the heat's on. He'll hang about for a couple of weeks, I should think, and if it's all quiet, he'll come back.'

'But if Farrell is not going to report it to police, he's got no worries, surely?'

'Not about us, no. He's probably waiting to see how Farrell will react.'

'But Farrell will go and get him in Spain if he wants him, won't he?'

Fox shook his head. 'They don't like working off their own patch, these bastards. No, Farrell will wait till he gets back here to sort him out, but Masters is waiting to see if Farrell has sussed him out.'

'Well, if you know, he'll know – Farrell, I mean . . . .'

Fox shrugged. 'They haven't got much imagination, these villains.'

'I think I'd better put you in the picture, Tommy,' said Gaffney slowly. 'Conway told me that Masters was having it off with Elizabeth Lavery.'

Fox's expression did not change one bit from the permanently cynical blandness that seemed a part of him. 'And you believe that crap?'

'There is some collateral.' Gaffney told him about the gold waist-chain and Lavery's story of his wife's visits to Spain, supposedly to advise on the making of a film.

Fox pouted. 'I still can't see Conway telling you all that, not if it's true. It'd be more than his neck's worth. Not that it's worth much anyway,' he added. 'But if you go down to Wimbledon and turn his drum over, and he gets wind of it, he'll never come back; unless you've got enough to extradite him.'

Gaffney shook his head. 'Not a bloody thing; he even paid for the gold chain. And if this story about him screwing Lavery's wife is true, that's no motive for topping her. What's the point?'

Fox gently tapped the arm of the chair with the flat of his hand. 'Unless the two are connected . . . .'

'In what way?'

'If the murder of Elizabeth Lavery and the screwing of this drum at Boreham Wood – on the same night, don't forget – are linked together in some way.'

Gaffney smoothed his hair with the palm of his hand. 'That's all I bloody well need,' he said. 'Coincidences like that!'

'It's *Miss* Diver,' she said in answer to Gaffney's query. He needn't have asked really; it was fairly obvious in her case. She had probably been quite attractive as a young woman, but decades of dedicated and largely unrewarding labour in the shadow of the great seemed not only to have deprived her of her looks, but also to have removed any sparkle of humour she may once have possessed.

'The Home Secretary suggested that you may be able to help us with regard to the late Mrs Lavery's trips abroad, Miss Diver.'

'Oh, did he now? Well, I don't know about that.' She was haughty: a strange mixture of defensiveness against any form of attack on *her* Member of Parliament, and an implication that she enjoyed a professional familiarity with him that was denied to others. 'What exactly was it you wanted to know?' Gaffney got the impression that when Miss Diver said 'exactly', she meant it. The immaculately tidy desk, the row of box files on the shelf behind her as regimented as guardsmen, the books descending in size order from the large Erskine May to the tiny Vacher's, all testified to her efficiency; all as carefully arranged as her faultlessly coiffured grey hair.

'I am interested in discovering when Mrs Lavery went to Spain.' There was no doubt in Gaffney's mind that he would have to mollify this hostile woman; if she didn't co-operate, there was no other way he was going to get the information he needed. There was certainly no power in law to secure a search warrant for execution within the precincts of the Palace of Westminster, and he did not care to contemplate the reaction of the Serjeant-at-Arms to a request that he be allowed to search the Home Secretary's office at the House.

'This is Mrs *Elizabeth* Lavery, I presume?' she asked.

'Yes, it is.' Gaffney detected a preference for the first wife.

'I see.' She sniffed and unlocked a drawer in her desk.

Gaffney knew instinctively that she would not have to rummage; that she could have found, blindfolded, the book she wanted. 'Now then, let me see . . . yes, here we are. She went to Spain on four occasions.' She looked at him directly. 'I suppose you want the dates?'

'That would be most helpful, Miss Diver.'

She drew a pad towards her and picked up her fountain-pen. Gaffney noted that the cap unscrewed; the pen must have been years old, and doubtless as well cared for as everything else around her. She handed him the piece of paper. 'Those are the dates of which I have a record,' she said. 'There may have been other occasions when she didn't seek my assistance, of course.' The expression on her face implied that such a course of action would have been extremely foolhardy.

'Thank you.' Gaffney folded the paper into his pocket book. 'As a matter of interest, Miss Diver, were all those trips made to Seville?'

'Do you mean did she actually go?'

Gaffney knew he should have made that clearer. 'No, I meant were the bookings to Seville, or did she have you book to anywhere else?'

'All the Spanish ones were to Seville from Heathrow, yes.'

Gaffney frowned. 'You made bookings for her to go elsewhere, did you?'

'Only two; both to the South of France.' She gazed at him levelly.

'Were they before or after the Spanish trips?'

'Both of them before.'

'Do you happen to know, Miss Diver, if they were all in connection with her filming assignments?'

'I really have no idea. I can tell you that they most certainly were not for official business, because she said that she would pay for the tickets. The Secretary of State is most particular about expenses. If it's government, the bill goes to the Home Office; if it's party, it goes to the constituency; but if it's a private affair either the Home Secretary pays or his wife does.' She hesitated. 'His late wife did, I should have said.' For the first time she smiled; Gaffney assumed it was a form of nervousness, to excuse one of her rare slips.

'You've been most helpful, Miss Diver,' said Gaffney, standing up. He glanced round the office. 'I must compliment you on how well organised you are.' She inclined her head slightly. 'You must have been Mr Lavery's secretary for a long time.'

'Since he became a Member.'

'Oh really? I thought that he had a secretary called Shirley at one time.'

'She was a temporary assistant,' said Miss Diver frostily. 'She was not at all satisfactory and left.'

'I see,' said Gaffney. Secretaries at the House not infrequently became second wives to MPs. He wasn't sure whether Miss Diver was opposed to this in principle, or whether she was piqued at never having been asked.

'Good day,' said Miss Diver.

Pete Roscoe flicked down the switch of his intercom. 'Yeah?'

'OSI USAF on the line, Mr Roscoe,' said his secretary.

'Thanks, honey, put them through.' He picked up the receiver. 'Roscoe.' It had been two weeks previously that Roscoe, the minute he had received the call from Daly in London, had contacted the Office of Special Investigations of the US Air Force in an attempt to get further details of the man Paul Cody that Scotland Yard were so anxious to trace. Roscoe was the Special Agent-in-Charge of the New York FBI office, and Daly had suggested that he handle the inquiry personally.

'Pete, it's Sam Delaney.'

'Hi, Sam.'

'We traced Cody's birth for you, but it's not going to help much. He was born at the USAF hospital at Prestwick in Scotland: 1951, April 17, son of Jackson Cody and his wife Martha, born Levenson. Sergeant Cody did a double tour and was repatriated Stateside in 1958 and took honourable discharge. I've gotten an address in Kansas City. After that – zilch.'

Roscoe jotted down the address, knowing that, thirty years on, his chances of tracing Paul Cody that way was an impossibility. He swore softly and then flicked down the switch of the intercom again. 'Get me Frank Robinson at the Kansas City office, will you honey?'

It was still dark, and snowing hard, when the car drew into the driveway of Masters' house in Wimbledon early on the Wednesday morning. In order to keep the visit as secret as possible, Tipper had driven the car, and, as well as John Gaffney, Tommy Fox had come along for the ride 'just to have a poke about', but had obligingly brought his locks expert with him. Normally, of course, they wouldn't have worried too much about damage caused in the execution of a search warrant – which Tipper had obtained from the Bow Street magistrate the previous afternoon – but they did not want to leave any trace of their entry.

'Hope it keeps snowing,' said Tipper, turning his back against the cold wind, 'otherwise these tyre tracks, and our footmarks, are going to be a dead giveaway.'

'It's going to thaw tomorrow, guv,' said the locks expert, a middle-aged detective constable from the Flying Squad, named Swann.

'How d'you know?' asked Fox.

'My seaweed's turned mildew.' There wasn't the trace of a smile on Swann's mournful face.

'Never mind all that crap,' said Fox, 'just get that bloody door open, will you.'

The constable surveyed the front door, and sucked through his teeth. 'I'll try the back,' he said, and walked down the side of the house without waiting for his chief superintendent's comment.

'Bloody prima donna,' said Fox, and slowly stamped his feet on the front doorstep, hunching his shoulders inside his sheepskin coat.

Five minutes later the door was opened by Swann. 'You rang, sir?'

'What took you so bloody long?' asked Fox acidly. 'I

think you're getting past it,' he added, and shouldered his way through the door.

It was undoubtedly what an estate agent would have described as a desirable, detached, four-bedroomed residence. There was nothing cheap about it; in fact its owner appeared to have been at pains to prove that he had money rather than taste, and there was an occasional gaudiness where patterns or colours clashed as though two different people had had a hand in its decoration, each unaware of the existence of the other.

But the detectives weren't judging it for an interior decoration prize; they were looking for information, for evidence. Unfortunately they were not having a lot of luck. There was a room filled with keep-fit equipment, enough to start a small gymnasium, and off that a sauna and a Jacuzzi. And downstairs was a fully fitted kitchen that looked as though it had never been used.

'This bastard's loaded,' said Fox enviously, 'and bent!' He stopped in front of a desk that occupied a corner of a room, the walls of which were largely taken up with bookshelves. 'I suppose he'd call this the library, if he could bloody well read. Here, Swann, you useless object, come here.' He pointed at the desk. 'See if you can banjo that without leaving splinters all over the floor.'

Swann nodded. 'Piece of cake, guv,' he said, and knelt down. After a few moments of operating his 'twirlers' – a bunch of skeleton keys, the possession of which by anyone else would have ensured their instant arrest – he stood up. 'There you go, sir.'

Fox opened the six drawers, one after the other. All were empty. 'Bastard,' he said.

'He must have some private papers somewhere,' said Gaffney.

Fox nodded. 'I'll put money on them being in a safety deposit box somewhere. What I wouldn't give for an hour or two poking about in there.' He looked thoughtful. 'Where's that Roller of his? In the garage?'

Gaffney shook his head. 'It's in the long-term car-park at Heathrow.'

'How d'you know that?'

'You've got DI Findlater of SO11 to thank for that. When our blokes told him that Masters had left for Seville, he got his lads to look in the most obvious place, and there it was.'

'Was there any—'

Gaffney shook his head. 'Clean as a whistle,' he said. 'Our Mr Masters is obviously a very careful man.' He looked around and shrugged. 'Well, Tommy, I don't see much profit in hanging about here. This is just a bloody show-house.'

Fox nodded his agreement. 'I'm afraid you're right, John. Where's that idiot Swann?'

'Here, guv,' said the mournful detective.

'Right. Let us out and lock up, will you.'

'Before you go, sir,' said Tipper from the doorway, 'you might be interested in this.' He held a brown manilla file in his hand.

'Where was that, Harry?' asked Gaffney.

'In one of the drawers in the kitchen.'

'What's more to the point, what is it?' asked Fox.

'It's a file of receipts, mainly household stuff: gas, electricity, telephone, a few repairs – that sort of thing; but there's also a receipt for a gold chain . . . .'

'Terrific!' said Gaffney. 'All we've found is what we already know.'

# Chapter Eleven

Gaffney turned from the window as Harry Tipper entered the office. 'What a waste of time,' he said bitterly. 'It wouldn't have been so bad if we hadn't had to get up so bloody early. I haven't done that for years; at least, not for the Metropolitan Police.'

'I didn't expect a result, sir. A villain like Masters is going to make damned sure that he doesn't leave anything lying about for the Old Bill to screw him with while he's sunning himself in Spain, is he?'

'Added to which,' continued Gaffney, 'the Prime Minister's principal private secretary – that little weasel Ronnie Mansell – has been on the phone to the Commissioner asking him what progress is being made, and reminding us that it was a week ago today that the murder occurred.'

'Happy anniversary,' said Tipper. 'What did the Commissioner say?'

'That enquiries are being pursued with vigour.'

'Oh good!' Tipper stretched out his legs and yawned again. 'I couldn't half go a cup of coffee, guv'nor; how about you?'

'I am wondering, Harry . . . ' Gaffney ignored Tipper's broad hint.

'Well don't keep me in suspense, sir.'

'I'm wondering if there's any connection between the break-in that Tommy Fox was talking about and our job, apart from Masters, I mean.'

'You've lost me,' said Tipper.

Gaffney stood up. 'Come on, we'll pay the Flying Squad a visit and have a chat with him. They might even give you a cup of coffee, too.'

'My word, this is an honour. We don't often get the gentlemen of Special Branch visiting us in our humble abode. Do take the weight off your plates, gents.' Tommy Fox reclined in an armchair in his office with his feet propped up on a coffee table which was protected from his elegant Gucci footwear by a copy of *The Times*. 'I dare say you'll take coffee?' He half turned and shouted out of the open door. 'Swann!'

'Yes, guv?' It appeared that Swann was not only Fox's locks expert but also his general factotum.

'Three cups of coffee, dear boy.'

'Yes, guv.'

'And make it the Brazilian. None of your instant muck.'

'Yes, guv.'

'He'll do anything to stay off the streets,' said Fox sympathetically. 'Now then, what can I do to help?'

'Yesterday morning, Tommy,' said Gaffney, 'when you came to see me with the sad news about Waldo Conway, you also told me about this break-in at Boreham Wood.' Fox nodded. 'I'm still wondering if there's any connection between that job and mine – apart from Masters, I mean.'

Fox spread his hands. 'No idea. How d'you propose to find out?'

'Go and talk to him.'

'Who?'

'Farrell.'

'What about?'

'It did occur to me,' said Gaffney, 'from what you were saying about his charity venture and the Commissioner, that he might have had some contact with Dudley Lavery.'

Fox snorted. 'More likely to cultivate the Chancellor of the Exchequer, I'd have thought.' He stood up and walked over to his bookcase, shuffled through a pile of old newspapers and eventually pulled one out. Opening it at the court page, he handed it to Gaffney. 'There you go,' he said. 'There's a picture of him at Mrs Somebody-or-another's Ball. Puts himself about does friend Farrell.'

Gaffney glanced at the photograph. 'Is it likely to foul up your job if I do make enquiries of Farrell?'

Fox shook his head slowly. 'Thank you, dear boy,' he said, taking a cup of coffee from Swann who had reappeared, adroitly balancing three cups. 'Close the door on your way out.' He put a saccharin tablet into his coffee and stirred it gently. 'As I said the other day, there's no job to foul up. Without a complainant – and Farrell has still not reported a break-in – we've got no crime. Christ, John, I know it's irritating, but I haven't really got time to go around drumming up trade.' He yawned. 'What does get on my wick is that Masters and his team seem to have hit on some smart-arse system of only robbing those blokes who aren't going to scream. Now, that interests me, that definitely does interest me. For two reasons. Firstly, it's time Masters got what he deserves – which is about fourteen years – and secondly, I don't like the idea of people like Farrell getting up to some sort of villainy while at the same time pretending that they're whiter-than-white.' He waved at the newspaper that Gaffney had put down on the table. 'Like that sort of caper, for instance. Mind you, like I said, he's cleverer at it than Masters. He's never been caught . . . yet!' He paused for a moment. 'What have you got at the back of your mind, then? That Mrs Lavery may have had something to do with this sort of blagging?'

Gaffney leaned forward and put his empty cup on the table. 'Tommy, when I first heard about her and Masters in Spain, I didn't believe it. Now, I'll believe anything. The only trouble is that I've damn-all proof, and I can't even talk to Masters; at least, not at the moment. The minute he lands on British soil, he's going to get lifted and talked to.'

'You've got that laid on, have you?'

Gaffney nodded. 'Enrico Perez has arranged that the moment Masters boards a plane at Seville Airport, I get a phone call. Then we'll have a reception committee waiting for him when he arrives.'

Fox scoffed. 'Excuse my mirth, John, but the first thing

that'll happen is that Masters will sit down, say sod-all, and demand his brief.'

Gaffney smiled. 'Ah, but he's never been arrested by Special Branch before, has he?'

'He's lunching with the London prison governors, Mr Gaffney. Then he'll go straight to the House.'

'Perhaps, Mr Stanhope, you would ask him if he has ever met a Mr Bernard Farrell. He's . . . ' He paused. 'He's an entrepreneur of some sort. If he has, I'd like to speak to him, the Home Secretary that is.'

'I'll get back to you as soon as I can,' said Lavery's private secretary. 'You'll be at the Yard, I take it?'

'Yes. If not, someone will take a message. And thanks for your help.' Gaffney replaced the receiver with a sigh. The problem with politicians had been summed up for him some years previously by an assistant secretary at Number Ten. 'By the time you've caught up with the Prime Minister,' he had said, 'he's somewhere else.'

Stanhope was as good as his word. He had spoken to Lavery in the car on his way to his luncheon engagement, and telephoned from the House.

Gaffney walked up Victoria Street from Scotland Yard, along Broad Sanctuary, through Parliament Square, and across St Margaret Street. He acknowledged the salute of the constable at the St Stephen's Entrance and made his way to that part of the House known as Back of the Speaker's Chair. It was here that Lavery had promised to meet him.

'Ah, Mr Gaffney.' Stanhope was waiting for him. 'I'll just signal the Secretary of State. It's only Foreign Secretary's questions.' He said that with a grin.

'You wanted to know about Bernard Farrell?' The Home Secretary appeared through the screen doors, touched Gaffney's elbow and steered him away from Stanhope.

'I wanted to know if you knew him, sir.'

'Well yes, but you intrigue me. Why are you asking? Is it something to do with Elizabeth's death?'

'Some information has come to me, sir, but it is unconfirmed. If you don't mind, I'd rather not repeat it, not at this stage at any rate.'

'My dear Mr Gaffney, how very mysterious. Come and sit down.' He led Gaffney across to a green leather bench-seat. 'I've had lunch with him a couple of times, along with a number of other people I may say.' He raised his hands in an attitude of surrender.

'Did Mrs Lavery ever meet him?'

'Ah, now that you mention it, yes. He was very keen to do something for released prisoners, a sort of charitable foundation. He held this private dinner party at . . . ' He flicked his fingers.

'Boreham Wood?'

Lavery looked sharply at Gaffney. 'That's right. There were about a dozen of us altogether, I suppose. He did us very well, but all perfectly above-board, you understand.' He said the last few words hurriedly as though afraid that Gaffney might think that he had been accepting hospitality that was unethical. 'I seem to recall that there were one or two industrialists, the Chief Inspector of Prisons, my permanent secretary . . . oh, and a Fleet Street editor. All very respectable and upright people.' There was a certain measure of relief in the way he said that, although Gaffney could not for the life of him understand why the Home Secretary, of all people, should feel it necessary to justify his actions to a mere chief superintendent. 'But I'm still interested to know what this is all about.'

'I think it may be nothing, sir, and as I said just now, I'd rather not start a hare running until I've learned a little more.'

'Of course, Mr Gaffney. I quite understand.' He paused. 'Are you trying to warn me, in an oblique way, that I ought to steer away from this fellow?' He looked a little apprehensive.

Gaffney smiled to himself. He never ceased to be amazed at the sensitivity of politicians' antennae, and their skill at moving adroitly away from anything, however remote, which might damage their careers in some way. 'If there is anything, sir, you may rest assured that I shall let you know at once,' said Gaffney.

Lavery patted Gaffney's arm. 'I should be most grateful,' he murmured. 'Most grateful.'

'I am talking to everyone who may have known Mrs Lavery, however tenuously,' said Gaffney.

Bernard Farrell advanced cautiously across his office. He was not a tall man, but had clearly tried to recover from his underprivileged childhood in Poplar; he now resembled a twist of tobacco: broad across the middle, but tapering at either end. His feet were small, almost dainty, and his head was pointed and narrow, its skin stretched like parchment over his skull. 'I wrote immediately I heard; what a tragedy. How can such things happen in a civilised country, Chief Superintendent?'

'Perhaps we make life in prison too easy,' said Gaffney drily.

Farrell avoided that; turned instead to his intercom and flicked down a switch. 'Hold my calls, Tracey, I've got the police – Scotland Yard – with me.' He turned back and rested his arms on the desk giving Gaffney and Tipper his undivided attention.

Gaffney was unimpressed. Any secretary worth her salt would know not to put a call through when her boss had visitors. He put it down as an example of Farrell wielding power, and letting everyone know that he wielded it. 'How well do you know the Home Secretary . . . or more particularly, how well did you know his late wife, Mr Farrell?' he asked, and sat back to await the lies he was sure would be forthcoming.

'Oh, very well, Chief Superintendent, very well indeed.'

'How did you come to meet him?'

Farrell's brief instructions to his secretary had given him time to collect his thoughts after Gaffney's little tilt about prison conditions. 'I have thought for a long time that half the problem with ex-prisoners is that we – by which I mean society – don't really care what happens to them when they come out—'

127

'Mr Farrell!' said Gaffney softly, and raised a hand.

Farrell stopped speaking and looked somewhat put out. 'What?'

'Could we get to the Home Secretary?' Gaffney didn't need a lecture on crime and punishment, particularly after learning how Waldo Conway proposed to speed up his chances of parole.

'Oh yes, of course. I'm sorry, I do tend to get carried away. I was merely trying to explain that it was this idea of mine that brought us together. I must say that Dudley Lavery was very keen.' Gaffney noted the way that he referred to the Home Secretary, implying a familiarity that was denied to policemen. 'Very keen indeed. It was he who arranged that we got the interested parties together, and . . . ' He interrupted himself by leaning over and pushing a silver cigarette box across the desk. 'I'm sorry, very remiss of me. Will you have a cigarette? I don't myself; gave it up five years ago, as a matter of fact. You know how it is: first my wife, then my doctor, getting on at me?'

'Not for me, thank you.'

'Very wise, very wise,' said Farrell, moving the box back into its place. 'Yes, the Home Secretary and various other good people helped enormously. As I said, he was very keen.'

'Perhaps it might help to save time if I tell you that I have already spoken to the Home Secretary . . . several times,' said Gaffney softly.

'Ah!' said Farrell, clasping his hands together and rocking back gently in his chair. 'Ah!'

'This dinner – at your house in Boreham Wood – was the first occasion that you met Mrs Lavery, I take it?'

'Er, yes, I suppose it would have been.' Farrell had appeared to give that some thought, but Gaffney was prepared to bet that he knew exactly where and when he had met anyone of importance; and that meant anyone who could further his career, which in turn meant anyone who could increase his wealth and influence. 'Yes. I had met Dudley several times before, of course, at various functions.' He waved his hand as if to encompass the whole of London, and nodded.

'But the first time you met Elizabeth Lavery was when she came to your house with her husband?' Farrell nodded. 'And that was also the last time?' Gaffney put a questioning inflexion into the last sentence.

'Alas, it was.' Farrell shook his head slowly. 'Dreadful, quite dreadful.'

'Yes, indeed.' Gaffney agreed with him and then paused. 'I understand that your house was broken into last week, Mr Farrell? While you were dining in the West End?' The question came suddenly and out of context.

Farrell stared at Gaffney for some seconds before replying. 'My house? My house broken into? I think you must be mistaken.' He smiled unconvincingly. 'That would be an event, Chief Superintendent, I assure you.' He recovered his poise and laughed outright.

'Really?' Gaffney looked sceptical. 'But you did go out to dinner last Thursday?'

Farrell made an expansive gesture with his hands. 'Chief Superintendent,' he said, 'my wife and I dine out most nights.'

'But last Thursday, you noticed nothing amiss when you returned?'

'Of course not. Do you think I would not report it to the police? I am puzzled. What makes you think this?'

'We rely a lot on informants, Mr Farrell.' Gaffney smiled. 'But informants are not always reliable. Perhaps they were talking about another house.'

'I think that must be the case.' Farrell nodded, a certain relief apparent on his face. 'But why the interest? What has this to do with Elizabeth Lavery?'

'Nothing,' said Gaffney blandly. 'But I am interested in burglaries at houses which are regularly visited by Cabinet Ministers.'

Farrell put the tips of his fingers together and smiled. 'Yes, of course. I see,' he said. 'I see.'

'Well, Mr Farrell, thank you very much for your time,' said Gaffney, rising from his chair. 'I can't think of anything else.'

He glanced at Tipper who had remained silent throughout the interview. 'Anything you wanted to ask Mr Farrell, Harry?'

'No thank you, sir.' Tipper nodded at Farrell who felt strangely disturbed by the taciturnity of Gaffney's colleague for a reason he couldn't explain. He wasn't to know that Tipper had that effect on a lot of people, particularly those with guilty consciences.

For a moment or two Farrell stared at the door after it had closed on the two policemen, then he walked across and unlocked a cabinet next to the bookcase. Inside was a direct-line telephone to which only he had access. Slowly he picked up the receiver and dialled a number.

Commander Murdo McGregor, head of the Yard's Criminal Intelligence Branch, smiled amiably at Gaffney and puffed a cloud of pipe smoke into the air. 'And what can I do to help now, John?'

'Bernard Farrell, sir. Does the name mean anything?'

McGregor pondered for a second. 'Runs some interesting business enterprises. But you obviously know that. What you're asking is whether he's bent, yes?'

'Yes.'

'Have you spoken to Fraud Squad?'

Gaffney nodded. 'Yes, I have.'

'And?'

'They say he's not bent, but he ought to be.'

McGregor laughed. 'What that means is that they're not clever enough to catch him at it.' He leaned back in his chair. 'As a matter of fact, John, we know of him, and we're not too happy about his operation. There's been a hell of a lot of rumour about his activities, but no proof; the typical policeman's dilemma.' He pouted. 'I don't know how much you know, but he's trying to organise some fool charity in aid of released prisoners. Quite frankly, I don't think he gives a damn about the prison population, but he's using it as a tool to increase his own power-base – and his influence – among people he sees as important.'

Gaffney nodded. 'Yes. Tommy Fox was telling me something about it.'

'As a matter of fact, I got a note from the Commissioner recently, saying that he'd been invited to dinner with Farrell, and did I think it was all right to go.' McGregor teased the tobacco in his pipe with the end of a dead match and then looked up. 'I warned him off. I don't know whether I did right, but there's just something about the man that makes me feel uneasy. Anyway, the Commissioner took fright and cried off with a diplomatic guts-ache. What's Tommy Fox been telling you about him?'

'Much the same as you've just told me, sir. Incidentally has Tommy told you why I'm interested?'

McGregor shook his head. 'I've been off for a couple of days . . . in the Highlands.' A distant look came briefly into his eyes. 'What's Tommy Fox got hold of now?'

Gaffney summarised what Fox had told him. 'But,' he said finally, 'Farrell denies all knowledge of a break-in.'

'Sure?'

'Certain. I've been to see him.'

'Then I would say he's at it.' McGregor scratched the side of his nose with the stem of his pipe. 'There are three things that I can think of that he might have that he doesn't want us to know about: cash, bullion or drugs. And,' he continued, giving Gaffney the benefit of his thirty-three years' service, 'the motive could be quite varied too. Let's give you an idea. Tommy Fox and his heathens lifted Masters a while ago for recovering certain goods—'

Gaffney nodded. 'He told me about that.'

'Now, the situation here might be similar. Supposing friend Farrell is a handler, but has either taken more than his share, or hasn't paid for services rendered. Masters does a repossession job – or takes payment in kind – and Farrell's left with nothing . . . and no redress. In those circumstances, a bloke like Farrell would be grateful he just got away with losing the gear. He could have got duffed-up as well. On the other hand . . . ' McGregor grinned; he was getting into his stride now. 'On the other hand, Farrell, who is in business on his own account – and I think this is more likely – is perhaps doing a bit of bent dealing on the side, in bullion or drugs, shall we say, and Masters gets wind of it. He goes and helps himself to some of the proceeds knowing that Farrell's not going to go waltzing down to the local nick to file a crime report.' McGregor laughed a short, malicious laugh, and swivelled his chair to and fro a couple of times. 'But I'm afraid they're all whispers, John,' he said. 'Certainly not enough to nick him for . . . or he'd have been nicked. Could even be someone putting the bubble in.' He laid his pipe on his blotter. 'We'll have to do better than that.' He smiled again. 'It could be that Tommy Fox's snout is spinning him a load of fanny. If I was Tommy, I'd go round and break all his fingers . . . just in case.'

'By the way, Claire, have we heard from Croft yet?'

'Croft, sir?' The woman Sergeant looked momentarily puzzled.

Gaffney laughed. 'Gotcha!' he said. 'The MP whose telephone number was found on an order-paper at the Home Secretary's house.'

Claire Wentworth laughed. 'Oh, him. No, sir, we've heard nothing so far.'

Gaffney nodded. 'Still in Ankara, I suppose. Keep trying.' He walked to the door and paused. 'By the way, have we got any result from that cab enquiry yet? You know . . . the cab that was heard by a neighbour in Cutler's Mews. . . .'

The Sergeant shook her head slowly. 'Not so far, sir.'

'Probably a waste of time,' said Gaffney. 'By the time they've done all the cab-ranks and caught up with the part-time journeymen drivers, and put it in their newspaper – or whatever they do – they'll have forgotten anyway. I have known it work, but not often.' It looked to Gaffney as though every avenue he explored brought him, sooner rather than later, to a dead end.

# Chapter Twelve

Gaffney gazed down on to the roof of London Transport's headquarters and pouted. 'The snow's beginning to settle again,' he said.

'So's this bloody inquiry,' said Tipper. He dropped the file on to Gaffney's desk and sighed. 'We're getting absolutely nowhere.'

Gaffney turned and sat down at his desk. 'All we've got so far is an uncorroborated relationship between Elizabeth Lavery and a main-index villain. Then there's the man Farrell who's had his drum screwed, but denies it—'

'If it's true.'

'What?'

'There's not much proof of that, is there, sir?'

Gaffney laughed savagely. 'I'm not sure that I want there to be. It makes this game too difficult. But either way, this man Masters seems to be the one who's got all the answers. And he's in Spain.'

'We could try talking to his associates, sir.'

'Look what happened to the last one we talked to,' said Gaffney and shook his head. 'The moment we did that, we could say goodbye to Colin Masters for ever. The bastard would stay put in Seville. What I want to do, Harry, is to make sure I know every one of them – and where he is – so that the moment Masters sets foot in the UK again, we can nick the bloody lot.'

'Bit heavy, guv'nor.'

'So what. We are investigating the murder of the Home Secretary's wife, after all. Who's going to argue?'

Tipper sniffed eloquently. 'All we've got to do is wait

for Masters to come home, and, when everyone's sitting comfortably, we can begin,' he said.

Gaffney chuckled. 'But I'm not going to wait, Harry. I'm going to tempt him home. In fact, I'm going to make him an offer he can't refuse.'

'So you want the help of the Flying Squad yet again, I hear?' Tommy Fox appeared in the doorway of Gaffney's office and smiled.

'Come and sit down,' said Gaffney, 'and give me the benefit of your advice.'

'How did you get on with Farrell?' asked Fox, lowering himself into one of Gaffney's armchairs.

'More or less as you predicted. He looked all blank when I mentioned the break-in. Must have got it all wrong, et cetera. He's a smooth-talking bastard, I'll give him that.'

'You don't get to make several millions by being dim. So what d'you reckon?'

'How many villains usually work with Masters?' asked Gaffney.

Fox looked thoughtful. 'There are five who regularly run with him. That includes Waldo Conway, of course, so there are four out and about. Why?'

'What sort of story could I feed to those monkeys that would get back to Colin Masters and make him angry enough to come home?'

For some moments Tommy Fox lay back in the armchair, his gaze fixed on the ceiling. Then he sat upright, a malicious smile on his face. 'I don't think we have to tell them anything. I think that just one telephone call will do the business.' He leaned forward and rubbed his hands together vigorously. 'Now,' he said, 'see how you like the sound of this for a scenario . . . '

Police Constable Richards had got the hump. In fact, he was beginning seriously to wonder whether his selection of the Metropolitan Police as a career had been altogether wise. The moment he had come on duty at six o'clock that morning, an irate sergeant had taken him to task about a report which had not been submitted as promptly as the sergeant would have wished. Secondly, there was no car driver to fill a beat which was definitely a car beat, and, as a result, Richards now found himself walking what would be about a five-mile round-trip. Thirdly, it was still dark, it was snowing, and it was cold. Richards was not happy, and was not, therefore, amiably disposed towards his fellow man. And that included postmen.

'Morning, guv.'

Richards ignored the niceties. 'You're not allowed to ride a cycle on the footway.'

The postman ignored the rebuke. 'I've just delivered to that house back there,' he said, pointing, 'and the front door's open; looks like it's been jemmied.'

'Anyone at home, was there?'

'Dunno!' said the postman. 'You're the one who deals with people who break the law. My job's to deliver letters. That's why they give me a bicycle,' he added, 'so's I can do it quicker. It's all a matter of economics.'

'Thanks,' said Richards sarcastically, and made his way up the drive.

The front door was indeed open, but to suggest that it had been jemmied was something of an understatement; to Richards' professional eye it looked as if it had been savagely attacked with a crowbar. The whole surround was splintered, large pieces were gouged out of the door itself, and the mortise-lock had been smashed right out of the woodwork. He shook his head in amazement; whoever was responsible must have made a lot of noise, but in this area – like most others these days – no one wanted to get involved.

Richards pushed the door wide and stepped inside. The beam of his pocket torch sought the light switch; he turned it on and illuminated the downstairs hallway. The first thing to meet his gaze was the telephone, ripped from its mounting and thrown into the centre of the carpet, but, as he looked around, he began to realise that everything movable had been wrecked. He went into the sitting room and again found wreckage everywhere: tables were overturned, pictures torn off walls and destroyed, the backs of expensive chesterfields slashed open, and the contents of the cocktail cabinet had been opened and poured over the carpet.

Richards toured the house. There was no one there, but all the rooms had been subjected to the same onslaught. Deep scratches on the dining table, mattresses torn open in the bedrooms; in another room an expensive desk had been prised open, drawer by drawer, and all the books had been taken from their shelves and heaped in the centre of the floor as if in preparation for a bonfire. Richards was not a detective, but to him it looked as though the thieves, having failed to find anything of value to steal, had taken it out on the absent occupant by smashing anything they could find. He stepped on to the front porch and called the station on his personal radio.

That Richards had not been a policeman for very long accounted for his not knowing who lived in this particular house. But the station officer knew, and the duty CID officer most certainly knew.

The duty CID officer rang the detective inspector at home. 'We've had a break-in, guv,' he said, 'at Colin Masters' drum. They've wrecked the bloody place.'

Detective Chief Superintendent Fox noted the message that had been received from the DI at Wimbledon about the break-in at Masters' house and walked down the corridor to the lift. He decided that there was no point in going to Wimbledon; he had after all inspected the property, so to speak, less than a week previously, and he didn't have time to gloat. Instead he made his way upwards, to the eighteenth floor and John Gaffney's office.

'Good news, my friend,' Fox said, pushing the door of Gaffney's office open wide.

'I'm glad someone has,' said Gaffney. 'D'you know Tommy, it's two weeks tomorrow since this bloody murder, and I'm not a step closer to an arrest than when I started. Anyhow, what is this good news of which you speak?'

'They took the bait. Colin Masters' drum has been done over a treat.'

'Really?'

'Been taken apart by all accounts. I am waiting by the hour for a full scientific report, but I'll lay even money right now that there'll not be a fingerprint to be found.'

'So what happens now?'

'Word will out,' said Fox. He grinned. 'Selected Flying Squad officers are this day about to advise certain well known conduits in what the popular Press laughingly calls the underworld, that there has been a happening to the detriment of one Colin Masters. And, if I was you, I would alert Enrico Perez at the Spanish Embassy that a villain we know and love is almost certain to board an aircraft bound for the United Kingdom very shortly.' He parted the slats of the Venetian blind and peered out. 'In the meantime,' he continued, his back to Gaffney, 'I am reliably informed that the CID at Wimbledon are making strenuous efforts to trace the owner of the property. Unfortunately,' he said, turning away from the window, 'contrary to all our advice about crime prevention, he appears not to have advised the local police that his premises were unattended.'

'Dear me,' said Gaffney. He had had doubts when Fox had outlined his plans for persuading Masters back to England, but had to acknowledge that the Flying Squad chief had a far greater knowledge of the criminal world and the individuals who populated it than he, a Special Branch officer, was ever likely to have. He had not enquired too deeply as to how Fox had known that Farrell had a private telephone in a locked cabinet in his office, or what its number was, but he would dearly like to have been a fly on the wall when Farrell had received the telephone call – anonymously, of course – advising him that there was a rumour being put about that it was Masters who had done his drum over at Boreham Wood, and that Farrell's property was to be found at a certain address in Wimbledon.

All in all, Tommy Fox was rather pleased with the result. It certainly ought to bring Masters home, but, more to the point, it proved that Farrell was at it. Exactly what he was at remained to be discovered, but that was a minor point so far as the Flying Squad was concerned.

The heavy Jaguar slid into the kerb and the police motor-cyclists deployed themselves in exactly the places which had been rehearsed several times over during the preceding week.

Detective Sergeant John Selway was out before the car had stopped and was quick to get hold of the handle of the Home Secretary's door before anyone else did, glancing rapidly around and upwards at the same time.

Dudley Lavery stepped out, left hand gently patting his hair, right hand extended, and his television smile fixed firmly on his face for the benefit of the Press – mainly local – who seemed to make up most of the crowd.

The Chief Constable tugged at the hem of his tunic, saluted, and half-inclined his body as though the Home Secretary were minor royalty. 'Good morning, sir,' he said as they shook hands.

'Chief Constable,' murmured Lavery. 'Good to see you again.' He could have sworn that he had never set eyes on the head of this particular force before, but he had been assured by officials that he had had a quite lengthy conversation with him at a recent conference of chief police officers.

John Selway knew that his principal had met the Chief Constable before, had assessed also that he wanted a knighthood and didn't mind how unctuous he had to be to get it. Lisle, Silvester and Selway, the three Special Branch officers responsible for Lavery's safety, had worked out a simple formula based on the hard experience of visits such as this one. If the Chief Constable was present in uniform, it would be a cock-up; present in plain clothes and there was a fifty-fifty chance of success; not there at all and things usually went off smoothly. In fairness of course – and Selway hated being fair to senior officers – Lavery had come to open a new divisional police headquarters, and the Chief Constable had no alternative but to be there in uniform.

It was a tedious business. The procession of senior police-men, led by the Chief Constable, supported by his deputy and flanked by the assistant chiefs, conducted Lavery round the new building, obviously under the impression that what the Home Secretary most wanted to see was the assorted new gadgetry which had been installed in the control room, the traffic unit and the computer centre. They had overlooked – or didn't care – that Lavery had seen it all before in a dozen different places, and that all he wanted was a gin and tonic, a decent lunch which – if his private secretary had done his stuff – would not include chicken, and then to get the hell out of it. Ironically for a Home Secretary, Lavery did not take to most of the senior policemen he met, finding them pompous and blinkered. On walks in the countryside around his Shropshire home however, he would often have animated conversations with Selway, the junior of his three bodyguards, about a whole variety of subjects . . . except the police force. Selway looked now at the top brass of this particular force and felt some sympathy for Lavery, a man whose natural courtesy obliged him to be polite . . . even to people he probably despised.

As if reading his detective's thoughts, Lavery glanced at Selway, walking, as ever, at his elbow, and said: 'Lot of people to thank today, John.'

Selway smiled. It was a private joke. On one of their regular visits to the constituency, a constabulary sergeant had discreetly drawn Selway to one side and asked him if he could persuade Lavery to thank the local chief superintendent each time he left. 'If he forgets,' the sergeant had said, 'the boss thinks something's gone wrong and we all get hell for a week.'

The Home Secretary had laughed when Selway had told him. 'You must remind me to thank him after each visit, John,' he had said and, turning to his private secretary, had added: 'And put him down for an MBE next time, Charles. We can't have him upsetting the troops.'

By the time the official opening ceremony was reached – a ludicrous ribbon-cutting affair at the main entrance – the retinue of hangers-on had increased, and among those lunching at the ratepayers' expense were chairmen of councils, mayors, other assorted dignitaries and the police authority in its entirety.

The Chief Constable, never more than a couple of feet from Lavery, had sat next to him at lunch and bombarded him with facts and figures which, roughly translated, were meant to imply greater efficiency at less cost, and added up to how clever a chief constable this particular force was lucky enough to have.

At last it was time to leave. The Chief Constable shook hands on the steps of the headquarters and again half bowed. The Home Secretary's car had not travelled more than fifty yards when a horrified Chief Constable saw a dustbin crash on to its roof.

John Selway didn't know what had happened and didn't intend stopping to find out. 'Put your foot down,' he said to the driver, and fingered the butt of his revolver.

'What on earth—' The Home Secretary twisted in his seat to peer out of the rear window.

'Get down, sir,' shouted Selway.

Lavery laughed. 'It's all right, John,' he said. 'It was a dustbin.'

Selway relaxed, but determined that he would not stop yet awhile to examine the damage. 'That's his knighthood gone for a ball of chalk,' he said quietly to the driver.

'I'll pretend I didn't hear that,' said the Home Secretary from the back seat. Selway glanced in his rear-view mirror: Lavery was smiling.

The dustbin had been thrown from the flat roof of a building on the opposite side of the road from the police headquarters; it was obvious that whoever had thrown it had had a clear view of the Home Secretary and his departure, and the incident could have been very much more serious had the attacker been so minded. The ground floor of the building was a large shop and five or six constables ran in through the door.

'How do we get to the roof?'

An assistant pointed. 'Through the fire exit and up the stairs,' she said.

Sitting on the roof, his back against the low retaining wall, was a man. His knees were drawn up to his chest and were encircled by his arms. The policemen stopped, surprised to see someone still there. In their experience, people who committed crime usually ran away.

An older PC took charge. 'Grab hold of him, lads,' he said. 'Don't want him chucking himself over as well. That would make a mess.' Two constables grabbed an arm each, dragging the man to his feet and pulling him away from the edge. 'You the bloke who just threw a dustbin off the roof?'

'Yes. Did I get him, that bastard Lavery?'

The PC smiled. 'Oh yes, you got him all right, leastways you hit his car. What's your name, pal?'

'Ernest Drake.'

There is a fallacy propounded by the Press, usually in the aftermath of an audacious or violent crime: 'Ports and Airports are being watched,' it proclaims, implying that it has some inside information on the matter, and implying also that such observations occur only spasmodically. None of this is true. The police are watching ports and airports all the time, or, more accurately, are watching the passengers who flow through them, as numerous travelling criminals have found to their cost.

It was a simple matter for Harry Tipper, when he received a telephone call from Enrico Perez telling him that Colin Masters had boarded Iberian Airways flight 616 at 11.30 local time, to pass that information to the Special Branch Unit at Heathrow Airport and still leave them about three hours to prepare a reception before he was scheduled to arrive at five minutes to three that afternoon.

For the tenth time since lunch, Detective Inspector Geoffrey Hall glanced at the monitor in his office at Terminal Two. Flight IB 616 from Seville was slowly moving up the list of expected aircraft, still estimated to arrive on schedule at five minutes to three. Hall walked out into the control area. There were five minutes still to go before touchdown, but he wanted to make sure that everything was ready. He had placed officers near the immigration desks, and between there and the 'finger' that would eventually be put in place when the aircraft's engines were switched off. There was no way that Masters was going to escape. He would be followed from the moment he stepped off the plane to the moment he presented his passport: always the best place to effect an arrest. Then he would be taken swiftly through to the Customs Hall where a previously-briefed preventive officer called Clancy – he refused to accept the Civil Service idea that he should now call himself an executive officer – would go through Masters' baggage and his apparel. After that he would belong to the police, having paid any duty for which he was liable, of course: Her Majesty's Customs and Excise were very particular about that.

Hall was determined that the arrest of Masters should present no problems. Seville at that time of year was not, it seemed, a popular place to leave, and the airline was expecting only seven passengers to disembark, less than the number of men that DI Hall had standing by. Two stewardesses walked through the Arrivals Hall, their neat little bottoms constrained by tight skirts, their stiletto heels clacking suddenly and sharply as they crossed the thermo-plastic flooring from one piece of carpeting to another. Hall watched them in an abstract way, trying to pretend that he wasn't watching them at all. They were followed by one of the airline men whose red cap indicated that he was the traffic despatcher. He nodded to Hall and laid one flat hand on top of the other, indicating that the aircraft was down. Hall nodded back. One of the stewardesses looked over her shoulder and smiled.

The passengers came through, seven of them as the airline had predicted. There were two obvious businessmen: one with his tie slackened off as if to emphasise his hard-working weariness; then a husband and wife: she with tired make-up and worn nail-varnish; two women in their mid-twenties came next, probably out-of-work dancers; and finally, a nun: there always seemed to be a nun. Two of Hall's officers brought up the rear. The senior of the two, a young detective sergeant, spread his hands, palms upwards. There was no sign of Colin Masters.

'Have you checked the aircraft?' asked Hall.

'Yes, sir. There's no trace of him—'

'Well, where in hell—?'

'—for the very simple reason that he got off the bloody aircraft at Valencia, sir. I showed the stewardess his photograph.'

'Terrific,' said Hall. 'Come into the office.' He had noticed, on the flight arrivals monitor, that the last stop was Valencia, but had paid little heed to it. There would have been no point in concerning himself that Masters may have got off there; the Spanish police should have thought of that. The British had only been told that Masters had got on the flight at Seville with a ticket that showed a booking to London Heathrow.

Hall telephoned Gaffney. Gaffney was not pleased, not at all pleased. Neither was Enrico Perez when Gaffney telephoned him. He swore volubly, first in English, then in Spanish, and promised to make several phone calls himself, after which he would ring back. Gaffney got the impression that he was about to reintroduce the Spanish Inquisition.

Perez was as good as his word. Quite what he said to whoever it was he spoke to in Spain, Gaffney never discovered. It was thorough, but ineffective because it was too late. Masters had got off the aircraft in Valencia, certainly, but had changed his ticket for one that would take him to Paris where he arrived at just about half-past five. Perez spoke to a contact of his in the Police des l'Air et Frontières in Paris who discovered that Masters had again traded his ticket and boarded a flight for London that left Paris at 1800 hours and arrived at Gatwick at eight o'clock. That interesting piece of information reached Gaffney at twenty-two minutes past eight. He rang the Special Branch at Gatwick. Yes, Masters had arrived, and they had reported his arrival – or would do as soon as the typewriter was free – on account of his being

143

a main-index criminal, but they didn't arrest him because no one had told them that he was wanted. Yes, they had checked with the Police National Computer but even that had said that he wasn't wanted. Gaffney cursed himself for not having anticipated Masters' deviousness, but that was the drawback with a confidential operation like the investigation into the murder of the Home Secretary's wife: you could be too secretive . . . and too clever.

Tommy Fox didn't attach too much importance to it all. In fact, he thought on reflection, it might all have happened for the best. 'We know where he's going, don't we, John?' he asked.

'We think we do,' said Gaffney grudgingly. 'But when?'

'If he's canny enough to change flights at Valencia and Paris and then come into Gatwick, then he's cunning enough not to go home to his pad in Wimbledon.'

'So where's he gone?'

'Quite simply, to ground,' said Fox, carefully removing a single hair from his jacket and dropping it to the floor. He sat up as if to take the whole thing seriously from now on. 'Look, John,' he said, 'he's got wind of Elizabeth Lavery's murder – couldn't be off knowing it, could he, with all the publicity?' Gaffney nodded. 'But there was no way that he was going to let friend Farrell tear his drum apart and get away with it, was there? No, you mark my words, Masters will fetch up in Boreham Wood sooner or later, or, if he doesn't, some of his team will. Either way we shall get to Masters. There's something very strange coming off here. And if you ask me, there's a bit more to Mrs Lavery's murder than meets the eye. Quite a bit more.'

Gaffney nodded slowly. 'What fascinates me is this reciprocal burglary business.'

'What?'

'Masters' mob turn over Farrell's place, but Farrell denies it. Question: what was Masters looking for, or what did he nick that Farrell didn't want police to know about?'

'Yes, that's about the strength of it.'

'Now, what story did you put about, Tommy?'

'Bit nebulous as you might say. I let it be known that something that Farrell wanted was in Masters' drum at Wimbledon.'

'Yes, but what?' asked Gaffney.

'Dunno!' Fox waved a hand in the air and grinned. 'Whatever you tell these bastards, they'll turn it into whatever they want to hear, so it doesn't really matter.'

'D'you reckon they found it?'

'Who? Masters or Farrell?'

'Yes,' said Gaffney, and smiled. 'D'you reckon there's any point in speaking to Waldo Conway again?'

Fox laughed sadistically. 'You can talk to him, but there's no danger of him saying anything, not after the last interview you had with him. I know his legs are in plaster, but for all you'll get out of him it might as well be his jaw.'

'How's the DI at Wimbledon getting on with investigating the break-in at Masters' place?'

'Not well, not well at all. He did pick up a partial that he's gone overboard about, but he hasn't got enough points to prove anything.'

That was always the problem with a partial fingerprint, and it was unusual for a skilled breaker to leave one anywhere, but, from what he had heard about the damage, it was more like an earthquake than a burglary, and it was possible that Farrell, if he was at the back of it, had used some front-line expendables. 'Is it enough for identification?'

Fox spread his hands. 'No idea. Fingerprint Branch are searching like mad at the moment, but it all takes time. After all, what is it? Somebody does over a main-index villain's drum. No one's going to get too excited about that.'

'Except me,' said Gaffney. 'Right now I'm clutching at straws and that may be the only hope I've got.'

# Chapter Thirteen

Gaffney's telephone call to the head of Fingerprint Branch ensured that priority was given to the search to identify the partial fingerprint, and it was the middle of the following morning when he got the message to say that they were ninety-percent certain that they had matched it.

'Who is it?' asked Gaffney.

'It's a hood called Watkins,' said the head of Fingerprints. 'Joseph Watkins. Hang on, I'll give you his CRO number . . . '

'He's got a string of previous,' said Tipper coming through the door. He waved the microfiche of Watkins' criminal record in the air.

'Like what?'

'Like every bit of petty villainy you can think of, starting off when he was twelve.'

'Same sort of form?'

'Nah!' Tipper scoffed. 'Anything that comes to hand. The only consistency is that he always gets caught.' He skimmed through the summary. 'Seems to use his head a lot.'

'Doesn't sound like it,' said Gaffney.

'For damaging other people with,' said Tipper. 'He's got two or three here for GBH – head-butting his victim and then robbing them.'

'Sounds like our man. I think we'll have a little chat with him, Harry.'

Detective Inspector Henry Findlater peered through his large spectacles. 'I've a team at Wimbledon, watching Masters' place, sir, and another at Boreham Wood, at Farrell's house. I must say that they couldn't have been further apart.' He shrugged hopelessly. 'Does make life difficult.'

'Never mind, Henry,' said Gaffney. 'You're doing a grand job.' Findlater sniffed. 'And I hope it won't last too long.'

'If Masters does turn up, d'you want him nicked, sir?'

'Most definitely, Henry. You'll have no problem identifying him, will you?' he asked with a smile.

'I'd like to have a pound for every mile we've followed him in the past,' said Findlater sourly.

'Joseph Watkins?'

'Who wants to know?'

'You're nicked,' said Tipper, 'official.'

Sometimes a policeman will get lucky. It doesn't often happen, but when it does he gets a warm feeling deep inside. Special Agent Frank Robinson of the Kansas City FBI office got this feeling of satisfaction when he found that Martha Cody, now sixty-three years of age, still lived at the address the US Air Force had turned up.

It was a dowdy apartment in a dowdy apartment-building just back of 35th Street, a building which displayed none of the aesthetic loveliness of the centre of Kansas City, with its tree-lined boulevards, its statues and its fine buildings.

'Who's there?' the voice, croaky with age, shouted through the door.

'FBI, ma'am,' said Robinson, hoping that the woman was not prone to a heart attack.

Bolts were drawn, locks were turned, and eventually the door opened an inch or two to reveal the face of the occupant. 'Who d'you say you are?' A heavy chain bridged the gap.

Robinson held up his badge. 'Frank Robinson, ma'am, FBI. From here in Kansas City. Mrs Cody, is it?'

'What d'you want?'

'I want to talk with you about your son, Paul.'

'What about him? He ain't done nothing wrong. What's the FBI want with him?'

'If I could just step inside, ma'am. It won't take a minute.'

The door closed briefly while the chain was released, and with evident reluctance Martha Cody admitted the agent.

'He ain't done nothing wrong,' said Mrs Cody again as Robinson followed her through to the sitting room.

'I didn't say he'd done anything wrong. We just want to talk with him.'

'What about?' She stood with her feet apart and her hands on her hips, challenging, and disinclined to ask Robinson to sit down. He didn't mind that; the chairs were old and filthy.

'It's about a lady he knew once when he was in London—'

'Pah!' she said vehemently. 'Ain't nothin' but trouble, women.'

'If you could just tell me where I can find him, ma'am . . . .'

'Broadway,' she said, her face cracking into a brief smile. 'He's a big star there. Here, look, mister.' She pointed to a framed photograph on the television set; it was the sort of photograph that embryo actors have taken and distribute in shoals to any agent, producer, backer or writer they think might employ them.

'Is he a good son?' asked Robinson.

'Sure he is. Why you asking?'

Robinson smiled. 'Just wondering, ma'am, just wondering,' he said. He doubted that a big star on Broadway would allow his mother to live in the obvious poverty that Mrs Cody's apartment indicated. 'What about your husband?' he asked tentatively.

'Died ten years back,' said Mrs Cody shortly. 'Why?'

'Just wondering,' said Robinson again.

'Strikes me you do a lot of wondering, young man.'

'Guess it's part of the job. Where can I find Paul. Broadway's kind of a long street.'

'Hell, I don't know. You'll just have to look for his name in lights, I guess.'

The news that Drake had been arrested was telephoned to Gaffney at Scotland Yard and he and Tipper left immediately to interview him. As Gaffney, dispirited by the whole inquiry, succinctly put it: 'We've bugger-all else to do.'

He was a little mystified that Drake had been moved from where he had been arrested to a station in the same town as the force headquarters. The reason became clear when they arrived and were met by the Detective Chief Superintendent of the force, an old friend of Gaffney with whom, long ago, he had attended a course at the Police Staff College . . . and drunk a lot of beer.

'The Chief'd like to see you, John, before you interview the prisoner.' He glanced around furtively as if fearing eavesdroppers. 'He's desperately worried about the whole thing.'

The Chief Constable's office was, if anything, slightly larger than that occupied by the Home Secretary, and it seemed to Gaffney that they had to walk a long way to reach his desk.

'Ah, Chief Superintendent.' The Chief Constable neither stood up nor offered to shake hands. 'You've come to interview the man Drake, I understand?'

'Yes, sir.'

'D'you think he's the man who murdered the Home Secretary's wife?'

It was evident to Gaffney that the Chief Constable was hoping to recover some of his tarnished reputation. 'Until I interview him I have no way of telling, but, on balance, I should think it unlikely.'

The Chief Constable looked at Gaffney sharply. 'Then why circulate his description to all forces?'

'Because he had written threats to murder the Home Secretary on numerous occasions previously, and he went missing from just before the time of Mrs Lavery's murder.' Gaffney smiled disarmingly. 'You will appreciate, sir, that we had no alternative but to circulate him. It doesn't make him guilty though, not by a long chalk.'

'Hmm!' The Chief Constable did not look happy. 'Does the Home Secretary know of this arrest by my officers?' He asked the question in a casual, offhanded way.

'Yes. I arranged for his protection officer to inform him the moment he returned to London.'

'Good, good. Say anything, did he?' Again an almost disinterested tone in his voice.

'Apparently he expressed the view that it would have been better if he had been arrested before he threw the dustbin, sir. I got the impression that the Secretary of State was not greatly taken with the security arrangements.' Gaffney could be extremely cutting when the mood took him.

The Chief Constable looked sick. 'Well, thank you, Chief Superintendent, and now if you'll excuse me . . . '

'Are you Ernest Drake?'

'Captain Drake, yes.' He put emphasis on the rank and sat down without being asked. The confidence of the army officer was still there.

Gaffney had read the details of Drake's court martial and his subsequent cashiering, and knew that he was no longer entitled to use the rank he had once held. There was, however, nothing to be gained by making an issue of it. 'Where were you on the night of—'

'If you're talking about the night that Lavery's wife was murdered' – Drake cut across Gaffney's formal opening – 'I was at Cutler's Mews.' He paused to give effect to his statement. Gaffney was about to intervene but Drake went on, giving him no chance. 'I know that I'm not obliged to say anything but that anything I say will be taken down in writing and given in evidence.' He grinned boyishly; it was evident that his knowledge of military law had not left him. 'I went to Cutler's Mews and I killed her.'

'I see.' Gaffney was leaning back in his chair, at an angle to the table; his left hand played idly with a pencil and he looked as though he was not much interested in what Drake was saying. 'And how did you murder Mrs Lavery, Captain Drake?'

'Why are you asking me that? You know, surely?'

Gaffney nodded and smiled. 'Oh yes, I know, Captain Drake, but you see,' he said mildly, 'I don't believe you.'

Drake considered that for some time. 'I strangled her,' he said eventually.

'And what time would this have been?'

Drake reflected on that for a few seconds, and then: 'About six o'clock, I suppose.'

Tipper had been sitting to one side of the room and now stood up. He brought his chair closer to the table, swung it round and sat down so that his forearms rested on the back. 'Stop poncing about, Drake,' he said sharply. 'You didn't kill Mrs Lavery, and we all know it.'

After the soft courtesy of Gaffney's questioning, Tipper's uncouth onslaught shook Drake, but he recovered almost immediately. 'Yes I did,' he said mildly.

'Why?'

'Because he killed my wife.'

'That's balls and you know it. He had nothing to do with the death of your wife. She committed suicide.'

Drake smiled patiently as though he had had to explain this elementary matter over and over again. 'If the judiciary had not put my wife in prison, she would be alive. Dudley Lavery is at the head of the Department of State responsible for prisons, so he is responsible. He killed my wife and I killed his. It's perfectly simple.' He leaned back and folded his arms.

'Why not kill the Home Secretary himself, if he's the one you hold responsible, then?'

'There's a certain justice in killing his wife, a rich irony.'

'But why didn't you kill him yesterday when you had the opportunity? From where you were on that roof you could have assassinated him quite easily. But instead you threw a dustbin at his car. Why a dustbin? You must have known that wouldn't harm him.'

'I didn't want him to think that he was that important,' said Drake. 'There's something rather insulting about having a dustbin thrown at you. It's belittling.'

'Well, Harry, what d'you think?'

'Mad as a March hare, guv'nor.'

It was obvious that Masters knew that Farrell was at home – he was that sort of thorough villain – and that he intended to do him some harm. What he did not expect though, was that Farrell's house would be under surveillance – or as he mistakenly assumed, under guard – by the police.

His arrival in a silver-grey Mercedes with three of his henchmen could have no other explanation than that of someone looking for trouble. But Masters was a shrewd villain – up to a point – which was how he managed to stay out of trouble for long periods at a time; and he seemed to have a sixth sense for detecting the Old Bill. The Mercedes drew up in the road outside Farrell's ostentatious mansion and Masters got out. Still holding the open door of the car, he peered round in the darkness; Findlater swore afterwards that he was sniffing the air – a statement which brought a ribald reaction from certain of his colleagues, policemen's humour being what it is – but whatever the reason, something warned Masters. He got back into the car – like a rat up a drainpipe, as one sage observer commented – and drove off at high speed even before the door of the car was closed.

That sort of behaviour tends to disconcert surveillance teams, but Henry Findlater responded with as much alacrity as his limited resources permitted. First of all he alerted the Central Command Complex at Scotland Yard through his main-force radio, then passed a spontaneously coded message for Gaffney, all while his driver tried desperately to keep up with Masters. There was not much chance; Findlater's vehicle was designed for static observation, not high-speed chases, but he did at least manage to gain the impression that Masters was making for the M1 motorway, presumably with the intention of getting lost somewhere in Central London.

Within minutes, every police vehicle in the Metropolitan Police District had a description of the car in which Masters was travelling, but they had been advised that there was a distinct possibility that Masters and his cronies were armed, and that they should only observe and report. One of the police cars which picked up the transmission was a powerful

Ford Granada containing Detective Inspector Denzil Evans of the Flying Squad and his deputy team-leader, Detective Sergeant Percy Fletcher. Not far away, in an equally powerful Vauxhall Senator, were another sergeant and a detective constable. Each of the cars was driven by a Metropolitan Police advanced driver, which proved to be unfortunate for Masters. There are two things you should never try to do to an advanced driver: one is to beat him at cards; the other is to outdrive him. Both are virtually impossible.

The obvious thing for Masters to do was to ditch the vehicle in which he was travelling, but that would put him in danger of being arrested, he thought, because he didn't know how close his pursuers were. He was angry, very angry, and he was going to kill someone for this. The people he employed were supposed to know about things like policemen watching houses in which he had an interest; that's what he paid them for. If he had known, he would have made alternative arrangements – like not going – or would have had another car placed judiciously in some side-street. Someone was in trouble and Masters let it be known. It created an uncomfortable atmosphere in the car.

The first police vehicle to spot the Mercedes was a traffic car pulling off the Scratchwood Services area on to the M1 and making south. The wireless operator switched on the double blue beacons and the siren, then grabbed the handset as the three and half litres of the Rover seemed to hit him in the small of the back. These two didn't give a damn about 'observe and report'; if there was a chance of stopping this monkey then they would do so. Anyway, he was exceeding the speed limit, and that was their department, whatever the Flying Squad might think.

Detective Inspector Denzil Evans and company were patrolling – or marauding, as Tommy Fox described it – in the same direction but on a parallel road. They were going south on the Watford Way having just unsatisfactorily executed a search warrant in Mill Hill; it was unsatisfactory because they hadn't found any stolen goods. 'Get on the bloody motorway,' said Evans to the driver of his car, and grabbed

the handset of the radio to instruct the other car to follow suit.

'How?' asked the driver.

'What d'you mean how? You're the bloody driver.'

'There's no access road, well, not officially.'

'What's that supposed to bloody mean?'

'Well, there is a road, guv,' said the driver, hunching
his shoulders and adjusting his position as the needle of
the speedometer crept past sixty miles an hour.

'Then use it, for Christ's sake,' said Evans. 'What d'you
think I'm going to do, summon you for a traffic offence or
something?'

They heard the whining siren of the traffic car as they
slowed down by the unofficial slip road and saw the white
Rover speeding down the overtaking lane.

'Reckon he's doing over the ton, easy,' said the Flying
Squad driver with a professional interest.

'Well, see if you can catch him,' said Evans testily.

The Granada accelerated on to the motorway and into
the outside lane, rapidly gaining speed. Evans was rocking
to and fro as if to urge the car to go even faster.

'Better book us on, guv,' said DS Fletcher from the back
seat.

'Do what?' Evans glanced over his shoulder.

'Tell the Yard we're involved in the chase, sir.'

'Ah, right, yes, good,' said Evans and seized the handset
of the radio once more.

It was Junction One that did for Masters' driver. The com-
plexity of the roundabout system where the M1 gets involved
with the North Circular Road and the Edgware Road was just
too much for him. Trying to select the right road and avoid
a bus at the same time was his undoing. The Mercedes ground
to a halt against a wall that tore most of the car's side out
and severely shook its occupants.

The traffic car pulled to the offside, its blue lights warning
of the accident; Denzil Evans and his sergeant were out of
their car before it had stopped.

The DI ran to the Mercedes and pulled open the door. His

154

pistol touched the ear of the driver. 'I think you've just had an accident, gents,' he said. 'Never mind, the RAC's just over there.' He paused. 'Oh, and by the way, you're nicked.'

'Don't forget the reckless driving as well, sir,' said the traffic car driver.

The pathetic figure of Joseph Watkins sat in the detention room of Rochester Row police station and contemplated the walls. Police station detention rooms were familiar territory to the petty criminal, but he had developed an immunity to the overawing effect that such places sometimes have on the more law-abiding, particularly those who have erred for the first time.

Tipper, however, was a very skilled interrogator, and the fact that he wanted information this time, rather than evidence, gave him a greater licence than the law allowed under normal circumstances. It is simply this: that a confession obtained under duress will be resisted by defence counsel when the case eventually goes to trial, and there is a good chance that the judge – judges being a bit of a soft touch these days – will exclude it. A verbal admission is, after all, only something which is destined to be denied at the trial on the advice of counsel.

But Tipper didn't want to charge Watkins with anything – not that he intended telling him that – merely wanted him to put the finger on bigger and better villains, and would be quite happy to release him from custody at the end of the day. In fact, he did tell him that. 'I've got Colin Masters locked up next door, and if I let the pair of you out together and he thinks you've been grassing, he'll probably cut your head off,' said Tipper conversationally.

'I ain't saying nothing.'

'On the other hand,' said Tipper, 'I could let you out at a different time, and no one need know you've ever been here.' Tipper thought it unnecessary to tell Watkins at this stage that Masters was in custody at Paddington, some three miles away.

Watkins looked foxily at Tipper. 'What's this all about?'

'That's what I want to know.' Tipper was aware that he was dealing with a foot-soldier, and the likelihood of his knowing very much was remote to say the least. 'But I'll tell you this for nothing: there's a murder charge at the end of it, and thirty years is a long time.' He paused to give that effect. 'Of course, this particular murder could easily be worth forty.'

That did it. 'I ain't had nothing to do with no murder. There was no one there.'

'Where?'

'But I thought—'

'Don't do that; it could seriously affect your health. Just tell me.'

'Some place down Wimbledon.'

'D'you know who it belonged to, Joseph?' Now was the time for friendliness and support.

'Dunno! Some geezer.'

Tipper didn't bother to point out the truism of that. 'It is the residence of a gentleman named Colin Masters, previously mentioned as being locked up here. Now do you get the drift?'

'Bloody hell,' said Watkins, which seemed adequately to summarise the situation in which he now found himself.

'Exactly so. Now, would you like to go on?'

'We was told we was looking for a package.'

'What sort of package?' Tipper knew that this was going to be hard work.

'Dunno! We was just told to look for it.'

'And what were you to do if you found this mysterious package?'

'Tell him,' said Watkins.

Tipper sighed. 'Tell who?'

Watkins realised the trap. 'I ain't saying nothing,' he repeated. 'I can't remember.'

'Oh dear!' Tipper made a move to stand up. 'In that case, I'll ask Mr Masters to step in and have a word with you in private. As you are prepared to take full responsibility for all the damage to his property, it seems only right that he discusses the question of compensation with you in person, doesn't it?'

'I've just remembered,' said Watkins. Tipper waited patiently. 'It was a bloke called Rogers.'

'First name?'

Watkins looked puzzled, as though unused to people having first names. 'Er—'

'We don't have to go through all that again, do we?'

'Charlie Rogers, it was.'

'And where do we find your friend Charlie Rogers, Joseph?'

'He's not a friend.'

'No. And he certainly won't be from now on. Where?'

'Up Finchley way. He hangs out in a boozer called The Stag, I think.'

'How old is he, this Charlie Rogers?'

Watkins pondered on that. ''Bout forty, I reckon,' he said at length.

Within the five-year bracketing of Charlie Rogers' estimated date of birth, the Police National Computer threw up – and that, in Tipper's view, was exactly the right phrase – five known criminals called Charles Rogers.

'Well?' said Tipper. 'What d'you reckon?'

Detective Sergeant Ian Mackinnon shuffled the computer printouts on which he had made his rough notes. 'One of them's in the nick at Lincoln doing five for aggravated burglary. One lives in Sheffield and another in Manchester. That leaves two in the London area. One . . . ' He paused to look at the papers in his hand. 'One has previous for buggery, attempted buggery, and falsely representing himself to be a private in the army. . . .' He looked at Tipper. 'Don't think he's our man, somehow.' He laid another printout on the desk in front of the Chief Inspector. 'I reckon it's this one, if it's anyone. Twelve previous – mostly petty – but a couple for robbery with violence.' He paused, and then said triumphantly: 'And he comes from Finchley.'

'Thank you,' said Tipper acidly. 'You could have saved a hell of a lot of time by telling me that in the first place.'

'Some people are never bloody satisfied,' said Mackinnon, but he waited until he was half-way down the corridor to say it.

# Chapter Fourteen

Gaffney decided that he would involve Tommy Fox in the next stage of the operation. He was unenthusiastic about it, realising that it seemed to be taking him further and further away from solving the murder of the Home Secretary's wife – a job he should not have been stuck with in the first place. Apart from anything else, the sordid world of ordinary crime was very much the Flying Squad's domain, and although Harry Tipper had a feel for it, resulting from his early experience in the force, it was SO8, as the Squad was known, which had the resources.

Tommy Fox was delighted. He had Masters locked up in Paddington police station – albeit facing only minor charges at the moment – and the prospect of being able to add to his collection was appealing. Apart from that, he had an abiding and ever-increasing interest in Bernard Farrell, whom he was convinced was at it, and felt that Masters was the man to lead him to this villainy.

It was the next day that the Brighton police telephoned Gaffney. Following the report of Drake's arrest which had appeared in that morning's newspapers, the administrator of a local hospital had informed the Brighton police that Drake had been brought to the hospital by ambulance at about midday on the day of Mrs Lavery's murder, suffering from an epileptic fit. He had been detained while the medical authorities pondered on whether his mental condition warranted compulsory detention under the legislation governing such matters. Twenty-four hours later they had decided that it did not and he was discharged.

'Well, that's effectively blown that job out of the water,' said Gaffney.

Tipper grinned. 'It had to be too good to be true, sir,' he said.

It was six o'clock in the morning when the Flying Squad, in the form of Detective Inspector Denzil Evans and his team, knocked at the door of Charlie Rogers' council flat. Mrs Rogers opened the door slightly.

'Good morning, madam,' said Evans, sweeping past her and straight into the bedroom.

'What the bloody hell – ?' It was rhetorical; she knew fine who they were.

'Shut it, missus,' said a detective constable, bringing up the rear.

'Don't hurt to keep a civil tongue in your head, bleeding filth,' said Mrs Rogers. 'What d'you want anyway?'

'We want Charlie,' said DS Percy Fletcher.

'You the Sweeney?'

'Can't you tell by the suits?'

'Bastards!'

James Marchant beamed as he came through the door of Gaffney's office. 'John, good to see you after all this time.'

Gaffney smiled half-heartedly. 'Whenever I see you, James, I get an awful sense of foreboding. What particular piece of grief are you bringing me this morning?'

Marchant waved a deprecating hand and sat down in Gaffney's armchair. 'Nothing you can't handle, John, I'm sure.' He felt around in his pockets and took out his pipe. 'D'you mind?' he asked.

Gaffney shook his head, mildly amused, as always, at Marchant's studied absent-mindedness; he knew from previous experience that the rotund and balding man opposite him had probably one of the sharpest brains in the Secret Intelligence Service.

'Colin Masters,' said Marchant. Gaffney raised an eyebrow. 'I believe you have an interest in him?'

159

'Now, what makes you think that, James?'

Marchant waved a hand and pipe-smoke eddied across the room. 'One hears these things, you know.'

'Go on, then.'

'A very strange tale, John – very strange indeed – concerning the said Masters and Elizabeth Lavery.'

'Yes, I know.'

Marchant looked surprised. 'Oh, you've heard!'

Gaffney laughed. 'You know bloody well I've got the man in custody.'

Marchant smiled. 'Yes, I know; just pulling your leg.' He became serious. 'You know about the liaison between the two, obviously?' Gaffney nodded. 'What you probably didn't know – although I don't suppose it will surprise you – is that the KGB in Spain had picked it up also.'

Gaffney sighed. 'I've got this awful feeling that you're about to complicate this whole bloody case, James. How did you know? Or mustn't I ask?'

'It's no secret,' said Marchant. 'The KGB told us.'

'You're joking!'

Marchant shook his head slowly. 'It happens from time to time. They knew about Masters and Elizabeth Lavery and were obviously bent on making capital out of it, and who's to blame them? They didn't tell us the whole story . . . ' He laughed cynically. 'They never do, of course, but their man in Seville, or wherever, disappeared without trace—'

'Defection?'

'No, I don't think so, or they wouldn't have mentioned it.' Marchant laughed again and spread his hands. 'Unless they'd sent him over deliberately and thought we hadn't noticed. I rather got the impression that this man of theirs had gone in a bit heavy and got his come-uppance somehow.' He looked enquiringly at Gaffney. 'This man Masters does have a reputation for being a violent criminal, I understand?'

'Yes, he does. Are you – or they – suggesting that Masters may have murdered him?'

'It's possible; such things have happened. Now, suppose for

160

a moment that that is what had happened, and then Elizabeth Lavery is murdered; that rather blows their little plan out of the water. But they're vengeful people, John. If they think that Masters killed their man, they're going to want to see justice. What d'you think?'

Gaffney laughed and shook his head. 'I don't believe it,' he said.

'Oh, I assure you, John, the information—'

Gaffney raised his hand. 'I don't mean I don't believe the information, James. What I don't believe is how this inquiry is getting so bloody complicated. Why me?' He paused to light a cigar. 'Are you saying that, because their plan came to nothing, they deliberately shopped Masters to you? Why not just take him out themselves?'

'That's too easy. They lost the first round, which I rather fancy was to persuade Elizabeth Lavery to spy for them or to persuade Lavery himself to do so. Blackmail! That plan's gone down the plughole, so they move on to Plan B: destabilise the British Government.'

'How so?'

'By letting us know that Lavery's judgement isn't all that it might be. Hinting that he was already a spy, perhaps; and leaving another question hanging in the air: are there any others in the higher echelons, et cetera, et cetera . . . everybody starts looking over his shoulder.'

'Bloody hell,' said Gaffney.

'I thought you'd say that,' said Marchant, and smiled.


Charlie Rogers was as unco-operative as Joseph Watkins had been, but it was clear to Tipper that he was certainly more intelligent. DI Evans wanted to have Rogers all to himself, but Tommy Fox had realised the possible importance of the man to Gaffney's inquiry, and Harry Tipper was having first bite at the cherry.

'You were concerned with others in breaking into premises in Wimbledon and committing several acts of substantial criminal damage.'

'Oh yeah?'

'What were you looking for?'

'I don't know what you're talking about.'

'Let me put it another way,' said Tipper. 'The owner of the property in question is none too pleased—'

'S'nothing to do with me,' Rogers still maintained.

'And when the owner happens to be Colin Masters, he's not much interested in proof . . . .'

Rogers sat up sharply, his countenance several shades paler than before. 'You're having me on, guv'nor.'

Tipper smiled tolerantly. 'Now, would I do a thing like that?' He studied Rogers for some moments. 'Are you seriously telling me that you didn't know?'

Rogers was sweating now, and ran a hand nervously round his chin. 'God's truth, I never knew.'

Tipper chuckled. 'You don't have to convince me, Charlie. But Colin Masters will suddenly take a great interest in your welfare as soon as he's told.'

'You mean he don't know?'

'Not yet . . . '

'Well, who's going to tell him, guv?' Rogers looked shiftily around the room.

'Me?' Tipper beamed at his prisoner. 'He's right here, banged up in this very nick.' That was true; Rogers had been brought to Paddington as well.

'Now look—'

'No! You're the one who's going to do the looking. You've got two choices. I'm investigating a murder, and you can have that, no problem. Or I let you out at the same time as Colin Masters – having had a little chat with him first.' Tipper swung off his chair and tucked it under the table all in one flowing movement. 'Please yourself, but don't bugger me about or you won't see the light of day for many a long year.' Tipper walked to the detention room door and rapped on it sharply.

'But guv'nor—'

'Stay fit,' said Tipper maliciously, and the detention room door swung to with a dull thud.

* * *

Tommy Fox stood, elegantly poised, in the doorway of the cell. He was holding a cup and saucer, and stirring his tea. 'Well, if it isn't Colin Masters. Is there anything you'd like to say to me, Colin?'

Masters scowled at the Chief Superintendent. 'I want my brief – now,' he said.

Slowly, Fox shook his head. 'So impetuous,' he said. 'Oh well, see you tomorrow.'

Having given Charlie Rogers time to come to the boil, Tipper had him brought to the interview room. 'D'you know how much I get paid an hour?' he asked.

'No.' Rogers, who couldn't see the point of the question, shook his head.

'A lot,' said Tipper, 'and my guv'nor doesn't like people who waste public money. And,' he lied, 'my guv'nor is Detective Chief Superintendent Fox of the Flying Squad.'

Rogers gulped. 'I been thinking,' he said.

'Yes – and?'

Rogers stopped again. 'Look, if I tell you this, will I get off?' He looked hopeful. 'You know what I mean, guv?'

Tipper nodded. 'I know what you mean, and you know also that I can't make any promises of that sort. I can make one promise though . . . .' He left the threat unspoken, but it registered.

'Drugs.'

Tipper masked his surprise. The inquiry had taken yet another turn. 'What about them?'

'That's what we were looking for.'

'Explain!'

'This geezer wanted us to turn over this drum. He said that there was a packet of cocaine in there and it was his, and the bloke whose gaff it was had had it away.' Rogers turned the palms of his hands upwards. 'Well, there's nothing wrong in that, is there?'

Tipper looked at the ceiling. 'Only about six offences for a start, each one of which is worth several years,' he said.

'Oh!'

163

'Go on. What sort of packet? Size, I mean.'

'He never said. Just said it was a packet of white powder. I asked him what it was, and he said it was cocaine.'

'What else did he tell you?'

'He give us the address and told us to find this packet, and, if it weren't there like, to give it a bit of a duffing-up, 'cos this geezer needed a little lesson.'

'Nice! What was this little job worth?'

Rogers looked down at the table and hesitated. 'Er—'

'Look,' said Tipper, 'I'm a copper, not a bloody tax collector. How much?'

'Fifteen hundred.'

'How many of you?'

'Just me.'

Tipper smiled. 'Uncharacteristic loyalty on your part,' he said. 'How many of you?' Rogers still paused. 'I've got one of them locked up already.'

'Oh yeah,' said Rogers, 'there was three of us done the drum, but it was only me what got the job.'

'I see,' said Tipper. 'You sub-contracted.'

Rogers face cracked into a slight grin. 'Yeah, sort of.'

'Right,' said Tipper, anxious to clear up loose ends. 'I've got Joseph Watkins; who was the other one?'

Rogers ran his tongue round his top lip and decided not to argue. 'Steel – Randy Steel. He's a coloured bloke from Wanstead. But don't let on I told you.'

Tipper smirked. 'Would I do such a thing?' He stretched and yawned. 'Now,' he said, 'let's get to the question you seem to be avoiding. Who did you do this job for?'

Rogers had hoped that that question wouldn't come; knew instinctively that it would. 'Look, guv, it's more than my life's worth.'

Tipper smiled. 'Right now, your life's worth sod-all, Charlie. Through that door is the charge room. You go on the sheet for murdering the Home Secretary's wife and I go home.' He folded his arms and sat back in the hard chair.

'Bloody hell!' Rogers had gone white. 'I never knew it

was that job.' Again he licked his lips nervously. 'You're having me on, guv'nor, aren't you?'

'Try me.' Tipper did not smile. There was a pause while he let Rogers sweat a bit more. If it didn't work, it didn't work, and that would be that. But the trouble facing villains like Rogers, was that they never knew who might have fingered them, or why; and alibis presented a terrible problem, too. In order to avoid a charge like the one Tipper had just offered him, Rogers would have to hold up his hands to a blagging in Tottenham, which unfortunately had occurred on the same night as the demise of Mrs Lavery. He thought it unlikely that his fellow robbers would be willing to come forward in order to exonerate him. And finally, he didn't know whether this chief inspector knew any of that anyway.

'Farrell.'

Tipper's face remained impassive. 'Who's Farrell?' he asked.

Rogers' hands were clenched together on the bare table, the knuckles showing white. 'He'll bloody kill me for this,' he said; the full impact of what he had just done suddenly descended on him.

If he doesn't, Masters will, thought Tipper, but deemed it impolitic to say so at that precise moment. He was certainly amazed that the name had come so easily. If it was true, and he had no reason to doubt it, and it could be proved, which was going to be much more difficult, it would spell disaster for Farrell; provided always that the jury believed a twelve-times loser rather than an ostensibly upright businessman and friend of the Home Secretary. Tipper thought of what Lavery's reaction would be when he heard, and smiled.

'It's not very funny, guv'nor,' said Rogers.

'You don't know what I was laughing at.' He looked at Rogers closely. He was the sort of villain you could see any day of the week at any one of a dozen Crown Courts. Shifty, undernourished for the most part, possessed of a certain element of pavement cunning but, at the end of it all, a loser. And Farrell was prepared to risk everything he had by taking a man like this into his confidence. And why? Greed, Tipper supposed, and the one dead give-away of the self-made man: if someone owed you, you couldn't let it go; you had to collect.

'Did you find this packet of cocaine?' asked Tipper.

'No. I reckoned it weren't there. Just an excuse like, to do this bloke's gaff over.'

'Don't see the point of that,' said Tipper. 'There's no profit in it. What did he say when you saw him next?'

'He was well pissed off. Asked us where we'd looked, and were we sure it wasn't there. Then he made us tell him all over again, where we'd looked like.'

'But he still paid you?'

Rogers grinned. 'Didn't have to. He done that first, see. Money up front, that's me.' He pulled down a lower eyelid with a grubby forefinger. 'Have to get up early in the morning to catch Charlie Rogers,' he said.

'We did,' said Tipper.

It is in the nature of things that the world of criminal investigation cannot function without information. For the most part this information – despite computers and all the other wonderful gadgets which the police now have – comes from informants . . . or snouts as the more earthy British detectives call them. But this method of acquiring information is not confined to Britain, and detectives operating in any part of the world will have a collection of such informants. The United States of America is no different, except that there the detectives refer to these mines of intelligence as snitches; but the principle is the same.

Pete Roscoe, the Special Agent-in-Charge of the FBI's New York office had been with the Bureau for more than twenty years, many of which had been spent in New York itself, and he had gathered around himself many such snitches. These snitches operated in diverse fields of criminal activity, and would from time to time pass snippets of information to Roscoe gratuitously; gratuitous only in the sense that they were unsolicited: not gratuitous in the sense that they were free. Snitches always expected to be paid for the information they provided – and sometimes they were – if it was worth it. Occasionally, however, an investigator would put out the word that he had a special interest in someone or something. A week or so previously, Roscoe had done just that, but the call he had from Frank Robinson in Kansas City had helped to narrow the field of enquiry. Or so he thought. Unfortunately – and it came as no surprise – Paul Cody turned out not to be a big star on Broadway at all.

In a sense there are two Broadways in New York: there is Broadway, and there is Off Broadway; and generally speaking those who are Off Broadway have only one object in life: to get On Broadway.

The Galaxy Theatre was definitely Off Broadway; in fact, it could almost be said to be Off Off Broadway, and looked as though it had started life as a garage or a warehouse . . . which it probably had.

Roscoe's snitch had told him that Cody was in a production at the Galaxy Theatre which the backers hoped might expand into a glittering Broadway extravaganza. The chorus – six men and six girls – could easily be expanded into a vast troupe of dancers that would not have disgraced the late Florenz Ziegfeld, said the producer hopefully: a view, sadly, not shared by the critics.

'Paul Cody?'

'Sure thing.' Cody smiled and showed his best profile. He obviously thought that Roscoe looked like an agent: a theatrical agent that is, not a federal agent.

'Name's Roscoe, Mr Cody. I'm with the FBI here in New York.'

The smile vanished. 'Look, I'm due back on in about ten—'

'Sure,' said Roscoe. 'It can wait.'

Twenty minutes later, Cody reappeared. 'What's this about?' he asked.

'Is there some place we can talk? D'you want to go into your dressing room, Mr Cody?'

Cody laughed savagely. 'You gotta be joking, mister. There is one dressing room here and we all use it . . . guys and dolls,' he said. 'I guess this is it.' He raised his arms to embrace the whole backstage area.

Roscoe shrugged and moved to what seemed a less public corner. 'What d'you know about a woman called Elizabeth Fairfax, Mr Cody?'

'Hell, man, what d'you want to talk about her for?'

'She's dead, Mr Cody.'

'Well, I'm real sorry to hear that. Real sorry. But what in hell's it got to do with me, huh?'

'Seems she was murdered.'

Cody shook his head. 'I've not been in England for more than five years. It ain't nothing to do with me. When was this, anyhow?'

Roscoe flicked open his notebook. 'Nearly three weeks back, I guess.'

'Yeah, sure. Well, for the past three weeks I been hoofing it every night – twice on Saturdays – and there's about four hundred people a night who can testify to that.' He jerked a thumb in the direction of the auditorium.

'Okay, okay.' Roscoe held up his hands and smiled. 'No one said you had anything to do with it, but Scotland Yard turned up your name. Seems you and she got on pretty good, way back?'

Cody looked down and kicked absently at a loose rope; then he tried to put his hands in his pockets, but realised that there weren't any in the costume he was wearing. 'Yeah, we did, until she cleared off and married this old guy.'

'Old guy?'

'Sure. About twenty years older. Some smart-ass attorney. He was a senator, too; whatever they call their guys in the Parliament over there.'

'What did you do then?'

'We split.'

'That come as a surprise . . . her marrying this guy?'

'You'd better believe it. We were in bed one morning when she told me.' He shook his head as though he still couldn't believe it. 'And we'd been screwing not two minutes back. I asked her why, and she said he could give her everything she wanted . . . and that was it.'

'She'd not mentioned this guy before?'

'Yeah, sure. Like I said, he was an attorney. There was some piece in a newspaper column, about six months before that, that said she'd slept with some guy – a producer on TV, I think – just so's she could get a part. I remember that—'

'Why?'

Cody looked incredulous. 'Why? For Christ's sake! Wouldn't you remember if the broad you was living with was in the newspapers for having slept with some other guy?'

'And had she?'

'Sure thing. We had one hell of a row about it. She came across with some crap about it wasn't for her, it was for me—'

'For you?'

'Yeah. She reckoned she did it to get a part for me. Load of goddam crap.'

'So what happened? She sue the newspaper?'

'Damn right she did. That's when she met this attorney. The next thing she's going to marry the guy. So we had another fight, right there in the bedroom. She was shouting and screaming, stamping about the place stark naked, waving her arms about. Our arguments were always like that, real Sarah Bernhardt stuff, like she'd rehearsed every goddam word ten times over. . . .'

A long-legged brunette in a brief costume and fish-net tights walked through backstage. 'Hi, honey,' she said to Cody, and winked at Roscoe; he noticed she had a hole in her tights.

Cody sat down on one of two crates. He pointed at the other. 'Want to sit down?'

'You get into a lot of arguments?' Roscoe's eyes narrowed, and he wondered – just briefly – whether Cody could have made a transatlantic trip; but then policemen were like that.

Cody nodded. 'Sure. Every time she made it with another guy.'

'Happen often?'

'Two or three times.'

'Why didn't you throw her out?'

Cody laughed bitterly. 'It was her apartment. I'd got no

place to go. Never had any money; I was out of work most of the time.'

'But she wasn't?'

Cody stared at Roscoe and shook his head. 'In this business a broad's got certain biological advantages over a guy. All the guys she went for had got money or power. Everything had to be for her. I remember one guy: I think he was a lord. He was in that smart-ass army outfit that spends all its time marching round London in fancy dress: the Guards? She pointed him out to me one day along that big street that goes up to Buckingham Palace. Big fur hat and a red coat; dab of rouge on each cheek and he'd have looked like the Chocolate Soldier. They all looked the same to me; I don't know how she knew it was him.'

'Name?'

'Huh?'

'What was his name . . . this lord?'

'Jeez, I don't know; she never said.'

'When d'you see her last?'

'The day we split. I'd had it. I came back Stateside. And here I am.' He waved his hand around the backstage area. 'Great, huh?'

Roscoe snapped his notebook shut and stood up. 'Thanks for your time, Mr Cody.'

'You're welcome.' Cody stood up too. 'If you're looking for a motive,' he added, 'I guess she carried on sleeping around even after she married that old guy.'

'You the director here?'

'So who wants to know?'

Roscoe flicked open the leather wallet containing his badge. 'FBI,' he said.

'So?'

'Cody, Paul Cody . . . '

'What about him?'

'Says he's been here every night for the past three weeks.'

'You bet your goddam ass he has.'

'Couldn't have gone to England then?'

170

The director laughed cynically. 'That guy don't even have the bus fare home; he walks. There's no way he could go any place.'

José Galeciras knew exactly where Masters' villa was; had he not been there several times before? But never with the *Teniente* who now sat in the front seat of the Land Rover, constantly smoothing his kid-leather gloves, and complaining repeatedly about the dust cloud which the vehicle made on the loose earthen track.

'It is over there, is it not?'

'No, señor, it is a little further yet.'

Galeciras kept driving with a grim determination. He did not need this dandy to tell him his job. But the *Teniente* was up to something. For one thing he had chosen not to explain to Galeciras or his partner why he needed a pickaxe and extra shovels placed in the Land Rover. He shrugged and stopped worrying. No doubt all would be made clear in due course.

They stopped outside Masters' now-deserted villa. The *Teniente* got out and stretched and then looked round, nodding. 'Come,' he said, and opened the gate. Galeciras grabbed the two carbines and issued an instruction to his partner to bring the shovels and the pickaxe. By the time they had caught up with the *Teniente*, he was standing at the edge of the pool looking down at the mirror-like blue water. After some moments he turned abruptly. 'We are looking for a body,' he announced, as if regretting that he had to impart this piece of information to his two subordinates, but he could see no way of setting them the task without telling them what it was.

'A body, señor?'

'That is what I said,' replied the *Teniente* curtly.

'The body of who, señor? Señor Masters?'

'No, not Señor Masters. The body of a man . . . another man.'

'You know where it is hidden, señor?'

'Of course not, dolt. That is why you are here . . . to look for it.' He cast his gaze beyond the pool to the grass, made

171

brown by the hot Spanish sun. Slowly he shook his head. 'I think not,' he said to himself. A body buried there would disturb the grass and would be easily found. He flicked his leg with his gloves. 'Here, I think.' He nodded as if to confirm his own thoughts on the matter. 'Yes, here I think.' He pointed at the flagstones surrounding the pool. 'Start there.' He pointed.

Galeciras was horrified. It was a hot, dry day – hot even for a Spaniard – and it was three o'clock in the afternoon. It was almost contrary to Galeciras' religion to work at such a time. He shrugged. 'What exactly do you want us to do, señor?' he asked.

'Take up the flagstones.'

'All of them, señor?' Galeciras could not keep the shocked tone out of his voice.

For the first time the *Teniente* smiled. 'No,' he said, 'not all of them. Just as many as it needs to find a body.'

Galeciras was not a very good policeman, and he would never have qualified as a detective, but he had a great instinct for avoiding hard work, particularly manual labour; his wife would happily have testified to that. He walked across to the part of the patio that was furthest from the villa and looked closely at the stones. Most were cemented into place, but several were surrounded only by earth that had been pushed into the cracks between them.

'What are you doing, Galeciras?'

'I think that this would be a good place to start, Señor Teniente.'

'Oh! Why is that?' The *Teniente* walked across to where Galeciras was standing and looked closely where the policeman pointed.

'See señor, there is no cement in those cracks there.' Galeciras felt quite pleased with himself. In favour with the *Teniente* . . . perhaps, and less hard work . . . maybe.

'Very well, try it. Here, you too.' The *Teniente* flicked his fingers at Galeciras' partner.

Reluctantly the other policeman walked across, carrying the two shovels. He placed the tips on the ground and leaned on the handles.

'Don't stand there, man, get on with it.' The *Teniente* looked first at the sun and then at his watch.

Galeciras took one of the shovels and forced its tip into the crack between two of the large slabs, leaning heavily on the handle to lever it out of place. Then he and his partner manhandled it and pulled it to one side, revealing the flattened earth beneath.

'Dig!' said the *Teniente* impatiently.

There was now no alternative, and, with a sigh, Galeciras bent his back to the ridiculous task of digging up Señor Masters' patio. After five minutes of intensive digging in the soft earth he stood up.

'Why are you stopping?' asked the *Teniente*.

'There is something here, señor.'

The *Teniente* moved closer and stared down into the hole. A large parcel wrapped in polythene sheeting and tied securely with rope had been revealed by Galeciras' exertions. 'Excellent. Get it out.'

That was easier to say than to do, but after several minutes' work, which included moving two other flagstones and digging some more, Galeciras and his partner eventually dragged the large plastic package clear.

The *Teniente* stood back. 'Open it,' he ordered. 'But carefully, it may be evidence.'

Galeciras smirked at that and watched as his partner withdrew his official-issue knife from his pocket, cut the rope and slit open the parcel. The body of the man which it had contained was now released from the confines of both the plastic wrappings and the ropes which bound it, and spread itself like a living thing, one hand slapping against a flagstone, its twisted grin staring up, sightless, at the searing sun.

'Good.' The *Teniente*'s face remained impassive but he withdrew a few feet. 'Break into the house and find a telephone,' he said.

'But we have a radio—'

'Dolt. Do you want to tell everyone that we have found a body?'

\* \* \*

173

The substance of the telephone call to the local headquarters of the *Guardia Civil* was passed immediately to Madrid and produced an electric effect. The *Teniente* was told curtly to do nothing but stand guard over Masters' villa and make sure that no unauthorised person interfered with anything. The *Teniente* tried to explain that he had found the body and that he should therefore conduct the inquiry. It was, after all, in the area for which he had responsibility.

He replaced the receiver firmly. 'It would not have happened when *El Caudillo* was alive,' he muttered darkly.

'What is that, señor?'

'Go and guard the gate,' said the *Teniente*.

# Chapter Fifteen

'We've got to have more than the word of some tuppenny-ha'penny tow-rag like Rogers before we can nick Farrell,' said Tommy Fox. 'Otherwise he'd laugh us out of court. What's more, with the team of mouthpieces he's got, he'd have a go for damages for wrongful arrest and false imprisonment as well.' He sucked through his teeth at the unfairness of the world.

'How do we get the evidence?' asked Gaffney. 'Always assuming there's any to be had. It might just be a malicious tale put about to discredit Farrell.'

'I thought of that,' said Fox, 'and I showed Rogers some pictures. He picked out Farrell as the bloke who gave him the job and paid him.' He shook his head. 'It's unbelievable that the man could be so bloody stupid.'

'Probably thought he was being clever. And perhaps he is. What have we got? Charlie Rogers! A petty villain, with form as long as your arm, fingers Farrell, a millionaire, and comes up with some bloody rubbish about being commissioned to turn over Colin Masters' drum because he's supposed to have a packet of cocaine that belongs to him.' Gaffney looked across the office at Fox with a half-smile on his face. 'Well, do you believe it?'

'Yes,' said Fox sullenly, 'but only because I want to.'

'I've checked with Fraud Squad to see if he's into any takeovers or the like, that would make it worthwhile putting round a story like that to discredit him, but there's nothing. At least, they've heard nothing. I can't see any point in anyone making that tale up just for the hell of it; it's too risky.' He glanced across at Tipper. 'What d'you reckon, Harry?'

'I agree with you, sir. Apart from anything else, Rogers was well-rattled after he'd come up with Farrell's name. I think he knew he was a big fish, and I think he knew he was into drugs. And let's face it: drug dealers are known to have long memories and short tempers. If anyone puts out the dirt on them, he'll get topped . . . and the same goes for anyone who bilks them.'

'That's given me an idea,' said Fox. 'I think I'll go and have a chat with Mr Farrell, informally as you might say. Fancy coming to listen, John?'

Tommy Fox did it all properly. He telephoned Bernard Farrell and made an appointment. When asked what it was about, he explained that the Home Secretary, no less, had mentioned Mr Farrell's name in connection with released prisoners. Fox then went on to say that he would very much like to speak to Mr Farrell about a specific released prisoner, but did not explain that the released prisoner he had in mind was Mr Farrell himself, or that that event – if Fox had his way – would not occur for some years.

'Gentlemen, do come and sit down. It's always nice to welcome representatives of the police force . . . .' He indicated a circle of leather armchairs near to a huge window. 'I was saying to the Home Secretary over dinner only the other day that I don't know how you fellows cope these days; crime rising all the time, everywhere you look.' He shook his head and then suddenly concentrated his gaze on Gaffney. 'Ah! We've met before, surely . . . ?' He was evidently disconcerted at Gaffney's reappearance, but probably less so than he would have been had Tipper been there too.

'Yes indeed, Mr Farrell,' said Gaffney with a smile.

Farrell forced a smile also. 'Of course. You came to see me about the Home Secretary's wife.' He laughed nervously. 'And now you want to talk to me about released prisoners.'

'Yes,' said Fox, crossing his legs and relaxing. 'Or more accurately, about one released prisoner in particular.'

'Oh?' Farrell looked at each of the policemen in turn before looking once more at Fox. 'Is this something I should know about?' he asked. 'I mean, this charity I was proposing is a general thing . . . ' He coughed: a dry, nervous cough. 'But, of course, if this is one man who needs special help, I'm sure that . . . '

Fox smiled and nodded. 'Oh yes, he needs help. You might be interested in his name, Mr Farrell. It's Colin Masters.'

There was just the slightest tightening of Farrell's fingers on the arms of his chair, otherwise there was no reaction. 'I don't know why that name should interest me; I've never heard of the man.'

'That's strange,' said Fox. 'He seems to know you. In fact, he claims to have done business with you in the past.'

Farrell furrowed his brow. 'Masters, Masters,' he said, slowly repeating the name. He shrugged. 'So many names, so many people I do business with; it's not easy to remember. I have to admit that I can't recall the name.' He nodded, although there was nothing to agree with.

'He's also claiming to have broken into your house, Mr Farrell.' Fox smiled pleasantly.

Farrell looked suitably mystified; it was very convincing. 'I know nothing about my house being broken into.' He shot out a hand in Gaffney's direction. 'I told this gentleman last time he was here: my house has not been broken into.' He laid great emphasis on the last few words. 'I can understand your difficulty, gentlemen, but I can only suggest that this criminal . . . what was his name? Masters, you say? I can only suggest that he must have made a mistake.' He spread his hands in a gesture of apparent hopelessness. 'I am more than willing to help the police, God knows that, but what more can I say?' He contrived a thoughtful expression. 'Did he say which house he broke into? Did he for example tell you the name of it, or describe it?'

'No. He just said that it was your house, Mr Farrell.' Fox smiled disarmingly.

Farrell shook his head. 'I am mystified, gentlemen. Is it so important though? I mean to say, if he has admitted to committing a crime, that's all you need, surely?'

'That's the problem, Mr Farrell,' said Fox. 'You see, what

177

I am telling you is merely underworld scuttle-butt. I've not spoken to this man myself; I don't even know where he is.'

'And of course that's not the only crime, Mr Farrell.' It was Gaffney who spoke as the two detectives rose to their feet. 'I'm investigating the murder of Mrs Lavery, as you know.'

Farrell looked at him sharply. 'Are you suggesting that there is some connection? Surely not.'

'Why are you so adamant that there couldn't be?'

Farrell backtracked. 'I didn't mean . . . obviously you know your job, gentlemen. It's just that it seems so amazing.'

'Why? Why amazing?' asked Fox.

'From what I understand your colleague to be saying, it is possible that a man who says that he broke into my house – without my noticing –' He laughed. 'That such a man could be involved in the death of the wife of my good friend the Home Secretary . . . .' He shook his head gravely. 'I don't know what the world is coming to.'

'Well, if you should hear anything of this man, Mr Farrell, or if he should contact you, I'd be grateful if you would let the police know.' Fox paused. 'As a public duty.'

'Well?' asked Gaffney. 'What d'you think?'

'Lying bastard,' said Fox.

'What now then?'

'We'll have a go at Masters.'

James Marchant smiled and closed the door of Gaffney's office behind him.

'Oh dear!' said Gaffney.

'Why "oh dear", John?'

'Because your appearance in my office usually means something ominous, James, that's why.'

Marchant spread his hands. 'My dear fellow,' he said, 'I've only come to help.'

'That's what I was afraid of.'

'You know that they've found a body . . . at Masters' villa?'

178

Gaffney nodded. 'Yes. I had a phone call from Enrico Perez. Is it the Russian?'

'As far as we can tell, yes.'

'Have the Spanish told the Soviet authorities?'

'Oh yes, but in the most formal way. Masters – if he was the murderer – didn't bother to remove the man's identity papers. Extremely careless for an experienced criminal. The papers were Spanish, of course, but it didn't take the Spanish long to discover that they were forgeries – very skilful forgeries – but forgeries none the less.'

'What did the Soviets say?'

'Nothing. They denied all knowledge of the man. Which is no more than I would have expected. They are hardly going to say that he was a KGB agent and that they knew he was there with forged Spanish papers, are they? They more or less threw the police out of the embassy and asked them kindly not to waste their time.'

Gaffney smiled. 'So what are the Spanish doing now?'

'I think that they might ask for the extradition of friend Masters to face a charge of murder, John.' He leaned back in his chair and smiled. 'So what d'you think of that?'

'Not a lot,' said Gaffney. 'Not a lot at all.'

'That's what I thought you'd say. I have seen "C" on your behalf and suggested that the Secretary of State intervenes with the Spanish Government to try to persuade them that it might be better all round if they forgot about it.'

Gaffney scoffed. 'Some hope.'

'Oh, I think they'll be amenable, John. And it'll give you an additional bargaining counter when you come to dealing with Masters, won't it?'

Gaffney pouted. 'Yes, I suppose it might,' he said. 'I should think that about forty years in a Spanish prison appeals to Masters even less than thirty years in an English one.'

'Thirty? D'you think there's a chance of your charging him with Elizabeth Lavery's murder then?'

Gaffney grinned. 'I wish I knew the answer to that, James. I really do wish I knew the answer to that.'

* * *

Apart from a carefully contrived air of injured innocence, Colin Masters betrayed no signs of nervousness at all.

'This is Detective Chief Superintendent Gaffney of Special Branch,' said Fox. 'He wants to talk to you.'

'Oh yeah.' Masters lit a cigarette. The lighter appeared to be of solid gold; so did the bracelet he was wearing which rattled as he put the lighter down on the table.

'You left the country on the next available flight following the murder of Mrs Elizabeth Lavery and went to Seville,' said Gaffney.

'What's that got to do with the price of fish?'

'She was a friend of yours, that's what.' Gaffney leaned forward slightly and met Masters' eyes.

'Who told you that?' Masters sat up slightly.

'You did.' Gaffney took a photocopy of the receipt for the gold waist-chain from a folder and laid it on the table.

Masters picked it up and gazed at it. 'And what's that supposed to prove?'

'That's a receipt for a gold chain that you had made and gave to Elizabeth Lavery. We found the receipt in your house, and the chain in hers.'

'I never met the lady.'

'Then how do you account for the chain being in her house?'

'I was robbed.'

'Are you suggesting that Mrs Lavery stole it?' Gaffney knew that Masters was playing a game, but was determined to play along with it; he could make it last longer than Masters could.

'I don't know. Has she got form?'

Tipper looked up from the book – the record of interview – he was writing in, and decided that he was going to join in the game too. 'Was that "form", that last word?' he asked, pen poised.

Masters looked at Tipper, then back at Gaffney, then across at Fox who was now sitting in the corner of the interview room reading a copy of The Times, apparently

180

uninterested in the proceedings. For the first time in many years, Masters was beginning to find an interview with the police a little disconcerting.

'Yes,' said Gaffney, looking at Tipper. 'Mr Masters said, "I don't know. Has she got form?"' He half smiled at Masters. 'I think that was it, wasn't it?'

Masters grunted. He didn't much care for this smooth bastard from Special Branch – didn't know why he was there anyway – but he was damned if he was going to ask for his lawyer. That would be a sign of weakness . . . in his book anyway.

'Why did you break your return journey at Valencia,' asked Gaffney, 'where presumably you hung around for an hour or so before catching a flight to Paris, hung around again and then flew into Gatwick?'

'Any reason why I shouldn't?' asked Masters. 'Anyway, what's it got to do with you?'

Gaffney glanced at Tipper, appearing to wait until he had written down Masters' latest contribution to the interrogation, and then turned once more. 'I don't think you quite realise the seriousness of your situation,' he said. Masters smiled sarcastically and put his head on one side. 'I have positive evidence that you consorted with Mrs Elizabeth Lavery on a regular basis, and that she visited your villa at Puente Alcazaba on more than one occasion. Furthermore, as I said just now, within hours of her having been strangled in her own home in Cutler's Mews, you left the country on the very next flight for Seville . . . ' Gaffney leaned back in his chair, the signal for which Fox had been waiting.

The head of the Flying Squad folded his newspaper untidily, like an unskilled housemaid disposing of a soiled tablecloth, and got slowly to his feet. Then he ambled across and pulled a chair into position on the third side of the table before sitting down between Masters and Gaffney.

'Bernie Farrell's put it all down to you, y'know, Colin,' Fox began amiably.

'I don't know what you mean, Mr Fox.' Masters was visibly jarred by the introduction of Farrell's name into

181

the conversation. He also knew Tommy Fox, knew that a detective chief superintendent who had got to be head of the Heavy Mob was a man to be reckoned with. Masters knew that anyway; he'd tangled with Fox before, and only escaped the consequences because of a very good lawyer . . . called Lavery.

'And there was me thinking that I always spoke fairly clearly too. Let me try again, Colin. Bernie Farrell was talking about the cocaine. The little consignment that you thought he had when you turned his drum over, and the same consignment he thought you'd got when he went through your gaff.'

'I don't know what you're talking about, Mr Fox, God's truth, I don't. I don't know nothing about no cocaine, neither.' He looked keenly at Fox. 'And who's Farrell?'

'He's the bloke whose house you stopped outside just before you changed your mind and took it on the dancers. Remember?'

'Oh, that Farrell,' said Masters lamely.

Fox smiled. 'Yes – that Farrell. What's more, Colin, he's put it all down to you, the whole lot. And why not. Respected member of the community; friend of the Home Secretary; something big in the world of high finance . . . ' Fox sniffed and looked down at his signet ring. 'And when he gets in the box at the Bailey, they'll hang on his every word . . . and believe it. And down goes Colin Masters . . . for about ten years at a guess.' He looked across at Tipper. 'About ten I'd think, wouldn't you, Harry?' he asked, as if discussing a suitable time for a meeting in a pub.

Tipper nodded thoughtfully. 'About ten, guv'nor, yes. Perhaps twelve if the judge's got a liver on.'

Fox nodded as if Tipper had made a valid point. 'Yeah, maybe, but either way it'll be a fair stretch, Colin.' He looked at Masters again and smiled benignly. 'And then he'll go out to dinner with his cronies . . . laughing, I wouldn't wonder.'

'Someone's been telling you wicked lies about me, Mr Fox.'

Fox tutted and shook his head. 'Happens all the time,' he murmured. 'It's a wicked world.'

'Can we have a little chat, Mr Fox?' Masters spoke quietly, almost conspiratorially.

'But we are having a little chat, Colin.'

'You know what I mean, Mr Fox.'

Fox smiled and put one arm round Masters's shoulders and the other round Gaffney's. 'You're among friends, Colin,' he said. 'You can speak freely.'

Masters was unhappy. 'Can we do a deal, like? Come to a sort of arrangement?'

'Such as?'

'Such as rowing me out, Mr Fox?'

Fox threw back his head and laughed. 'You always were a bit of a card, Colin. I have concrete evidence from the upright Mr Farrell that you're well at it. No doubt Mr Farrell, with a little gentle persuasion – like a subpoena – will come along and repeat what he has already told us. And you want me to row you out? Oh dear!'

Masters stared at his packet of cigarettes, probably considering his health, but not in relation to smoking. He took one and lit it. 'I arranged the couriers for Farrell,' he said shortly.

'Yeah?'

'Shouldn't you caution me?'

'Get on with it.'

'To get the stuff back here.'

'Always cocaine?'

'Mostly. Sometimes heroin. I don't know. I never asked.'

'How often was this?'

'As and when.'

'What's that supposed to mean?'

Masters looked unhappy. He realised what was happening and was by no means sure of Fox. He would just as likely screw him for every bit of information he'd got and still stick him on the sheet, probably for conspiracy as well. But what choice had he? It was a gamble. Perhaps Fox would let him turn Queen's Evidence; on the other hand he might just be inviting him to screw himself further into the mire than he was already. 'About six times altogether.'

'Over how long a period of time was this?'

''Bout a year, maybe eighteen months.'

'And how much each run?'

'Never more than a kilo.'

'Mmm! Anything you say will be taken down in writing and may be given in evidence.'

'Thanks,' said Masters, and pointed to the tape-recorder. 'I suppose you're only saying that because the gismo's on.'

'It's not,' said Fox. 'My friend Mr Gaffney here has excluded it under the terms of the Official Secrets Act.'

'What's that got to do with it?'

'You'd better ask him, but it's pretty powerful stuff, and you've got involved in the death of the Home Secretary's wife.'

'But I—'

Fox held up his hand. 'Can we deal with one thing at a time? Where did these drug consignments come from?'

'I don't know,' said Masters. Fox sighed and looked up at the ceiling. 'Honest, Mr Fox, I don't know. They was delivered to my place in Seville, and I arranged for them to be brought here.'

'How?'

'All sorts of ways.'

'I'm beginning to feel more like a dentist all the time,' said Fox, playing a little tattoo on the table with his fingers.

Masters looked nervous. 'You're asking me to put a lot of people in the frame here,' he said.

'Yes,' said Fox, and looked sympathetic. 'Well, you can take it on your own if you prefer, Colin. Farrell seems to think you will anyway.'

'Bloody Farrell. If I go down, he comes with me.'

'That's the spirit,' said Fox, beaming. 'That's what won the Empire.'

'Sod the Empire,' said Masters with feeling. 'I'm not having him walk out of this one, I tell you that straight, Mr Fox.'

'Well you'd better go into a little more detail, eh?'

'I'd get it carried across from Seville and deliver it to him in London, or wherever he wanted it.'

'What happened to the last lot then?' Fox reached the crux.

And Masters knew it was coming. He sighed loudly. 'I don't know.'

'I hope you're not pussyfooting about again, Colin.'

'She took it, but what happened after that—'

'Hold on, hold on,' said Fox. 'Who's this "she" you're talking about?'

'Liz Lavery.' Masters spoke resignedly.

'Are you suggesting that the Home Secretary's wife was a drugs courier? Is that what you're saying?' Fox looked quite nasty.

'I'm not suggesting it, Mr Fox, I'm telling you.'

'You'd better tell me some more, then.'

Masters licked his lips; he realised that he was getting into serious business here. 'She didn't know of course. It was better that way. I put the packet into her case before she left Seville and marked the outside. The plan was for Farrell's people to pick it up from her at Heathrow.'

A sardonic smile of disbelief crossed Fox's face. 'Really?' he said sarcastically. 'And how was that to be done . . . without Mrs Lavery knowing?'

'I telephoned Farrell from Seville once she was airborne, and one of his people – a loader, I suppose – was going to nick it from her at the airport. Couldn't be easier.'

'So what happened?'

Masters shrugged. 'I don't know. I never heard from Farrell.'

'Should you have done?'

'Too bloody right. I should have got my cut.'

Fox laughed. 'Oh dear, what a shame. Have you over, did he?'

'It's not funny, Mr Fox. I took a lot of risks there.'

'So you went and took your share out of his drum at Boreham Wood, eh?'

'Is that what Farrell told you?' Masters' eyes narrowed.

'No! There's nothing in the crime book at Boreham Wood; in fact, Farrell denies ever having had a break-in.'

'Well, in that case, I never done it,' said Masters.

Fox leaned menacingly across the table. 'Don't get clever with me, Colin. I've still got a murder charge sculling around waiting for someone.'

Masters coughed. 'I never done no topping job, Mr Fox, stand on me.'

'Well, someone did, my friend, and right now you're the one I've got in custody.'

Masters looked desperate. 'Look, Mr Fox, there'd be no point in topping her. I was on to a good thing there. Farrell's the one you should be looking at.'

'We're not talking about Liz Lavery now.' It was Gaffney who spoke, and Masters darted a nervous glance at him. 'We're talking about a certain gentleman who the Russians mislaid, and whose body the *Guardia Civil* found crawling out from under a stone at your villa at Puente Alcazaba.'

'I don't know nothing about that.' Masters licked his lips; that had come like a bombshell. 'You couldn't never prove it, anyway,' he said desperately.

'Wouldn't even try,' said Gaffney airily. 'And I'll tell you this: the KGB won't worry too much about proof either. All I need to do is release you and tell the Soviet Embassy where and when I'm going to do it.'

'Or tell Farrell,' said Fox amiably. 'So it might be a good idea for you to give us a hand to screw him down, don't you think?'

Masters was now very rattled, and knew instinctively that he was in serious trouble on more than one front. And that bastard Fox just sat there smiling. 'You mean you want me to turn Queen's Evidence?'

Fox leaned back in his chair and smiled. 'I must warn you about the risks of that . . . unfortunately. If you make a full confession and the court accepts it, it will only convict Farrell if other, corroborative evidence is forthcoming. And sadly, if the court doesn't like your confession – that is to say, they think it's a pack of lies – they might still convict you. There, got that have you?'

Masters looked very unhappy. It was time to surrender. 'I want to see my solicitor.'

'Yeah, okay!' said Fox. 'But not before I put you on the sheet for drug smuggling, and other assorted offences . . . ' He looked across at Gaffney. 'I suppose you'd like to tack your murder on, just for good measure?'

Gaffney shrugged. 'Why not?'

Masters held up his hands. 'All right, all right, but this is bloody duress, you know.'

'You could well be right,' said Fox. 'I'll send for Amnesty International, if you like.'

'We'd arranged a few runs over, but it's bloody dicey . . . '

'But worth it?'

'Yeah! Then I met this Liz bird.'

'By which I take it you mean the Home Secretary's wife?'

Masters smiled. 'Yeah! It was dead lucky an' all. It was after that job you did me for.'

'The one you got away with, you mean?'

'No, straight, Mr Fox, that was a diabolical liberty, and you know it.' Fox raised his eyebrows and waited patiently. 'Yes, well, the day I was acquitted' – he laid heavy emphasis on that word – 'she was at the Bailey to meet her old man, Lavery, what defended me.'

Fox nodded. 'Yes, Colin, I do remember.'

'Well, I reckon she fancied me—'

'You are a conceited bastard,' scoffed Fox.

Masters looked hurt. 'Well, I proved it, didn't I?'

'How was that?'

'After that traumatic experience—'

'What traumatic experience? And where d'you get a word like that, anyway?' It was skilful interrogation – a matter of nice judgement – to let Masters think that what he was saying was not too important, but Fox was careful, always, not to overplay it.

'After the trial. I went off down the South of France for a bit of a break. Play the tables, an' that.' Masters grinned. 'Down some place called Le Trayas' – he pronounced it 'lee trays' – 'for a few weeks like.' He paused to lick his lips. 'Well, I was walking along the beach one morning, and I see her, this Liz bird.'

187

'Doing what?'

'Nothing. Just lying there. Sunbathing.'

'And?'

'So I sat down beside her.'

'And frightened Miss Muffet away?'

'No. I just says to her, "Remember me?". Well, she gives me the once-over, pretending she don't know me from Adam. So I says to her like it was up the Bailey, and give her a reminder. Then she says yes she thought she remembered.'

'Yeah, go on.' Fox looked sceptical.

'I asked her what she was doing out there, and she says she'd been doing some filming. Then I remembered that she'd been an actress . . . so I heard.'

'So I heard, too,' said Fox. 'What happened then?'

'I asked her if she was on holiday after that.'

'What are you talking about now, for God's sake?'

'No, sorry. She said that the filming was finished, see. Sorry, I missed that bit.'

'All right, get on with it.' Fox looked across at Gaffney and shook his head wearily.

'She says she was staying at some earl's place – friend of her old man's – Earl Barclay. So I says what about a few sherbets—'

'Just like that?'

'Well, you know me, Mr Fox.'

'Unfortunately,' murmured Fox.

'So we went to a bar and got a few down us, and then I invited her up the villa—'

'What villa? We are still in the South of France with this little yarn, aren't we?'

'Oh yeah. I'd took a villa, see. Well, it's more private than a hotel. Anyway, people nick things in a hotel.'

'God Almighty!' said Fox. 'Doubtless you will now tell me that one thing led to another.'

Masters grinned obscenely. 'Had a very nice little week in that villa, I can tell you. Couldn't keep her hands off of me. Fair wore me out she did.' He glanced at his fingernails. 'Like a bit of rough, some of these high-class birds,' he said.

'So I've heard. What then?'

'She had to go back to the Smoke, to her old man. So I says why not come down the villa in Spain. Well, she jumps at that and says when. Course, it struck me then . . .'

'What did?'

'What a bloody gift she was. Put a kilo of cocaine in her gear and we're home and dry. No bleeding Customs is going to turn her over, not the Home Secretary's missus.'

'Don't you believe it,' said Fox. Privately, he thought it was a very good idea. 'How did she explain that away to her husband – a week in Spain?'

'She spun him some fanny about advising on a film that was being made. At least, that's what she said she'd told him.'

'And was there a film?'

Masters laughed scornfully. 'No, of course not.'

'And how many times did she bring a consignment back here?'

Masters looked pained. 'Only the once, and that's the bastard that's gone adrift.'

'And what happened about the pick-up at the airport?'

'Well, like I said, I give Farrell a bell and he was supposed to get some finger to nick her case at Heathrow.'

'And how many times d'you think that someone was going to get away with nicking her case before she started to notice?'

Masters looked slightly shocked. 'Oh, it was only a one-off,' he said. 'Mind you, I did think about putting it to her straight; asking her to take a parcel back for me . . .'

Fox laughed. 'You're a bigger prat than I thought,' he said, but he wondered, nevertheless, whether Masters might just have got away with it. He stood up suddenly. 'Right,' he said. 'I shall come back and talk to you again later. Meantime, we'll have a statement typed up for you to sign.'

'Eh?'

'You heard. It's all going down in writing. If you're think-ing about denying it all in the future, at least I'll have your signature on a bit of paper.' Fox paused at the door. 'By the way, Colin,' he said, 'the other tape-recorder was on.'

# Chapter Sixteen

'I've got an idea,' said Fox.

'It's more than I have,' said Gaffney.

'If Masters hasn't got that cocaine, and Farrell hasn't got it, and setting aside that anyone working for either of them would have taken the suicidal course of nicking it, the chances are that it is still somewhere in Elizabeth Lavery's possessions.'

Gaffney looked thoughtful. 'She wasn't a user,' he said. 'There was nothing in Pamela Hatcher's report about traces of coke in the body.' He paused. 'And we didn't find it at the scene of the crime.'

'You weren't looking for it, were you? If you'd been searching the Home Secretary's house for drugs' – he broke off and laughed sharply – 'it would have been a different story. But what did you have? You started off with terrorist overtones – which might still come to something, I suppose, but that's your department – and then considered a disturbed burglar. Anyone else would have taken the same sort of action. You were looking for evidence that would enable you to convict a murderer, not a drug-runner, for Christ's sake. And let's face it, John, there was not the remotest suggestion at that stage of the game that it would come to this.'

Gaffney nodded slowly, unwilling to admit that he had erred. In all conscience, he knew that he hadn't; that any other detective would have taken the same line of investigation that he had. 'So what do we do? Look for it?'

'Got to, haven't we? Is Lavery back in residence yet?'

'Yes . . . but it's only a *pied à terre;* he's hardly ever there, I gather.'

'Can you see him; ask if we can have another look round?'

'Sure. Do we tell him why?'

'No, I don't think so. He's matey with Farrell, isn't he?'

Gaffney laughed, remembering his last interview with Lavery. 'I'm not too sure about that. I think Farrell thinks he's matey with the Home Secretary.' He glanced at the clock and sighed. 'I'll start with the Home Office. It's never easy to track him down.'

They were lucky. Dudley Lavery was at the Home Office and had given permission for the police to have another look round his house without even enquiring why they wished to do so. Tommy Fox had summoned his car and driver and, pausing only to collect the keys from Charles Stanhope at Queen Anne's Gate, he and Gaffney had driven straight to Cutler's Mews.

'Where shall we start?' asked Fox. They had decided not to involve drug-detecting dogs in their search of the Home Secretary's house. As Fox had put it: 'That would be too much to expect them to keep under their helmets; you know what coppers are like for gossiping.'

'If it's here,' said Gaffney. 'And if it was, it strikes me as being a bloody good motive for murdering Elizabeth Lavery. Worth a few bob on the open market, a kilo of cocaine.'

Fox nodded. 'That had crossed my mind, I must admit. But we'd better make sure it's not here before we go off on that particular tangent.'

'What does anyone do when they come home from holiday? They unpack their suitcases and put them away wherever they keep them, I suppose.'

'Mine go in the loft,' said Fox. 'But I can only afford one holiday a year. These people are probably rushing off every five minutes.' He paused. 'Well, we know she was.'

Gaffney smiled. 'I've just thought of something quite irrelevant. D'you remember Masters saying that he met Liz Lavery on the beach at Le Trayas . . . ?'

'Yes.'

'And that she was staying with Earl Barclay – who incidentally is not an hereditary earl – he's an American banker or financier, or some such thing?'

Fox nodded. 'Yes.'

'I just wondered if Lavery was there when Liz was having it off with Masters down the road.'

Fox chuckled. 'I wouldn't put it past her, not from what we know of the lady. And I certainly wouldn't put it past Masters. Incidentally, do we know how long she'd been back from Spain before she was topped?'

'Yes.' Gaffney flipped open his pocket-book. 'Lavery's secretary gave me the dates, or some of them . . . ' He glanced down at the list. 'Five days before she was murdered.'

'That means that Masters must have virtually followed her back, probably the day after, to collect his cut from Farrell.' He nodded to himself. 'It's beginning to come together. Farrell denies having had it; Masters swears that he must have done, because he sent it. I reckon they came to the same conclusion, but separately, that Elizabeth Lavery had still got it.' He drove his right fist into the palm of his left hand. 'And one of those two bastards – or one of their employees – killed her for it. That almost takes us back to the theory of the disturbed burglar.'

Gaffney nodded slowly. 'He could have come here – probably wouldn't even have thought about breaking in – and tried to persuade her to part with it. She refused – or didn't know what he was talking about, which he didn't believe – and chop!' He drew a finger across his throat. 'It doesn't take much to work out that Dudley Lavery's not at home; only got to hang around the House of Commons, see him in, and you know you're safe.' He spun his paper-knife in the centre of his blotter. 'Anyway, we know that Masters has got a sophisticated line in surveillance, don't we, from what you were saying about when he screwed Farrell's house?'

Fox nodded. 'But why resist?' he asked. 'It wasn't hers, and she like as not didn't even know what it was.' He paused thoughtfully.'Or she did know, and got all arsy about parting with it.'

'Doesn't matter, not now anyway,' said Gaffney. 'Whether it was Masters or Farrell, they would have had to kill her: she knew them both.'

'True,' said Fox, 'but my money's on Farrell. She knew that Masters was a villain, and seemed not to care. She'd met him at the Bailey; knew her old man had defended him. Anyway, from what Waldo Conway told you and Tipper, she'd have been under no illusions about him after one of his little parties in Seville. No, John Gaffney, my old gentleman-detective, I reckon it's down to Farrell.' He rubbed his hands together. 'Come home, Bernie Farrell, uncle wants to talk to you.'

'There's only one problem,' said Gaffney. 'Proof!'

'Trust you to throw a spanner in the works . . . to wreck a beautiful dream . . . '

'And apart from anything else,' continued Gaffney, 'if the cocaine's still here, it'll blow the whole lovely theory out of the water.'

'Not necessarily,' said Fox, 'but it does mean that we'll have to think again.'

They started with the suitcases which were stacked neatly in a cupboard in a spare room. The third case they opened, which had a small yellow sticker on the outside, revealed a packet of white powder, probably about a kilo in weight.

'Bloody terrific,' said Fox, throwing himself down into Gaffney's armchair. 'Now what?'

'Firstly,' said Gaffney, sitting down at his desk, 'I fill in this form and get the damned stuff across to the lab. We'd look a bit silly if it wasn't cocaine.'

'I know bloody cocaine when I see it,' said Fox moodily. 'I suppose we'll have to hand this over to the Drugs Squad now.'

'No! Not yet.' Gaffney shook his head. 'The Commissioner wants Liz Lavery's murderer before anything else. We go ahead and do whatever needs to be done to effect an arrest. I'm to keep the Drugs Squad apprised, and they

193

can have what's left. The Commissioner's words, not mine.' He grinned and put his pen back in his pocket.

'So what do we do now?' asked Fox. 'Well, I say "we"; perhaps I'm rowed out.' He yawned. 'I suppose I am really.'

'Oh no you're not. I need your expertise. The plan is this: as your Colin Masters is so keen to turn Queen's Evidence, he's going to have to work for it. Supposing we arrange a meet between the two, having first got Masters to ring Farrell – monitored, of course – and tell him that he's got the cocaine, and does Farrell want it or not? Along will come Farrell, and into our waiting arms . . . we hope. How's that grab you?'

Slowly a beatific smile spread across Tommy Fox's face. 'Oh, my dear boy, I do like that. I like that very much. Have you ever thought of making the police force a career?'

Detective Inspector Henry Findlater walked into the foyer of the hotel looking exactly as if he belonged. He wore a navy-blue Crombie overcoat, open to reveal a dark grey suit with an albert across the waistcoat. His horn-rimmed spectacles clung to the end of his nose, and tucked beneath his arm was an untidily folded copy of the *Daily Telegraph*.

The linkman had touched his hat and murmured a respectful greeting as Findlater had entered, and now, as he stood staring absently around the foyer, the hall porter nodded in his direction, convinced that he had recognised a valued guest.

Findlater was not, of course, the absent-minded businessman that the staff appeared to have mistaken him for; Findlater was checking to see that his officers were in place. He had been entrusted to let Fox know when Farrell appeared and made his way to the lift. He already knew that Farrell had taken the bait, following Masters' reluctant telephone call, and was now on his way to the hotel that Masters had nominated. There was little doubt – and no great concern – that Farrell would arrive at the appointed hour. What was concerning Fox and Gaffney more – and therefore Findlater – was that he might arrive with a number of henchmen, tooled-up. The last thing that the police wanted was a shoot-out in a good-class West End hotel. As Fox had succinctly put it at the briefing: it does tend to bugger up the decor.

Tommy Fox was a shrewd detective – he would not have been in command of the Flying Squad otherwise – and he had arranged for a number of his officers to be armed and strategically placed, just in case. Fox and Gaffney themselves were in a room next to the one occupied by Masters, so that they could listen to the bugging devices which had been so carefully installed; and of course to allay the suspicion that would be aroused were Farrell to spot the two officers, both of whom he knew by sight.

'On his way up in the lift now.' Findlater's voice crackled through the radio and Fox smiled. They had deliberately chosen a room on the sixth floor to allow themselves adequate notice of Farrell's arrival, and so that the officer who was in Masters' room could warn him and have time to leave before Farrell walked into the trap.

The communicating door opened to admit a detective sergeant who immediately closed it behind him. 'All set, guv,' he said to Fox.

'Right.' He looked round. Apart from the DS who had just appeared, there were three other Flying Squad officers in the room, two of whom would move into the corridor to cover the other door to Masters' room as soon as the listening devices told them that Farrell had entered. Fox rubbed his hands together and grinned at Gaffney. 'I do believe we're going to get lucky,' he said.

'What the hell are you playing at, Masters?' Farrell's voice, clear and easily identifiable, came through the earphones.

'I'm covering my back, that's what,' said Masters.

'And what's that supposed to mean? You tell me that you've put the bloody woman on a flight to Heathrow from Spain, with the cocaine, and she doesn't arrive.'

Masters' shrug was almost audible through the headsets that Fox and Gaffney were wearing. 'Is it my fault if the plane gets diverted to Gatwick because of fog? You should tell your hooligans to listen to the travel news. If you paid more, you'd get a better class of hood.'

'He never said anything about a bloody diversion, the bastard,' said Fox in a whisper.

'Well, where is it?' Farrell's voice again.

'Right here, in this room.'

'What took so long?' There was clear suspicion and mistrust in Farrell's voice.

'What took so long was you cocking everything up.' There was malice in that.

'Meaning?'

'Meaning that, if you hadn't been so bloody impatient, you'd have got the stuff without all this hassle.'

'What are you talking about, you bastard?' Farrell was clearly getting angry.

'I do love it when thieves fall out,' said Fox in an aside to Gaffney. He was obviously enjoying himself.

'What I'm talking about is you sending your thugs down to see Liz Lavery and bloody well topping her, that's what I'm talking about, Mr Big Shot.' Masters' voice had risen and it was fairly obvious to the listeners that he had gone beyond playing the part for which the police had briefed him; he now actually believed that that was what had happened. Fox and Gaffney had had an open mind until then, but were prepared to attribute the murder of the Home Secretary's wife to one or the other of the two main actors in the drug-smuggling business. 'You couldn't wait, could you? You go in, heavy-handed, and because you can't find it, and she doesn't know what you're talking about, you have her fixed so she won't be able to give evidence against you.'

There was a lengthy pause before Farrell replied in very restrained tones. 'They told me I shouldn't get involved with scum like you, Masters, and they were right. I don't know if that's the way you conduct your business – going around murdering people – but it isn't mine. You don't kill the goose that lays the golden egg. If anyone killed that girl, it was you; that's the sort of thing you hoodlums do. Anyway, that's your problem, for your conscience; I've come for my package.'

'Your package?' Masters had remembered what the police had told him to say.

'The cocaine.'

There was an audible slap as Masters hurled the package on to the table.

Fox walked swiftly through the communicating door, flanked by the two detective sergeants who had remained with him and Gaffney. 'Mr Farrell—'

Farrell assessed the situation in a moment. He had already put the packet of cocaine into his overcoat pocket, and had his hand on the doorknob. He recognised the Flying Squad chief and wrenched the door open. Immediately outside, standing shoulder to shoulder, were the other two DSs from the Flying Squad; Farrell could not avoid cannoning into them.

'Now, now, sir,' said one of the sergeants benevolently. 'That's what we used to call assault on police in the bad old days.'

Farrell turned to face Fox, and looking over the detective's shoulder, said: 'You bastard, Masters.'

Fox tutted gently. 'D'you know, Mr Farrell, just for one moment there, I thought you were running away.' He paused, and then: 'Bernard Farrell, I am arresting you for the unlawful possession of a quantity of cocaine. Anything you say will be given in evidence, and I must warn you that other charges may follow.' Farrell said nothing and Fox turned to the two sergeants. 'You may remove Mr Farrell to the comfort and convenience of West End Central police station,' he said. 'I shall be down later to charge him.' To the other two sergeants he said: 'And friend Masters here can be taken back to Paddington. I don't want these two tapping out messages to each other on the radiators.'

'That never did work,' said Masters sullenly. 'You've been reading too many detective stories.'

'Discounting Earl Barclay, sir,' said Claire Wentworth with a grin, 'there was only one peer of the realm that we came across.' She thumbed through a list of names. 'There was a telephone number that was found in the small leather diary in Mrs Lavery's handbag. It was just a number – no name – but

197

we traced it back to a private line into an office somewhere. It went out to a Lord Slade.'

'Lord Slade?'

'Yes.' The word was drawled out.

'This is Detective Chief Superintendent Gaffney of New Scotland Yard, Lord Slade.'

'Yes.'

'I should like to come and see you in connection with a matter I'm investigating.'

There was a light laugh from the other end. 'You're not from the Fraud Squad I hope.'

'No, sir; Special Branch.'

'Oh, I see. When did you have in mind, Chief Superintendent?'

'Now?'

'I am rather busy at the moment. Look, could you make it this evening, by any chance? I live in London.'

'Will Lady Slade be there?'

'Yes, of course. Why d'you ask? Is it something to do with her?'

'I am investigating the death of Mrs Dudley Lavery, Lord Slade.'

'Ah!' He paused. 'In that case, perhaps we should make it at my club – say lunch-time?'

'Will you come this way, sir? His lordship is waiting for you in the withdrawing room.' The steward led Gaffney into a large room and across to a small table in the window. 'Your guest, m'lord,' he murmured.

Lord Slade was of medium height – a bit small for a Guards officer, Gaffney thought – and levered himself out of the deep leather armchair with difficulty. 'Mr Gaffney? How d'you do? I'm Roger Slade.' He shook hands and waved towards the other chair. 'Do sit down.' He nodded to another steward. 'Will you have a drink?' he asked Gaffney.

'Just a Perrier water, if I may.'

'Of course,' murmured Slade. He turned to the steward.

'And I'll have a brandy and soda.' He faced Gaffney again. 'Well now,' he said as they sat down, 'what d'you want to talk about?'

'Mrs Lavery.'

'Yes, of course. What an awful business.' He looked at the centre of the table, and then looked up again, smiling. 'I suppose you'll want me to account for my movements on the night in question?' He paused. 'Which I can, of course.'

'Why should I want you to do that?'

Slade looked momentarily nonplussed. 'Well, er – isn't that the sort of thing you chaps ask?'

'Only if we suspect someone,' said Gaffney, smiling. 'Should I suspect you?'

'Well, I . . . ' Slade paused to sign the chit for the steward, and to sip his brandy and soda. 'I suppose I thought that . . . I mean, because we were having an affair.' He leaned forward confidentially. 'We can be adult about this, can't we, Mr Gaffney?'

Gaffney reached forward and took a sip of his Perrier water. 'I didn't know that,' he said.

'Oh!' Slade had the good grace to smile. 'What you might call a bit of an own goal, I suppose.'

'But now you've mentioned it, perhaps you should tell me about it.'

'Yes, but, if you didn't know, why have you come to see me?'

'Because I have been told that you knew her before her marriage to Dudley Lavery.'

'Good God! How on earth did you know that?'

'Let's just say that I do know.'

Slade shook his head. 'Well, I must say,' he murmured, but then didn't say anything for a moment or two. 'That was years ago,' he said eventually, 'when I was in the army.'

'So I gather,' said Gaffney.

'It was some party I went to – you know the sort of thing – when you've . . . ' He broke off. 'Perhaps you don't know,' he said vaguely. 'But when the battalion was on public duties they tended to live the high life, you know. Probably still do . . . ' He spoke as though he were a retired general, but Gaffney knew from the entry in *Who's Who* that Slade was not yet forty. 'I've no idea where she came from. One of our ensigns seemed to know an awful lot of actresses and showgirls – that sort of thing – and he brought a crowd along to this thrash.'

'And that's the first time you saw her?'

'Yes. I have to admit that the whole business was a bit hazy. Champagne was flowing, and . . . ' He broke off as if unsure how to describe what had happened next. 'I woke up next morning in someone's flat . . . in bed . . . with her. I suppose I'd, well, you know . . . '

Gaffney nodded. 'Yes,' he said. 'I think I do.' He was rapidly coming to the conclusion that Lord Slade was a pompous arse.

'It was a Saturday morning, I seem to remember. We showered and eventually . . . ' He chuckled. 'Eventually we went out for a champagne breakfast . . . about lunch-time.'

'And you continued to see her?'

'Only a couple of times, or so. Until the battalion went to Germany.'

'I see. Did you meet – or did she mention – someone called Cody, Paul Cody?' Gaffney was not much interested in whether Slade knew him or not, but it was part of his ploy to encourage him to talk. It was surprising what came out of mundane chatter.

'Oh yes. Liz lived with him.'

'I see. And that didn't concern you?'

Slade smiled. 'Why should it? She said their relationship was purely platonic.'

Gaffney smiled. 'And you believed her?'

'No!' Slade laughed. 'Guards officers are always painted as being rather stupid, but they're not, you know.'

'But you didn't care anyway?'

'No, not really. As I said, I only saw her a few times and then we folded our tents and disappeared into the night.'

'To Germany?'

Slade nodded. 'Exactly so. Actually, she brought him up

to see the change at Buck House one morning. At least, I presume it was him. This chap was standing beside her and she waved. In The Mall, it was.' He picked up his glass again. 'I didn't wave back, of course,' he said seriously.

Gaffney thought he was joking. 'No. I imagine they discourage that sort of thing.'

'Oh yes. Absolutely.' Slade did not smile.

'How did you meet her again, then?'

'We'd finished our tour in Germany and came back to Windsor. More public duties,' he added with a sigh. 'And I was walking down the High Street one morning and I saw her name on a sign outside the theatre there. I forget now what she was in – *Lady Windermere's Fan*, I think. Never did like Sheridan—'

'It was Oscar Wilde,' said Gaffney quietly.

'What? Oh yes, quite probably. Anyway, I went to see it, just for old times' sake as you might say. After the show I went round to the stage door and took her for a drink.'

'She was staying in Windsor presumably?'

'Yes, in some awful theatrical diggings.' Slade slipped a gold cigarette case out of his pocket, and opened it. 'Do you?'

Gaffney shook his head. 'No thanks.'

Slade tapped the tip of the cigarette slowly and reflectively on the case. 'We spent the night in a hotel,' he said. 'In fact we spent the remaining four nights in a hotel . . . until she went back to London.'

'Was she still with Cody at that time?'

'Don't know. Didn't ask.'

'And then?'

'And then we went to Northern Ireland. The battalion, that is.' He smiled briefly. 'It was while I was there that I read in the paper of her marriage to Lavery. I thought, well, that's the end of that. Then I thought: jolly good luck to you, girl.' He grinned. 'Did pretty well for herself. Mind you, the outcome was tragic.'

'What d'you mean by that?' Gaffney spoke sharply.

Slade hesitated briefly. 'Well, she might still be alive if she hadn't married him, mightn't she?'

'Are you saying, Lord Slade, that her death is in some way attributable to her marriage . . . or her husband?'

Slade pondered on that for a while and finally lit the cigarette with which he had been playing for some moments. 'Not really. It's just that if her life had taken a different course, she may not have been killed. Fate, I suppose.' Gaffney remained silent, compelling Slade to continue. 'She and Lavery were very remote from each other, you know.'

'Really?'

'Oh yes. He neglected her terribly.' He looked round as if afraid of being overheard in the near-empty room, and lowered his voice. 'Sexually, I mean.' He breathed in deeply, as though purging himself of some awful memory. 'But then he was twenty years older than she.' He paused. 'It seemed to me that his only interest in her was her value to him as a decorative consort. I don't think there was any emotional attachment at all. She was just a part of his collection really: like the car, the chauffeur, his suits, and the high office he held; all designed to impress. And mark my words, he'll replace her now he's lost her, just as he would his car if it had got smashed up. His only problem would be how quickly he could do it. One always got this awful impression that if Liz had run off and left him on a day he was dining at the Palace, his real worry would have been having no one to go with. I know all that sounds pretty damning and that sort of thing, but quite frankly that was the impression I got from what Liz said.' He shook his head sadly. 'Damned shame.'

'By this time you had renewed your affair with her, I presume?'

Slade looked ill at ease. 'Sounds awful in the circumstances, doesn't it?'

'How did that start again?'

'I'd resigned my commission by then; had enough of guard-changes and Trooping the Colour.' He smiled. 'I bumped into her in a restaurant. She was lunching with her husband. I wouldn't have said anything, of course, but as I passed their table she said "Hallo, stranger" – something like that – and insisted on introducing me to Lavery. Frankly I didn't much care for him; bit of a cold fish, and much older than Liz. Well, I said that, didn't I: twenty years older. Had the damned audacity to ask which side of the House I sat on.' He shook his head. 'As if there could have been any doubt. Anyhow, when Lavery went out for a pee, she sent the waiter over with a note – I was lunching with a business friend – with her telephone number on it, and something like "Ring me – with caution".' He laughed at the memory. 'Well, a nod is as good as a wink, as they say . . .'

'So you got in touch with her?'

'Yes, of course.'

'Were you married by then?'

'I'd got married about six months before, yes.' He said it in matter-of-fact tones, as though it were an irrelevancy.

'You saw her fairly regularly after that, I take it?'

'Yes.' He paused. 'But it was over when she died.'

'When did you last see her?'

Slade thought about that. 'I don't know, offhand. About six weeks ago, perhaps.'

'What happened . . . to end the affair? I presume that something did?'

'She asked me if I'd marry her.' He laughed. 'Well, I pointed out that I was married already . . . and so was she.'

'What did she say to that?'

' "Get a divorce" is what she said. "If you will, I will." She made it sound like a nursery game; and quite honestly, I think she thought it was that easy.'

'But you refused?'

'Certainly I did. When you've as much money as I have, a divorce settlement can cost you a fortune.' He smiled wryly as if expecting sympathy, and Gaffney thought what an unscrupulous bastard he was. And an illogical one.

'She presumably saw no problem in getting a divorce from Lavery?'

'On the contrary, she said that he wouldn't give her one.'

'Well then—'

'She said that she was quite prepared to be named.'

'I take it you didn't think much of that?'

'Frankly no. I said that I didn't want to be involved in a divorce case with the wife of the Home Secretary. I should think that that really would have ruined my standing.'

And that, thought Gaffney, would have served you bloody well right. 'What did she say to that?'

'She said that in that case she would commit adultery with someone else and make sure it got out.'

'Was she joking?'

'I hoped she was, but I really think she was serious.'

'And that was the last time you saw her?'

'Yes, it was. It was starting to get a bit tedious. I don't mind a simple affair – a bit of fun on the side, as you might say – but women are funny things; they always want to complicate it. They fall in love; all that nonsense.'

Gaffney couldn't imagine anyone falling in love with this insufferable, noble prat opposite him, but, as his lordship had said, women are funny things. 'Perhaps,' he said slowly, 'it might be as well if you told me where you were on the night she was murdered.'

'Oh, I say,' said Slade. 'I really was only joking. You can't possibly believe that I had anything to do with it. I mean to say, I don't mind sharing a bed with someone else's wife, but I do rather draw the line at killing her.' He laughed nervously.

'Well, in that case, you've nothing to worry about, have you?'

Slade looked unhappy. Eventually he spoke: 'I was with another woman,' he said.

That came as no surprise to Gaffney. 'Who?' he asked coldly.

'D'you mean you'll go and see her?'

'Yes, I do.'

'Oh God!' He ran a hand through his hair. 'You will be discreet, won't you?' he asked after some time.

Gaffney smiled. 'Of course,' he said.

★ ★ ★

The next morning, Gaffney walked through the incident room and into his own office in a mood of deep depression. Tommy Fox, in high humour, had charged Farrell with several offences in connection with the smuggling of drugs and he and his team were now, with the aid of the Drugs Squad, pursuing further enquiries with vigour, as they are apt to say in police circles.

'You're not looking desperately happy with life, sir,' said Harry Tipper, putting his head round the door of Gaffney's office.

Gaffney laughed a short, cynical laugh. 'It's a blow-out, Harry. Come and sit down.' He stared moodily at the centre of his blotter. 'Mr Fox has arrested Farrell – got him bang to rights – and he'll either charge Masters or use him for the prosecution; that depends on the Crown Prosecution Service. Unfortunately, there's not a shred of evidence that would support a charge of murder against either of them, and, of the two, I fancied Bernie Farrell.' He sighed deeply and nodded towards the papers that Tipper was carrying. 'What have you got there, Harry? Anything interesting.'

Tipper riffled through the file he was balancing on his knees. 'They've traced the cab-driver, sir.'

'What cab-driver?' asked Gaffney in a tired voice.

'The one that one of the Cutler's Mews residents claimed she heard . . . the night of the murder.'

Gaffney looked surprised. 'Any good?'

Tipper handed over a couple of pages. 'That's his statement. Wisley took it last night.'

Gaffney skimmed through the closely written document and tossed it on the desk. 'That's not worth the paper it's written on,' he said. 'What the hell made Wisley ask that particular question, incidentally?'

Tipper shrugged. 'I suppose it was an obvious question to ask in the circumstances,' he said, 'although I don't know what made him ask it, but . . . ' He paused to extract another piece of paper and pass it across. 'Put with that, it becomes quite interesting. Walter Croft, the MP whose telephone number we found on that old order-paper, has come home at last.' He nodded at the message form which Gaffney was now reading. 'I spoke to him about twenty minutes ago. That information, incidentally, hasn't been recorded anywhere else.'

Gaffney looked up and grinned. 'Christ Almighty, Harry,' he said. 'You realise what this means, don't you?'

'Livens it up a bit, doesn't it?' Tipper was non-committal.

'When can we see him – Croft?'

'This morning, sir. I've made an appointment for ten-thirty, if that's all right?'

'That'll do fine. Then, Harry, you and I will make some further discreet enquiries.' He leaned back in his chair. 'Anything else?'

Tipper smirked. 'Yes, sir. The Commissioner would like to see you as soon as possible to give him an update, and the Home Secretary wants to see us at five this afternoon for the same reason.'

Gaffney smiled. 'Does he now? Well, that could be just about the right timing. Let's hope we'll have something to say to him.' He stood up and stretched. 'Harry—'

'Sir?'

'Get one of the lads to go down to the Commissioner's library for me, will you?'

'Yes, sir . . . ?' Tipper looked puzzled.

'See if they've still got a copy of Fred Cherrill's autobiography.'

'Who's Fred Cherrill, guv?'

Gaffney smiled. 'Probably one of the greatest fingerprint men ever. He was detective chief superintendent in charge of Fingerprint Branch years ago, well before our time. But I've just had an idea. It's a long shot, but when you've got nothing else . . . ' He walked across the office and put the file he had been studying into his safe. 'When you've done that, we'll see Croft, and then we'll go clubbing.'

'At this time in the morning, guv?'

'Not quite. We've a call to make first, just to eliminate a suspect.'

★ ★ ★

The woman who answered the door was about thirty-five years of age. She wore black leather trousers and a white silk blouse with long voluminous sleeves. Her red hair tumbled about her shoulders and she was holding a glass of red wine. She looked vaguely at Gaffney and Tipper. 'Yes?' she said.

'We're police officers. Mrs Anne Tremayne, is it?'

'Yes,' said the woman again, making no move to admit them.

'I understand you know Lord Slade . . . '

'Oh! Perhaps you'd better come in.' She led them into the sitting room and refilled her glass, neither offering the policemen one, nor inviting them to sit down.

'During the course of certain enquiries,' Gaffney explained, 'Lord Slade accounted for his movements on the last Tuesday of last month by telling us that he spent the afternoon and evening with you.' He glanced down at his pocket book. 'He said that you lunched together, then spent the afternoon here. He went on to say that you then both dined here and spent the night together.' Gaffney looked up. 'Are you prepared to confirm that, Mrs Tremayne?'

Mrs Tremayne contrived to look both astonished and angry at the same time. 'He actually told you that he'd spent the night with me?'

'Yes, he did,' said Gaffney.

'Well, that's bloody rich. And I thought he was supposed to be a gentleman.' Anne Tremayne banged her glass heavily on a side-table. 'Well, as a matter of fact he did,' she said, 'but it'll be the last bloody time he does.' She took a cigarette out of an open packet on the table, lit and pulled on it. 'We went out to lunch, way out in the country somewhere. That was so that none of his friends would see him and report us to his wife, I suppose.' She stubbed the cigarette out viciously. 'I don't know why I ever got mixed up with him,' she said half to herself. 'Yes, then we came back here and went to bed. We got up, had a bit of supper, and then went back to bed.' She folded her arms tightly and stared out of the window. 'I've a good mind to ring him up and tell him I'm pregnant.' She turned to face the two detectives. 'Or, better still, ring up

207

his wife.' She took another cigarette. 'So much for a discreet affair,' she said.

'End of a beautiful friendship,' said Tipper when they got back to the car.

'End of another suspect, too,' said Gaffney.

# Chapter Seventeen

At ten past five, Gaffney and Tipper were still sitting in the waiting room near the Home Secretary's office at Queen Anne's Gate.

'Bloody marvellous, isn't it?' Tipper spoke in low tones. 'He makes the appointment for five, and then keeps us waiting.'

Gaffney was leaning back in his chair, legs stretched out, arms folded and eyes closed. 'He's a politician,' he said, which in his view was sufficient explanation. He was feeling reasonably happy about the day's work; the results of his enquiries were the best that could be hoped for, but the next half-hour or so would be the testing time.

After what seemed an age, Charles Stanhope, Lavery's private secretary, appeared in the doorway. 'I'm sorry to have kept you waiting, Mr Gaffney,' he said. 'The Home Secretary will see you now.'

The only illumination in the darkening office was a brass banker's lamp which cast a pool of light on the desk and gave the eerie impression that Dudley Lavery was headless.

'Detective Chief Superintendent Gaffney, Home Secretary,' said Stanhope.

Lavery rose from the desk with a weary smile. 'Ah, Mr Gaffney, come and sit down; you too, Mr Tipper.' He glanced at Stanhope. 'Charles, perhaps you'd put the overhead lights on.' He peered across at the high windows. 'Still snowing, I see.' He indicated the little circle of chairs with a gesture. 'Oh, and Charles, could you arrange for us to have some tea?'

'Yes, Home Secretary,' murmured Stanhope. He switched on the lights and walked across to the window. 'I'd better just draw the blinds,' he said, 'or I shall have these gentle-men complaining that you're being exposed to assassins on rooftops.'

'Do make yourselves comfortable,' said Lavery. 'Perhaps you would excuse me just for a few moments while I sign these papers.' He resumed his seat behind the large desk.

The tea arrived, and Lavery walked across to join the two detectives. 'Well, Mr Gaffney?' He sat down, took a cup of tea and gently stirred it. 'What progress have you to report? I understand that you've made an arrest?'

Gaffney nodded. 'As a matter of fact, we have about five or six persons in custody, sir, yes.'

Lavery leaned forward earnestly. 'That is good news, Mr Gaffney. Many congratulations. I assume that one of them is the man who—'

'We haven't got to that stage yet, sir. There are a few things that I have to check. Perhaps you can help me with them?'

'Of course, of course.' Lavery leaned back, relaxing, and letting his forearms lie flat along the arms of the chair.

Unprompted, Tipper opened his brief-case and handed a sheaf of papers to Gaffney.

'I have here,' began Gaffney, 'a copy of the statement which was made by Detective Sergeant John Selway . . . ' He glanced up at the Home Secretary. 'One of your protection officers, of course.' He smiled and Lavery nodded. He turned a couple of pages until he found the paragraph he wanted. 'He says here that you left the House at six-fifty on the evening of your wife's murder and arrived at the Chesterfield Club at about a minute to seven.'

Lavery gestured with his hands. 'I'm sure that's right. If John Selway says that was the time, then so be it.'

'He then goes on to say,' continued Gaffney, concentrating once more on Selway's statement, 'that you remained there until nine-twenty when you left to return to the House.' He paused before looking up. 'And you arrived at the House at half-past nine.'

'I'm sure that's absolutely right. But why are you going

over these times again, Mr Gaffney? Has one of the men you have in custody . . . Masters, perhaps . . . ?' Lavery had been advised of the arrests by DCI Lisle, his senior protection officer. 'Has he said something – made some statement – that is germane to those times?' Lavery spoke in a detached way, politely, as though, in his capacity as the police authority, he was listening to a senior officer's account of a crime with which he was unconnected.

'No, he hasn't.' Gaffney glossed over that, but he was interested that, out of all the men in custody, Lavery should have selected that name. Not even a mention of Farrell, whom he claimed to know on a social level. 'Why Masters in particular, sir?' he asked.

Lavery smiled blandly. 'I defended him once,' he said. 'Ironic, isn't it?'

'Perhaps you'd just have a look at this, sir . . . ' Gaffney waited until Tipper had handed Lavery the order-paper. 'This is a House of Commons order-paper . . . '

Lavery smiled tolerantly and took the document, turning it over in his hand. 'I have seen one before you know,' he said. He returned it after only a cursory examination. 'Does that have some special significance?' he asked, with a puzzled expression on his face.

'It may have, sir. You will see that it has a telephone number written on it.' Lavery nodded. 'Our enquiries show that it is the home telephone number of Mr Walter Croft, MP.'

'Ah, Wally Croft,' murmured Lavery and nodded.

'Do you remember his giving it to you, sir?'

Lavery raised his hands and then let them fall again. 'My dear Mr Gaffney,' he said, 'how on earth can you possibly expect me to remember a thing like that?' He shook his head and stretched out a hand. 'May I?' He studied the order-paper once more. 'Well, I suppose the date is some indication, but it was a week before my wife's death,' he said, and returned the document to Gaffney. 'It was probably on that day.' He said it with an air of lofty indifference. 'Look, is this really of any importance?'

'We found it in the bedroom at Cutler's Mews on the

night your wife's body was discovered there,' said Gaffney quietly.

Lavery waved a deprecating hand. 'That's Edna for you,' he said dismissively. 'Cleaning women are so damned difficult to find these days, you just have to put up with what you can get, or do without.'

'Mr Croft remembers quite clearly when he gave you that order-paper, sir. He states that he gave it to you at about five o'clock on the afternoon of the day that your wife was murdered.' Lavery opened his mouth as if to speak, but Gaffney went on: 'He's quite adamant about it.' Tipper passed another written statement across. 'He says that he spoke to you on the matter of one Joseph Ellis, a constituent of his, about the treatment of Mr Ellis's son while serving a term of imprisonment. According to Mr Croft, you undertook to make some enquiries and telephone him urgently. He gave you his home telephone number, written on the back of that old order-paper, because he would not be attending the House again prior to leaving for Ankara for an Inter-Parliamentary Union meeting.' Gaffney paused. 'He also says that you did not ring him back . . . '

There was a long pause before Lavery spoke again. When he did, the old politician's smile was firmly fixed on his face. 'I think there must be some mistake here, Mr Gaffney. I don't recall having seen that before.' He gestured towards the order-paper which Gaffney was still holding. 'Why has it taken so long to produce this rather odd piece of . . . I suppose you'd call it evidence?'

'Very simply, sir, because Mr Croft didn't get back until yesterday.'

'Ah!' Lavery let out a long sigh. 'Well, what are you suggesting?'

'I'm not suggesting anything, sir,' said Gaffney slowly. 'I'm just curious to know how it managed to get from your pocket – which is where Mr Croft swears he saw you put it – to beneath your bed near the body of your wife, when you claim not to have been home that evening.' Gaffney leaned back in his chair, waiting for the storm to break. There was little doubt in his mind that his career, by that question, had been laid firmly on the line.

Lavery smiled owlishly. 'Poor old Wally,' he said. 'He is getting a bit past it.' He leaned forward slightly, false concern on his face. 'I wouldn't want you to repeat that, of course.' He appeared visibly to relax and surveyed Gaffney for some time before speaking again. 'I hope, Mr Gaffney,' he said, his voice conveying an element of threat, 'that you are not suggesting that I – the Home Secretary – would have done anything untoward.' He smiled as if to soften the menace. 'You will know, of course' – he gestured towards the pile of statements resting on Gaffney's knees – 'that John Selway was at the Chesterfield with me all that evening.'

Gaffney had the feeling that he was being dragged under. One of the things that he had learned early on in his days at Downing Street, looking after the Prime Minister, was that you didn't joust with a politician unless you were absolutely sure of your facts, and not even then if it could possibly be avoided. 'John Selway was there, sir, but not with you.'

Lavery smiled blandly. 'Are you suggesting that I slipped out of the back door then?' he asked jocularly.

'I have made enquiries at the Chesterfield,' said Gaffney heavily. 'I can find no one, no one at all, who can remember seeing you between a quarter past seven and half-past eight when you went in for dinner.'

'I was in a private room upstairs. I told you I went there for some peace and quiet to read the Prisons Bill.' He frowned. 'Look, Mr Gaffney, I have been as co-operative as possible, but I have to say there comes a point when this whole thing gets too bizarre for words. I can only suggest that you get back to this man Masters and charge him with my wife's murder.'

Gaffney spread his hands in an attitude of resignation. 'I apologise, sir, but I'm sure that you – more than most people – will realise that when inconsistencies of this nature arise they have to be resolved.'

'Of course, of course.' Lavery smiled magnanimously. 'It is rather irksome though.'

So now it came to it. Now was the point when Gaffney

had to gamble. And not only to gamble on the inquiry he was conducting, but with his career, too. If he lost, he would be looking for a job; there was no doubt in his mind about that, and that meant leaving under a cloud. Even if he stayed, having failed to find the murderer of the Home Secretary's wife, it wouldn't do his professional career a great deal of good. It would certainly banish all hopes of his ever becoming a commander, and would tarnish the reputation of Special Branch as well. There would be pointing fingers, the laughter, and the suggestions that the inquiry should have been given to a real policeman.

'Masters didn't murder your wife, sir,' said Gaffney quietly.

Lavery affected a surprised look. 'Oh? Are you certain?'

'Absolutely.'

'But how can you be so sure? From what Lisle told me – indeed from my own knowledge of the man – Masters is an out-and-out criminal . . . '

Gaffney relaxed. There was no point in being tense now that he had made his bid. 'Some years ago, sir, well before my time, there was a detective chief superintendent at Scotland Yard called Cherrill who was head of our Fingerprint Branch.' Lavery raised an eyebrow, clearly wondering what relevance this had. 'And in 1941,' continued Gaffney, 'he was called to investigate the murder of a young woman called Maple Church . . . in Camden Town, I believe—'

'Strange name,' murmured Lavery.

Gaffney wasn't sure whether Lavery was referring to Maple Church or Camden Town. 'The interesting thing about it,' he continued, 'was that he found the imprint of a finger-mark on the body: an identifiable fingerprint. It was the first time that such a mark had been discovered on a body. . . .' He paused. 'But not the last.'

Lavery glanced at his watch. 'I suppose all this is leading somewhere,' he said, his face showing no emotion.

Gaffney was impressed by Lavery's control. 'And it has happened in the case of your wife's murder.' Gaffney spoke quietly and precisely. 'That is how I can be so sure that Colin Masters did not kill her.'

Slowly the Home Secretary sat up, his eyes fixed gimlet-like on Gaffney's face, as if willing him to say no more. 'Well, who did?' He frowned intently.

'I don't know,' said Gaffney. 'You see, sir, the killer's fingerprints aren't on record; he has no previous convictions.'

'Why did you arrest Masters, then?'

'We arrested him on drug-smuggling charges, sir,' said Gaffney, varnishing the truth only a little.

'Good Lord!' Lavery looked genuinely astonished. 'Well, what are you going to—'

'I propose to take elimination fingerprints from everyone who may have had contact with your wife, sir, however tenuously. I was wondering if you would set an example by giving us your own to start with. The others could hardly refuse then, could they?'

Slowly Lavery stood up and walked across to the window. He parted the slats of the vertical blinds and for an age stared out. 'It's still snowing,' he said absently. Then he turned and focused his gaze on the detective's face. 'There is no need, Mr Gaffney,' he said. 'It was I who killed my wife.'

Gaffney, conscious of the uniqueness of the situation, waited silently, expecting the Home Secretary to say something else. But Lavery remained still and silent, arms limply at his sides, gazing unseeing at his desk, just the occasional twitch of his bottom lip betraying the emotion of the drama. Finally Gaffney spoke: 'Dudley Lavery, I am arresting you for the wilful murder of your wife, Elizabeth Lavery. Anything you say will be given in evidence.'

At last the Home Secretary looked at Gaffney, staring him in the face. 'Of course, of course,' he murmured. Even in his anguish he could not forget that he was the political head of the police force of which Gaffney was a member. 'You should go far in your chosen profession, Mr Gaffney. You are a brilliant detective.' He smiled ruefully. 'Which is more than I can say of my career; I only asked the Commissioner to have Special Branch investigate the murder because I didn't think they'd solve it. Just shows how little I know of your abilities.

Shouldn't have judged you all by Lisle, I suppose.' Suddenly he looked younger, years younger, as if now not only free of the guilt of his crime, but also of all the burdens of the office which he knew instinctively, from that moment, were no longer his. The unfinished minutes would now be completed by another. The pending decisions would be taken by someone else. In a strange paradox, his arrest marked his freedom. All that remained was a prison – and he was more than familiar with prisons – where he could sit and read, and be free of all the passions, the ambitions, the cut-and-thrust of politics, the backbiting, and the worry of re-election in a seat that had become marginal since the boundary changes. No more money-worries, no more concern about the social niceties, the protocol. No more need for leadership; no more aspirations for leadership. He was abdicating it all.

Then the terror of it struck him: incarceration, for the rest of his life probably. The disgrace, the sagely shaking heads and, above all, the deprivation of liberty.

He appeared not to have heard Gaffney's caution, despite having acknowledged it; either that or he chose to ignore it. 'She was impossible,' he said. 'I didn't suspect for a long time. Perhaps I did and couldn't bring myself to face it. I know she was an actress, but I never imagined that she'd become involved with a man like Masters, not a criminal. When I found out, I still couldn't believe it, but I confronted her. She just laughed at me and said, "So what?" I asked her why; what could he possibly give her that I couldn't. D'you know what she said? Sex! – that's what she said. She said that Masters was alive and vibrant and treated her like a whore, and that was what she wanted. Not to be on a pedestal with everyone bowing and scraping just because she was the Home Secretary's wife. I idolised that woman; gave her the best of everything. There was nothing she wanted for.'

'How did you find out?'

'I have a friend – his name's Earl Barclay – who owns a villa in the South of France, at Le Trayas.' Gaffney nodded. 'We've often stayed there over the years—' Lavery broke off, interrupting himself. 'He's not an English earl, this Barclay.

216

It's his name; he's actually an American, an American financier.' He seemed to think it important that he should clarify that. 'We were staying down there –' He broke off again. 'As a matter of fact, Elizabeth had gone down ahead of me. I'd not been long in office, and something had arisen that meant I couldn't go until a day or two later. I flew down to Nice and motored along the coast from there. It's about thirty miles, I suppose. Very pleasant in the summer.'

'Yes, it must be.'

'What?' Lavery looked startled, as if surprised to find that Gaffney was still there.

'I said it must be. Pleasant in the summer.'

Lavery nodded slowly. 'Yes, oh yes. We were driving along the front at Le Trayas, almost there, as a matter of fact, when I saw her coming out of a bar with a man. I recognised him instantly as Masters.' He shook his head, still unable to believe what he had seen that day.

'What did you do?'

'I got to the villa and asked Earl where she was, as if I hadn't seen her. He told me that she had left the previous day. Some story about an urgent filming assignment that they had phoned about. She'd just packed up and left, so Earl said.'

'But she knew you were coming down?'

'Of course, but she didn't know when. I think I told her it would be a few days later than it actually was, but whatever it was that had held me up in London didn't come to fruition, so I left. It must have been pure chance that I saw her. I didn't see her again in Le Trayas, even though I kept my eyes open.'

'Did you tackle her about it, the next time you saw her?'

'Oh yes.' Lavery nodded seriously. 'She said that it was a case of mistaken identity, that it wasn't her at all. She said that she'd already left by then.'

'And you believed her?'

'Yes, I did, but only because I wanted to. I tried to reason with myself, believing that my wife would never do a thing like that.' He shook his head sadly. 'Can you imagine? The wife of the Home Secretary consorting with a known criminal. It would have put paid to my parliamentary career; my legal one too.'

Gaffney refrained from making the obvious retort: that that had happened anyway. 'I suppose so,' he said. 'What did you do then?'

'At first I didn't know what to do. I couldn't very well get Five to look into it. The result would have been the same . . . if they'd confirmed it of course. So I got hold of a fellow who'd done occasional inquiry work for our chambers in the past, swore him to secrecy, and paid him well.'

'And?'

'I'm afraid he came back with just what I didn't want to hear.'

'Yes?'

'He'd found out that she'd spent a week in Spain with the man Masters, at his villa. She was supposed to be there – in Spain I mean – but advising on a film. At least that's what she told me.' He paused. 'And that's what I told you. . . . '

'Then what?'

'When she got back I confronted her again.'

'Go on,' said Gaffney. 'If you wish to.' He was conscious of not really being entitled to ask questions.

'She was so truculent about it. Asked what I proposed to do. Funny that: what did I propose to do? I told her that it was what she proposed to do that was important. Then I told her that she would stop seeing him.' He shook his head sadly. 'She laughed and said "Make me". So I tried to reason with her; make her see sense. I explained what it would do to my career if it got out – and it would have done – but she said they wouldn't dare publish it. I told her that Home Secretaries weren't immune from the attentions of the Press, and she said that that was quite right, but that Masters was. It seems that he had threatened to kill any journalist who mentioned him or her in his newspaper. Then she said she wanted a divorce. I asked her if she intended to marry Masters . . . '

'What did she say?'

Lavery looked up, an expression on his face that was

half smile, half sneer. 'She said no: she wanted to marry someone else.'

'Did she say who?'

Lavery shook his head. 'No, she wouldn't tell me. Frankly, I didn't believe that. I think she did want to marry Masters, and was just piling on the agony.'

Gaffney wasn't so sure of that, remembering his conversation with Lord Slade, and also what Desmond Marshall had said about Liz Lavery being unhappy that her husband wasn't to be made Attorney and, therefore, a knight. 'What did you say? When she asked for a divorce.'

'I refused, naturally. Then she flounced out and said that she would see him as often as she liked.'

Gaffney glanced across at Tipper and waited until he had lifted the point of his pen from his pocket book. 'What happened on the night of the murder?' he asked.

It was as if Lavery hadn't heard that, intended going at his own pace. 'I couldn't have that, you see. Not a second divorce, not in those circumstances. I'm afraid that there's a tendency these days for the public to say that a man who makes bad decisions in his private life is just as likely to make them in his official one.' Gaffney felt that the public was probably right. 'I rang her from the club that night, as I told you. She said that she'd had enough, that she was going and wouldn't be coming back, and that I could do what I liked. I knew then that I had to see her, talk her out of it. You were quite right, Mr Gaffney, I left by the back door.' He smiled ruefully.

'I know,' said Gaffney. 'You walked out of the back door of the Chesterfield, into South Molton Lane and caught a cab to Cutler's Mews. It's a miracle you weren't recognised.'

'I turned up the collar of my coat, and I stole a hat from the hatstand.' He smiled at that. 'I suppose you'll want to take that theft into consideration?'

'Why go to all that trouble?' Gaffney thought he knew the answer. The answer was that Lavery had returned home with the specific intention of murdering his wife, hence the elaborate plan to evade his protection officer and at the same time give himself a first-class alibi.

'I didn't really want to take John Selway with me. I think he would have sensed that things weren't all that they ought to be between Elizabeth and me. It's very difficult, and at times very embarrassing, having your every footstep dogged by a bodyguard.'

'Yes, it must be.'

'Anyhow, I went home—' He broke off as a thought came to him. 'D'you mean that the cabbie remembered me?'

Gaffney shook his head. 'Not you personally, no, but we did trace a cab-driver who remembered taking someone from the junction of South Molton Lane and Davies Street to Cutler's Mews that night. Couldn't identify you positively; just said that it could have been you.'

'Mmm!' Lavery paused again. 'Anyway, I went home and she was still there. I tried reasoning with her, but to no avail. She wouldn't listen, and I grabbed hold of her shoulders. I don't know what she thought I was going to do, but she started struggling quite violently.' He paused reflectively and took a deep breath. 'I don't know what happened then, but the next thing I remember was that she was lying on the floor, dead. I panicked, I'm afraid, and then realised that if I went back to the club, through the back door, I might just get away with it.'

Gaffney smiled to himself. Knowing juries, he thought, you might just get away with it yet.

'Not very gallant, I'm afraid,' said Lavery. He looked round his office, knowing that he was seeing it all for the last time. 'I wonder if I might have a moment or two to myself, Mr Gaffney?'

Gaffney watched Tipper close his pocket book and put it and the statements into his brief-case before standing up. Then he looked back at Lavery. 'I'm afraid that is out of the question, sir,' he said. 'You see, you are now in my custody.'

# Chapter Eighteen

'What?' There was outrage in Tommy Fox's voice.

'I think *nolle prosequi* is the Latin term,' said Gaffney mildly. 'What it means in short is that the Director of Public Prosecutions, on the instructions of the Attorney-General, is not going to prosecute your friend Masters, in exchange for which the latter will keep his mouth shut about the goings-on in Spain, particularly in relation to the late Elizabeth Lavery's infidelity and the interest the KGB took therein.'

'It's bloody diabolical,' said Fox.

Gaffney laughed. 'I don't know what you're getting all worked up for. After all, Tommy, you thought it was a good idea that he should be used to trap Farrell, and you did suggest that he be allowed to turn Queen's Evidence. And when you think about it, thanks to him, there's one KGB agent less to worry about.'

'What about Farrell, then?' growled Fox.

'You're not going to like this, Tommy, but there's a chance he won't be tried either . . . at least not here.'

'Why the hell not?'

'For the same reason.'

'Bloody hell!' Fox was clearly disgusted.

'But all is not lost,' said Gaffney. 'We've refused to give up Masters to the Spanish for murder, which means he'll never be able to use his villa again . . . unless he wants to get nicked. But as a sop, it has been agreed that Farrell should be extradited to Spain to stand trial there for drug-smuggling. I don't think we'll be seeing a lot of him for about the next thirty years.'

Tommy Fox's face broke into a grin. 'I think I shall send him a get-well card,' he said.

\* \* \*

'I didn't know that you'd got a fingerprint off Elizabeth Lavery's body, John,' said Commander Frank Hussey. 'You didn't tell me that.'

'I didn't tell you for the simple reason that there wasn't one there, sir,' said Gaffney.